PITCH BLACK
VI CARTER

WARNING

This book is a dark romance. This book contains scenes that may be triggering to some readers and should be read by those only 18 or older.

NEWSLETTER

Join my newsletter and never miss a new release or giveaway:

Scan the QR code to
sign up

CHAPTER ONE

WILLOW

Two doors face me. They are wooden, polished, and I know they are heavy in my hands as I have drawn them back many times before. They are pretty harmless. They are, after all, just doors made from wood. I fidget with the pleated skirt that skims my knees.

If they are so harmless, why are you hesitating, Willow?

I'm unsteady as I draw the doors back and step into the room that is my stepbrother's domain. The green wallpaper, with its golden diamond-shaped pattern, gives the room an almost pleasant feel. That is, until you take in the large paintings that are placed around the room. To me, the images look like someone took buckets of paint and splashed them across a canvas. People declare these a masterpiece; I don't.

My gaze darts to Rian as he steps out from behind a dark wooden partition that covers half the room. Blood drips from his fingers and splashes onto the oak flooring. I hold my head up high, and my arms cross tightly behind my back. I hope the beat of my heart isn't penetrating through my blouse and cardigan.

His moss-green eyes smile at me. Shivers skitter down my spine. Rian reaches behind the partition and brings out a white towel that he uses to wipe off the blood from his fingers. It should bother me, the amount of blood, but my brain refuses to acknowledge what's right in front of it. I think it's my brain's way of protecting me.

"Willow." My name from his lips always sends fear pulsing through me along with something else, which I immediately push away.

"Your father asked me to find you." I can't look away as he takes controlled steps towards me. He continues to rub his hands on the cloth. His gray shirt sleeves are rolled up to his elbows. The closer he gets, the more blood I spot — flecks of blood coat his tattooed neck. My heart continues to hammer in my chest. It's right there on the tip of my tongue: the question I want to ask, but I don't—whose blood is coating your arms?

This is my world now. I might not like it, but I can't question it.

Rian steps up to me with only a foot separating us. He's taller, making me feel smaller than my actual five-foot seven-inch frame.

"Why couldn't he come himself?" Rian's words are distracted as he picks up one of my blonde curls in his bloodied fingers and rubs it softly. "Or maybe you wanted to see me."

His moss-green eyes flicker to mine, and that mocking smile he seems to reserve for me spreads across his face. More shivers assault my body as I step away from his touch. He releases my hair, but not before I see his bloody fingerprints on the strands.

"It's my mother's birthday; he wants to make sure you're present."

Rian flashes me another smile and steps towards me again. His fingers are covered in rings, gold rings that are coated in someone's blood. My gaze flickers to the partition, and my pulse spikes. Is the person dead? Are they lying in a pool of their blood? What had they done to deserve such a fate?

Warm, strong fingers grip my chin, drawing me back.

The heat from his fingers burns through my skin, and heat races through me all the way to the tip of my ears. My body feels like it's going to catch on fire from how he is looking at me. I'm ready to ask him to let me go; I'm even willing to ask him nicely when he leans in and sniffs me.

"I'd like to fuck you."

His words are designed to have my mind scattering, and it has the desired effect. I want to run away from him. He's vulgar and a maniac. Yet, I'm still standing here, with blood in my hair and his hands on my face.

"I'll pray for you," I tell him and step out of his touch again. My nostrils flare as I grapple for air. I hate the effect he has on me. It doesn't matter how little or often I'm around him; I can never seem to keep it together. And he knows the effect he has on me.

He grins. It's quick. Rian returns to drying the blood from his hands.

"I can picture you, Willow, on your knees..."

I cut him off as my face blazes. It shouldn't. I should be used to Rian's foul mouth at this stage, but he always has a way of penetrating all my armor, no matter how heavily I put it on.

"Seven o'clock. Don't be late."

I turn, and each step takes a lot of force to keep me upright. No one speaks to Rian like that, but for some reason, he lets me. He knows my fear of him, yet he lets me, just like he taunts me with his foul mouth and dark promises.

My body has cooled down long after I've returned to my bedroom. I move past the large four-poster bed that's been neatly made. The red bed covers are the only color in my whiteout room. My mother hates color, and each time she enters my room, her gaze always zooms to the bed, and her lips curl in distaste.

I enter my bathroom that's also decorated in all white. Here I didn't get to add color. The water turns pink as I wash the blood from my hair. I can't meet my eyes in the mirror. I don't want to see what reflects in them. My fingers tighten around the cold porcelain sink as I close my eyes and take calming breaths.

My heart skips a beat as I look up and meet my eyes in the mirror, and I watch as my control fades. Pushing away from the sink, the feeling of sand slipping through my fingers has me wiping my hands repeatedly on my skirt. I want to bite the flesh of my palms to make the deeply-rooted itch leave.

"Willow." My mother's soft voice is a whip that has me standing straight and stepping into my bedroom. Her gaze skims across my structure before she steps up to me. Her fingers reach out and fix the silver cross that dangles from around my neck.

"You look perfect." She flashes me a wide smile and steps back. Pride shines in her brown eyes, the same color as mine. My mother's blonde hair sits perfectly on her slim shoulders. People say I'm a carbon copy of her. On the outside, I'm sure I am. Inside, I feel like I'm rotten to the core. Black as ink that reflects more darkness. A darkness that I can never let anyone see. She knows I have it in me. She knows what happens when it's let out. So I let her control the darkness in me. If that means being a good Catholic girl, then that's what I will be.

It's not easy living in a place so coated in sin that it's dripping all over everything. But for my mother, I have to try. Rian tests my restraints, but what we lost and how far we've come is a stark reminder to stay on this path.

"Thank you, mother." I smile sweetly, and her smile widens.

"I'm the luckiest woman alive." My mother leaves my room, and I follow. "I have the best daughter." My mother stops and touches my face; I hold still as she caresses it. "And the best husband."

I don't blink until she releases my face, and we make our way down the left staircase. Tonight is a private party for my mother—just the four of us. Tomorrow night, this house will be alive with the elite of our neighborhood.

We enter the foyer. The space is buzzing with life. Florists arrive with large bouquets of flowers and huge plants that graze the top of the front double door frame.

Mark, our party planner, directs every one. Caterers arrive with so much food that it looks like it could feed an army.

"How many people are coming?" I ask as my mother walks through the chaos.

"One hundred and fifty guests. A small gathering. You know I don't like anyone making a fuss over me." My mother pauses and stops a lady from entering the kitchen.

"Don't bring that plant through my kitchen. It smells funny. Bring it out the back."

The lady is ready to leave, but my mother stops her again.

"Actually, take it away. I don't want it."

There is a moment when the florist's gaze ping pongs between my mother and me. I have no idea why she is looking at me. She finally nods and leaves with the offending plant.

"Mark." My mother signals Mark with two fingers, beckoning him forward.

I glance down at the large white tile I'm standing on. It's large enough that both my shoes fit into the square. The black polished shoes reflect my face. Feet move around me as my mother makes it clear to Mark that no plants with any type of odor may enter through the kitchen.

I want to exhale loudly or jump up and down, just do something that allows my stiff body to move. The familiar click of his shoes has my head snapping up. But I don't look in Rian's direction. My mother's stance shifts slightly. She's aware of him, too, yet she keeps speaking to Mark.

"Catherine." Rian's voice has that sing-song tone to it that's dipped in annoyance like he's about to hand out his final warning.

I don't direct my attention to Rian. He's to my left. I'm aware of the space he fills. I'm aware of his smell.

Too aware! My brain screams.

"Yes, Rian." My mothers' dislike for him is evident in her tone. When I glance at my mother, she wears a perfectly practiced smile. Mark leaves and orders anyone with plants to go outside for an odor test.

"The noise level, Catherine, is distracting me from my work."

Work!? He means hurting people.

"I'll tell them to keep it down." My mother raises a brow in question. "Anything else?"

I want to look at Rian. I want to see the expression on his face, but I glance around at all the moving bodies. A man carries a crate of wine. I don't drink alcohol. I've often thought about stealing a bottle and letting go, but letting go is dangerous for a person like me.

"No, Catherine." Rian shifts, and some part of me breathes at the expectation of his departure.

He doesn't leave, and when I give in to the urge to look at him, he's staring at me. The gray shirt he wore has been replaced with a dark purple one. Moss-green eyes bore into me, and I'm frozen while being dragged into the vortex of Rian.

He never says anything inappropriate in front of our parents. I honestly don't think it's because he cares what they would say. I think he does it for me. My cheeks blaze at my stupid analysis.

"Willow." I tighten my hands into fists and give him one of my own perfectly practiced smiles. It sits in my inventory for moments, just like this—moments where my mother is watching my reaction.

"Rian," I speak his name clearly.

His lip tugs up before he turns on his heel. Everyone parts like a wave to let him walk through. He doesn't have to pause in his footing or ask anyone to move. It's like everything is repelled by him.

"Willow." My mother is waiting for me, expectantly.

I've been watching Rian for far too long. I give her a softer smile, and she says no more as I follow her to the ballroom where the party will be held tomorrow night.

I sit on a lone chair to the left of the large room as my mother instructs everyone on what she wants to be done. My two feet are firmly on the oak floor, my hands in my lap, and my back straight. This is what keeps everything in me at bay. This is the discipline that will help me keep control. These are my mother's words.

I will sit here for hours and try to blink as little as possible. Every once in a while, my mother will glance at me and give me a nod of approval. I want her approval because each time I get that nod, it's like it restarts my clock, and I'm ready for another hour. I'm aware of how the staff steals glances at me, and like a battery-operated toy, I smile at them on cue.

CHAPTER TWO

RIAN

Catherine's party is in full swing; the room is full of people who made it onto the list. Their fake laughter rings out through the room that I scan. I stop a waiter passing and remove a flute of champagne from the tray he carries before letting him move on. Taking a step deeper into the room, I hide my smile behind the glass as Willow comes into view. She's a vision of light and darkness. Everyone sees the light in her angelic appearance. Even now, she's in a cream gown that flows over her curves. It nearly touches the ground. Long blonde hair billows out around her in soft curls. Her skin is as flawless as she pretends smiles that she automatically gives to everyone who approaches.

It's her eyes, dark brown eyes that swirl with pain, hidden secrets, and darkness, that I want. I take a second sip and step even closer. Half the room divides us, but watching Willow is a pastime that relaxes me. She's an enigma that I desperately want to solve.

I sense another set of eyes on me and fire my gaze at Catherine. She hates how I watch her daughter. I raise my glass to her, and she flashes me a smile of her own.

"Tell me again why I have to be here?" Hearing this, I release Catherine from my gaze as I turn to Calum. I would never call him Calum. He goes by the name Blitz. He likes to make things go boom, or in his own words, he likes to Blitz things.

"We are networking," I speak to him as I try to find Willow in the mass of people. It's not hard. She stands out.

"You expect me to talk to these people?"

I glance at Blitz and give a sharp nod before moving the glass to my other hand. "This is how you keep your head above water."

He selected a black tux for tonight. It's stretched across his huge frame, and I grin. "Try not to move too quickly in that suit. It's looking a bit tight."

He pushes his glasses back upon his face and smiles as a female approaches us. I walk away and let him do the talking.

Willow smiles, yet it never touches her eyes. Her small hands curl into fists, and I want to laugh. She knows I'm watching her, and she's trying not to look at me.

I empty the champagne glass and place it on one of the large tables that have been placed sporadically around the room.

A preppy boy is talking to Willow, and his chest is puffed out, his mouth moving too fast. She nods and smiles at him like he's very entertaining. He has no idea how bored she is. But I do.

"You look ready to combust into flames; I thought I would rescue you." Willow stiffens before her long dark lashes lift, and her gaze fixes on me.

The preppy boy is about to say something. I cut him a look, and he sucks in his chest and leaves.

"That was rude." Willow's tone is meant to sound monotone, but I hear the hitch of nerves in her words.

"No, he was rude, boring you to death." I stop another waiter and remove two champagne flutes.

"To Catherine." I hand one to Willow, and she takes it hesitantly. She's careful not to let our fingers touch.

I tip my glass against hers and drink, but she doesn't. She never drinks.

"That dress doesn't leave much to the imagination." I grin when her cheeks turn a nice shade of pink. I take a step closer and lower my voice. "I've always wondered what's underneath."

A vein flickers along her neck before her lashes flutter closed. Cutting me off.

"Rian, Willow." My father approaches, and I take a step away from Willow, but I can't take my eyes off her as my father speaks to us.

"Your mother is having a great time, so thank you both for coming."

Now I flick a glance at my father. He knows I'm not here for Catherine. I'm only here to make sure all the important people know my face and know never to cross me.

"She looks happy," Willow speaks truthfully for the first time. Her gaze flickers to me before returning to my father. He really likes Willow. I can see how he looks at her. He sees her as a good daughter.

"I know this isn't the time or place, but since I have both of you..." My father fixes his cuffs before jutting his chin in my direction. "Catherine wants Willow to start working in the family business."

I don't speak. I take a drink and watch Willow place her glass gently on the table like she can't hold it much longer.

My father is watching Willow expectantly. I have no idea what Catherine is playing at by placing Willow in our field of work, but I don't like it.

"Of course." Willow folds her hands in front of her and smiles at two guests who pass but don't linger.

"She can help me out." I offer up to my father, and surprise flitters through his moss-green eyes.

He raises a brow. "You?"

"In the market, she can help some of the sellers." I'll have to find one who will take Willow on—and keep the worst of them away. I won't be able to keep the underworld hidden from her, as we'll be directly in the black market, but every other area of our business won't work for Willow.

"I never thought of the Market." My father smiles.

"What's the Market?" Willow's voice shakes, and I have the urge to step closer to her and reassure her.

"I'll educate you tomorrow when you start."

Her nostrils flare as she glares at me. The sense of victory I feel has me smiling at her. My father is taken away by one of his guests, and it's just Willow and me again.

"I don't want to work with you." Her words are low and said through a smile as she glances around the space.

"That's not very nice, Willow."

Her gaze snaps to me, and her pink lips part slightly. Lips I want to taste. I've never desired anyone like I desire Willow.

She drops her gaze, and I take a step closer to her. I know I'm too close, especially in public, but it's sometimes hard to keep away from her. Her scent swirls around the space, and I want it to cling to me.

"I think you secretly want me."

Her chest rises and falls, and I love the reaction I get out of goading her. The small silver cross that she never takes off dangles down the front of her dress. I'm tempted to reach out and touch it.

"I think you're deranged." Her sharp words make me laugh. I pull back as Blitz approaches us. He gives Willow a quick nod before standing shoulder to shoulder with me.

"Where's Fox? How the hell did he not get roped into this?" Blitz folds his arms, stretching the suit. He changes his mind and stuffs his hands into his pockets. Any female in the room that spots him gives him a second glance. He doesn't notice. He's too busy scouring the room for Fox. My attention returns to Willow; she doesn't even blink in Blitz's direction. Instead, she's looking around the room, and I notice that she's getting ready to leave me by the shift in her stance.

"See you tomorrow, Willow." Her shoulders stiffen, but she doesn't turn back to me; instead, she leaves, and I watch her depart.

"What's tomorrow?" Blitz asks.

I spot Fox the moment he steps into the room. So does everyone else. His seven-foot thin frame pauses in the doorway as he scans the crowd. His hair is darker, making his complexion appear sickly. He nods when he spots me and Blitz and steps into the room. Fox is cunning and has come up with some ingenious plans in the past. He is my most trusted partner. Blitz isn't as privy to things, but he runs a very close second. That's my circle. I let no one else in.

"You're late," I say to Fox the moment he arrives.

"He was doing his hair." Blitz sneers.

Fox glares at him. "You look like you're ready to bust out of your suit. You look stupid."

Blitz cracks his neck like he might start something here with Fox.

"I agree with Fox," I say, knowing that will end the argument. "Now go mingle." I pat both of them on the back before walking off into the crowd. My eyes follow Willow from across the room for a while. She's aware of me, but she never meets my gaze. Tomorrow she will have no choice but to be close to me. I don't imagine that's what Catherine expected to happen when she suggested her daughter works with us.

"Rian Steele?" I didn't notice anyone approaching. A young redhead stands to my left in an emerald green dress. She reminds me of an Irish dancer, with her milky skin and height.

"I'm Celine. My father's the mayor."

I take her outstretched hand. "Nice to meet you, Celine. How is your father?"

She rolls her eyes. "Still with us."

I grin at her wicked tongue.

She's smiling up at me, and I know that smile. I know her next words will be an invitation to leave with her.

"You want to ditch this so-called party and have some fun?"

I smile at her. "That sounds so enticing, but right now, I can't. Maybe later." I give her the false promise, and her disappointed eyes slowly re-light.

"I'll find you," she says.

No, you won't.

My attention is dragged to Willow, who slips from the room. Taking Celine's hand, I shake it.

"Nice meeting you." I leave quickly, weaving through the crowd and leaving the room. A few people linger in the hallway, mostly staff waiting for instructions.

Willow's cream dress flows behind her as she enters the kitchen. I follow and hover at the door as she leans against the counter with her palms firmly pressed into the marble. Her head is bowed, and I have no idea if she's crying or praying. She steps back, and I spot a glass in front of her. It's filled with a clear liquid. She picks it up and sniffs it before spilling it down the sink.

"Not to your liking?"

She jumps, and the glass releases from her fingers. It rolls a few times in the sink without breaking before coming to a halt.

"There was a fly in it."

I take a step into the room and shove my hands into my gray trousers pockets. "You know you don't have to lie to me."

Her eyes dull further and she stands straighter. "I'm not lying." Her lie sounds almost convincing.

I take another step, and she juts out her chin. Being around her is dangerous, but I like this game she plays.

I close the distance between us. I think she's holding her breath as I reach around her. Our faces are close, and if I thought she would allow it, I would kiss her. My fingers tighten around the glass that I step away with and sniff.

"Vodka."

Her cheeks darken. "What do you want, Rian?"

I hold the glass high. "I want to know why you poured it down the sink."

"I told you there was a fly in the glass." She steps away from the counter, and I could stop her from leaving the room, but I'm aware that we are no longer alone. Two waitresses linger at the door, unsure if they should come in or not.

I glance at them as Willow flees for her life.

I nod at the staff. "You can enter." They do, and I sniff the glass one more time before placing it in the sink.

Tomorrow she won't be able to run from me. That thought has me returning to the party with a slight bounce in my step.

CHAPTER THREE

WILLOW

What does one wear to a black market? I'm staring at three nearly identical outfits that I have laid out on my bed. I've been up for far too long. My long blonde hair is tied back in a high ponytail. Each move I make has my hair brushing across my bare back, making my skin itchy.

Pulling on the white blouse, I button it up to the neck before pulling out my cross. The gray cardigan fits snuggly over it. Instead of a skirt, I select gray pants and a pair of sensible brown shoes. I take one final look in the mirror, meeting my muddy brown eyes. They are so dull, and I hate what I see. My room needs one final check. I straighten the sheets on the bed again and put away the clothes I'm not wearing. Once everything is back in its place, I make my way down to the kitchen.

I can smell his cologne before I even enter the room, and I pause in the doorframe, imagining my steel armor building itself around me. Once it's all on, I step into the kitchen and walk up to my mother, who looks like she's been up for hours. Her blonde hair is in a tight bun. She smiles and places a kiss on my cheek after giving my outfit a once over. A slight nod of her head in approval has me smiling back.

I don't acknowledge Rian as I pick up the coffee pot. A small tap on my hand has me putting it down.

"It's not good for your skin." My mother explains her reasoning for slapping my hand.

I take the steaming cup of green tea from her and sit down at the table. I know Rian is watching me, but I refuse to look up. A bowl of chopped fruit is placed in front of me, along with a spoon. I thank my mother and start to eat.

"This black market…" I glance up at my mother as she speaks to Rian. "Please educate me on what Willow will be doing?"

I'm eager to hear this, too. For the first time, I look to Rian, and he's staring at me.

"It's in a private airport that I own." Rian grins and wipes the corners of his smiling mouth with a white napkin. His black attire today makes him appear dangerous. I remember to breathe but make sure it's controlled and level.

"There are hundreds of stalls set up daily; it's guarded at all times." Rian is still watching me, and I can't seem to look away.

"What do they sell, exactly?" My mother asks, and Rian releases me and turns to my mother. He picks up his coffee and sips it before answering her.

"Guns, bombs, anything a criminal might need. We have some of the deadliest people on the planet come through our doors. Everything is illegal." Is he trying to make her keep me here?

I'm waiting for my mother to say I'm not going, and a part of me would be okay with that. Instead, she sips her own coffee and smiles at Rian.

"Perfect. I can assume security is at its highest there."

Rian nods his response.

They smile hatefully at each other, and I'm picturing trying to sell a gun to some guy who wants to rob a bank. *This is what little girls' dreams are made of.* I pull away from that thought, knowing this fate was brought on by my actions.

"Are you ready?" Rian asks while standing.

I glance at my mother, and she nods.

"Yes," I answer, standing up. My mother approaches me and fixes my cardigan before placing a kiss on each cheek. "Have a great day."

"I'm sure I will."

Rian's laugh isn't quiet as he grabs his keys off the counter.

"Let's go, Willow." The way Rian says my name has me wanting to hunch my shoulders forward. It's too personal in front of my mother.

I give her a final smile of reassurance before following Rian out to his car. This will be the first time I've left the property with him. My nerves jangle, but I refuse to let them show.

Climbing in, I close the door and am ready to put on my seat belt when Rian leans towards me. I freeze, not sure what he's going to do. He leans too close as he opens the glove compartment and removes a slick black device that he hands to me. I don't take it at first, but as he continues to hold it out, I remove it from his fingers, making sure mine don't touch his.

"I'm programmed under Rian. If you need me at any time, all you have to do is give me a ring."

My fingers curl around the sleek device. "Thank you, Rian." I've never had a phone. I don't want it. I don't want access to anything that could make me slip. I place the device on my lap and put on my seatbelt. When I glance at Rian, he's watching me, only this time; he isn't smiling like he normally does. I can't decipher what I see on his face, but he turns away from me and starts the car.

"You stay beside me from the moment we enter. We will walk around the whole area and let everyone see you."

The world moves so fast past the window that I want to reach out and make it slow down. This is too fast for me.

"I want everyone to know you are with me."

I press my palm against the glass. My heart hammers a little quicker as the gray buildings give way to large green trees.

"Once people see you are with me, no one will ever harm you."

I remove my hand from the glass and watch the imprint of my fingers slowly disappear.

"Are you listening to me, Willow?"

How could I not? His voice, his smell, his closeness. I'm aware of every single cell that makes up Rian.

"Yes, stay beside you and I'll be safe." I sit back and glance at him.

His moss-green eyes are smiling at me again. "Have you any questions for me?" He glances back at the road before looking back at me.

His hands are coated in gold rings. His large fingers wrap around the steering wheel. I have so many questions for Rian.

"No, I think my mother covered everything."

He snorts. "I think Catherine needs to let you have a bit of breathing space."

I want to laugh at that. He has no idea. "My mother is looking out for me. Always."

"Controlling you is more on point."

I return to looking out the window. His stare is too intense. The trees fall away, and the landscape grows barren before we pass a station and take a left just after it.

The road we drive down has metal fencing on either side and in the distance, I can see several planes and large hangers. Everything grows bigger the closer we get. I reach down and touch the black device. We are stopped before entering the compound. Rian rolls down his window, and the gates are lifted. We are granted entry. He drives close to a side door, and my stomach roils.

"Why didn't you go to college?"

Rian's question has my head snapping up to him. I'm shaking my head. "I didn't want to."

He unbuckles his seat belt and faces me. One hand is placed on the steering wheel, and all the air slowly leaves the small space.

"You don't have to lie to me." He leans in, and fear has black dots dancing in front of my eyes. The click of my seat belt has me glancing down as he unbuckles my belt.

"You're nervous." His voice carries a hint of joy.

I let my eyelids flutter up and meet his gaze. He's too close.

He reaches out and touches my hair. "Your hair is so soft. What shampoo do you use?" He's teasing, and I hate the reaction he ignites in me.

He continues to roll a piece of hair around his strong fingers.

"You intrigue me." His moss-green eyes flicked up to mine, and I slowly move away from him. He releases my hair.

"I shouldn't," I answer, and immediately hate that I did. I know it's always best to say nothing.

He laughs. "Yet, you do, Willow." He's smiling like it's some private joke. There is an element of confusion on his handsome face, and I glance away.

I shouldn't think of him as handsome. I grip the phone and stare out the window, counting the cars. I get to thirty-two when Rian finally gets out of the vehicle. I get out and walk around to his side before following him to the large building. Fear starts to choke me, and I stop walking and quickly turn my back on Rian. I can't let him see my fear. Closing my eyes, I reinforce my armor. I picture the walls around my emotions, blocking them. When I open my eyes and turn around, Rian is watching me with curiosity. He didn't ask me what I was doing.

The moment he opens the steel door, the noise from the hangar is deafening. The sound lessens as Rian steps in with me close behind him. He places his hands behind his back, and we do as he had said we would. We walk around the hangar. Everyone stops and acknowledges Rian—their gaze holds respect—that is until it bounces to me and their eyes light up with questions.

Rian glances back at me every few stalls, and I give him a curt nod to assure him I'm fine. The walk feels endless. Rian wasn't lying when he said the stalls sold guns and armor that criminals use. A large guy with a Mohawk picks up a bazooka off the table and places it on his shoulder. What could he possibly want with that? I quickly look away from him to another stall that sells knives. These aren't pen knives or anything I've ever seen before. They remind me of hunting knives that would gut an animal. *Or a human,* my mind whispers.

The click of a gun has me swinging to the left where a man holds up a handgun checking it out. Rian stops close to the back of the room where the first female I've seen gives Rian a toothless smile. She has several layers of clothing on, none of them make sense—jeans with a skirt and underwear over the skirt. I count five different colored tops. Her greasy hair hangs in clumps around her shoulders.

"This is Margie," Rian says, stepping aside so I can get a better look at her.

Margie continues to grin at Rian. "She makes jam."

I notice all the pots filled with purple jam. The lids are paper with rubber bands around them.

"Margie, this is Willow, and she will be working with you."

Repulsion courses through me as I glance around the space. "Let me work with him."

I point at a guy who has a table filled with watches. It looks innocent enough, and he appears clean.

Rian whistles, and the guy I'm pointing at looks up. "Willow wants to work with you, Reggie. Is that okay?"

Reggie stares at Rian, and I have no idea what passes between the two men but Reggie glances at me.

"No."

"I tried," Rian says, but his voice holds too much humor.

"You could make him."

Rian steps closer to me. "You want me to force him to let you work at his stall?"

What would force entail? I remember where I am and who I am speaking to. "No. I'll work with Margie."

"Thief!" The roar from a man has everyone within hearing distance turning to where he is pointing. Rushing towards us in a panic is a man dressed all in denim, the goods he lifted are held firmly to his chest. His eyes are wild with fear as he moves closer to us. Rian steps out in front of me and hits the man squarely in the face. He sails back and hits the ground heavily as all the stolen goods scatter across the floor. Blood immediately pours from his nose.

He glares up, and his eyes widen. Horror fills his paling face as Rian steps closer. I'm aware of the pure silence, and that's when I look up to see everyone in the hangar is watching to see what's going to happen.

CHAPTER FOUR

RIAN

His fear grows as I stand over him. I grin over his trembling form.

"A thief." I laugh at the irony. "You never steal from a thief." I kneel down and soak up his fear. It's such a genuine emotion. You can't fake fear. That's what makes it so addictive. Fear and pain, they can't be faked.

I stand up and glance out at the waiting crowd. They know the penalty for stealing. I step up to the closest stall that has a large selection of knives. Picking up a butcher knife, I hold it up for all to see—anticipation courses through the hangar.

I turn to the thief, who scatters away from me on all fours. A large foot clamps down on his shoulder, stopping him from leaving. I flick a quick glance at Blitz, who keeps his huge foot on the man's shoulder while pushing his dark-rimmed glasses back upon his face.

I turn to Willow, and the excitement that bubbles through my system erupts as I see the horror in her stunning brown eyes. I want to keep staring at her and savor her fear. It's worth so much more to me than the thief's. I turn away, knowing I have an audience to entertain.

Glancing out at the crowd again, I meet a few gazes before walking towards the thief who's being dragged off the floor by Blitz. Blitz slams the man's arm on a nearby table and holds it firm.

"Now, you lose your hand," I tell the man, and he tries to pull away from Blitz. He's frantic in his desire to get away, but he can't make Blitz's huge frame budge, not even an inch.

"If you don't hold still, I'll take your head off." The man falls numbly onto the table and starts to sob. "I won't ever come here again." His voice is low and carries a note of hopelessness.

"I know you won't, because if you do, I'll take your other hand."

Blitz shoves the man harder onto the table, and I'm so very tempted to look at Willow again. I want to see all her forms of fear. I raise the butcher knife, and the man screams long before the sharp blade cuts through flesh and bone, dislodging his hand from his wrist. Blood sprays and pools out onto the floor and I stay where I am as his screams of horror turn to labored sobs. Blitz releases him, and he falls onto his back, cradling the stump as blood continues to ooze out of the wound.

Two security guards pick him up.

"My hand." His words are weak, but his eyes are on fire with pain.

One of the security guards looks at me, and I shake my head. "His hand is mine."

Hate fills the man's eyes briefly before they are consumed with agony. I would stay longer and really soak up all that pain, but I'm aware of Willow behind me. I turn, and her arms hang at her side. Her small hands are balled up into fists, and I'm surprised at the numbness I see in her pretty eyes. I take a step towards her, and her gaze snaps to me. This is the part of Willow I can't figure out. She juts out her chin, her golden hair swishing at the sharpness of the movement.

I'm waiting for the questions that don't come. Noise starts to rise, and soon the market is bustling again. I glance at Blitz as he stuffs the hand into a plastic bag and holds it up to me.

"You really want to keep it?"

A shake of my head has him leaving with the severed hand. I don't want it. I just don't want the man to have the opportunity to have it put back on. Once I take something, it's mine for good.

"Where were we?" I ask Willow.

"I'm working with Margie." Her words are controlled, and I want nothing more than to see what's really going on inside her head.

I close the distance between us, and her gaze flickers to my arm. I peek down at my arm and can see the flecks of red liquid.

"It's not the cleanest job," I say to Willow.

Her gaze jerks back to me. "Is it really only jam that Margie sells?"

She's refusing to talk about the thief or what she just witnessed. "Yes, but it's not any jam." It's a deadly poison, and with one small dollop on bread or dessert, the person would be dead.

I reach in and pick up a golden curl. Willow is quick to step away, showing me she isn't as unaffected by what happened as she's letting on.

"Can I start now?" She swallows before glancing at Margie.

"Do you have your phone?"

She holds out the black device.

"I'll be here if you need me. If you can't see me, just ring."

She turns her back on me and moves towards Margie. I'm aware Blitz is waiting for me.

"What is wrong?" He isn't one to linger.

"Not here." We leave the hangar. Each stall we pass has the sellers looking up and nodding with respect.

Outside, the air is heavy. "I think there's a storm coming," I speak to the sky as I inhale deeply.

"I think you're fucking right." Blitz pulls off his brown jacket and throws it on the ground before taking a pack of smokes and a lighter from his pocket. "The Rat Pack has taken another shipment that arrived last night. There are members in that fucking room." Blitz points at the hanger with a jab of his finger.

"What do you suggest we do? Shut it down?" I'm willing to listen to Blitz. The Rat Pack is like an infestation that I can't get rid of.

A car pulls up close to us and Fox climbs out. His skin is paler in the light of the day. He doesn't help himself with his dark clothes and hair.

His limp affects his left foot as he walks towards us.

"The Rat Pack stole again last night," Blitz informs him before taking a large inhale from his cigarette.

"Again?" Fox looks at me with a raised brow.

"What about shutting down the market until it's solved?"

Fox sneers. "That's not how you get rid of rats. They will use the opportunity to grow."

Fox rubs his chin, and this is why he's my right-hand man. He's thinking and plotting on how to fix this problem.

"How do you kill rats?" Blitz asks before crushing the cigarette under his black military boot.

"You kill them." Fox laughs and shrugs when Blitz doesn't join in.

"I mean it." Fox's serious tone and expression are directed towards me. "Small bombs. Placed in six locations around the market."

"You want me to blow up our number one source of income?"

I step closer to Fox, seeing his plan expand and develop in my mind. "We blame the Rat Pack. Say they targeted us."

Fox grins and nods.

"We'll kill our own people?" Blitz still hasn't caught on.

I glance at him. "But we might kill theirs too, and spreading bad feelings amongst the people is what we want. There will always be a sacrifice in war. Right now, we need the Rat Pack to look like the enemy,"

Blitz shakes his head. "I don't like this." He rubs his clean-shaven jaw. "When do you want it done?"

I glance at Fox, and he smirks crookedly. "No time like the present."

If they're doing this now, I need to get Willow out of here.

"Okay, boys, get to work." I leave Blitz and Fox and re-enter the market, making my way to Margie's stall.

Willow is standing rigid along the side of the stall. Her gaze keeps skimming across the jam like it might grow legs and take a run and dive at her.

"We have to cut our stay short."

Willow jumps slightly before reigning in her emotions. She doesn't question me, but steps away from the stall. I want to touch her again, but she's mentally further away than she normally is.

She follows me out of the hangar. When we get outside, Blitz and Fox are nowhere to be seen. I unlock the car, and Willow climbs in. She's staring out the window again like I don't exist, or it's her first time seeing the world, and she doesn't want to miss a moment.

Once I'm in, I reach across and touch her hair. She doesn't turn to me or pull away, and having no reaction from her has me releasing her hair and starting the car.

I drive with no destination in mind. I'm not returning her to her gilded cage. I'm not ready to let her go. I have other jobs to do. Glancing at Willow, she's still staring out the window. "Do you like flowers?"

Her attention is drawn to me, and I love the look that often flashes in her eyes when she looks directly at me. It's like it's her first time seeing me, and she's taking in every detail. I can't stop the grin that coats my lips.

"Yes."

"Okay." I know where to take her, and I can get some work done too.

The large, green, double gates open slowly, and I drive in. Willow sits up straighter, and I drive slowly. I'm impressed with what I've built here. Flowers burst between the bushes, colors complement each other, and I know the overall effect is stunning.

Willow rolls down her window, and I stop the car. She looks at me. "A garden center?" I take the keys out of the ignition and get out of the car. She does too, and I walk around to her. She seems cagey now, and I stop a few feet away.

"It's my garden."

Her eyes narrow slightly, and she looks out across the acres of landscaping that I had spent years creating.

"You garden?" Her voice rises slightly, and I take a step towards her.

"I do."

"Why, what's in it for you?"

I laugh at her words, and her cheeks darken. She's right, I have reasons for my garden, but that isn't something I'll be sharing with her.

"The sheer joy of taking a seed and watching it grow, only because I planted it."

"You think of yourself as a God?"

More laughter falls from my lips, and I move closer to Willow. I want to kiss her. "If I thought of myself as a God, I'd just have my way with you."

Her eyelashes flutter closed, and she looks out into the rows of flowers before glancing back at me.

"What am I doing here?"

I step away from her. The monotone is back, and I do have work to do. "I have some jobs to do, so take your time and look around. Enjoy."

Her eyes narrow ever so slightly, and I want to capture her lips in between mine. I'm staring at her mouth for far too long.

The rise and fall of her chest grows faster, and I take a step back towards her. She quickly pushes her hands behind her back before taking a step away from me.

"If I get lost, I'll ring you." She turns on her heel, and I watch her until she disappears between white rose bushes. I have a few bodies to burn, and then I'll find her.

CHAPTER FIVE

WILLOW

I can't move. My legs have turned to jelly as I glance around me. It's like I'm dreaming. I know what's just happened, but my brain once again won't let it register. I'm aware that Rian just cut off a man's hand right in front of me. I'm aware of the amount of blood that was spilled. But that seems to be it. I'm aware but not reacting like I've got a broken heart.

I move and step deeper into the rows of flowers. To think he could create something like this. The sky is cloudless as I throw my head back and inhale deeply. I want something to fall from the sky and break me, wake me up.

The red rose bushes to my left spill over the fencing, trying to keep them in to no avail. I step closer and wrap my hand around the stem of the roses. The thorns pierce my skin, and the pain ignites quickly in my hand. Along with the pain comes a flash of fear that dies far too quickly. Once I let the rose go, the pain dies along with my fear.

I tighten my fist as warm liquid pools in my palm. Roses turn to shrubbery before it reduces to small wildflowers that release their lavender scent and a tinge of oranges catches on the soft breeze. It's a picture-perfect day. If I saw this in a painting or captured in a scene, I would think it was picture-perfect. I stop when a large red brick structure comes into view—soft gray billows of smoke puff from the double chimney. Rian closes the front door of the furnace. My stomach twists as I walk towards the sinister structure. I'm thinking the worst, and I know I'm right, too.

Rian turns around and assesses me slowly.

"What are you burning?" I ask as the smell of something else mingles with the scent of the flowers. The flowers are more powerful, but still, I can taste the saltiness on my tongue. We aren't near the sea, but that's kind of what it smells like.

"Bushes." Rian takes a step towards me. "I scatter the ashes on the clay, and it helps the flowers grow." He grins. "But don't tell anyone. It's my little secret."

Rian is sharing a secret with me. My heart gallops as his gaze roams across my face and settles on my lips. I've wondered a million times what it would feel like to have a man like him kiss me.

"You don't have to look so fearful. I'm not going to hurt you." His words aren't delivered with any encouragement that I *shouldn't* fear him. I think he likes the fear that I always try to hide.

"I'm not afraid," I lie.

A lie he reads too easily. "You're afraid of something." He takes a step towards me. "You're hiding something. Something big." He grins like this is a little game.

My stomach hollows out. "I've nothing to hide. I most certainly wouldn't hide anything from you."

His laughter sends my heart fluttering. The smile on his face transforms him. His teeth are perfectly straight and white. He's perfect. It really shouldn't be so. I wonder again what it would be like to laugh just like him. My lips twitch like I'm trying it out, and I can't stop the wobbly smile that erupts out of me.

His laughter dies, and he stares at me.

A wave of confusion slices through my system, and I swallow the smile, trying to keep the tsunami in me at bay. I wrap my hands around my stomach as pain blossoms too.

"You're beautiful." He says the words so off-handily—like it's okay to say such things. The ringing of his phone has him digging into his pocket and answering it. He doesn't look away from me. "How many are dead?"

I catch my breath and hold it.

"They must have been large bombs." His statement isn't said with any care, really, and I frown as he hangs up.

"The market was attacked. Over a hundred are dead."

I hold my hands behind my back as he slips his phone back into his pocket. "The market we just left?"

"Yes. Thank God we got out."

The moment of horror washes over me but quickly dies away. Rian watches me closely, and now I step away from him.

"When I start to think you're good, I realize I'm wrong. You came here because you knew those bombs would go off. Did you plant them?" Does it matter? What am I doing? I shouldn't ask questions. It opens a window allowing him to see what I don't want him to see.

"I'm not good, so don't ever think that." His words are a matter-of-fact, and he takes a step closer to me.

My body grows stiffer, keeping me in place. "I won't make that mistake again," I tell his chest, refusing to meet his eyes.

His warm fingers lift my chin until I'm looking into his eyes. "I would be good to you if you let me."

I frown at his offer. He has no idea what he's saying. I want to laugh, I want to accept, but I need to remember I'm alone in all this, and I need to stay that way.

"No." I pull away from his warm touch, and he doesn't seem put out by my rejection.

I want to reach out and touch something. I'm a little unsteady. He makes everything tilt and warp, and I'm not sure if that's a good thing or a bad thing anymore. I turn away from him and start to walk. Opening my hand, a small amount of blood escapes.

"You cut yourself?" Rian falls into step beside me.

I don't answer him but remove my cardigan and use it to soak up the small amount of blood.

"Good Riddance."

I flicked a glance at Rian.

"I hate that cardigan. I need to get you a work uniform."

I feel exposed in just my white blouse.

"It's my favorite cardigan," I speak quickly.

"Really?"

No, not really. It's my mother's favorite cardigan.

"I like red." I give up something about myself and regret it the moment Rian stops and takes my hand in his. He pulls the cardigan away from my palm, and my fingers open up instantly like a flower blooming.

"Like blood?" He isn't looking at me; he's staring at the wounds. He runs his finger along the wound and brings it to his mouth.

Horror fills me as he licks my blood from his finger. "I could have a disease."

"Do you?" Amusement flashes in Rian's eyes.

Heat pulsates through my body. "No. But you don't know that." I blink several times and pull my hand behind my back.

"I see your fear again." Rian's too close, and he's taking up all the air. "I think you're afraid of what you feel for me?"

"I feel nothing for you, Rian." Lies slip so easily from my tongue.

"A kiss would end this debate."

My stomach rolls, and I want to step away from him, but that would prove him right. He would think I'm afraid, and I can't let any of my wounds be exposed to him.

"There is no debate."

"If I kiss you, and you honestly feel nothing, I will leave you alone." His serious tone has my heart pumping harder. I've thought of kissing him too many times, and right here, and right now, I can see exactly how it would feel.

"This is silly." I don't move.

His feet come into view, and I tilt my head back so I can meet his eyes. "If it's silly, then why not just do it?" He takes a step away. "Or I'm right, and you are afraid of feeling something for me." He shrugs like he's won this.

I know he's goading me.

"One kiss, and if I feel nothing, you stop touching my hair and all your crude comments."

His eyes light up. "I promise." His gaze flickers to my lips.

"Fine." I stand taller. It's only a kiss. No one will know. I stomp on the excitement that's bubbling up inside me. All I have to do is tell him I feel nothing, and maybe I *would* feel nothing. He might be a horrible kisser.

Rian grins as he steps closer to me. I have no idea what to expect. He takes my face in his large hands and tilts it back. His eyes dance across my face. "Are you ready?"

He's trying to build the suspense. "Just do it."

His grin widens, and his hands tighten on my face. "You can't rush these things."

"I think you're the one stalling now." I'm ready to smile in victory when a savage look flashes across his eyes, and he presses his lips against mine. It jumpstarts my heart, and I'm thrust into a whirlwind of emotions that shake and rattle my bones. His hold on me becomes more demanding, and the hardness of his chest under my hands makes me realize I'm gripping him like he's an anchor that will keep me from drowning in pain and want. His hands run down my neck, and I know I have to stop this; I can't shatter in Rian's hands. My fists slam into his chest as I shove him away from me.

I try to control my breathing. I don't want him to see that he is undoing me. "Nothing." The word is angry and breathless, and I know straight away, I am a fool. I know before his shaky laughter has me looking up at him.

"Nothing." Is gritted out between his teeth.

"That's what I said." I push my hands behind my back and jut out my chin. "Nothing," I repeat, and it sounds steadier now, even as everything in me crashes and batters against my flesh like it's craving release from its hold.

"That was everything." He takes a step back. "I know you felt it too."

Before I can speak, he presses a finger against my lips. "Don't lie to me." His words are a warning that I've never heard before. "I proved my point."

He steps away from me, and my lips are buzzing.

"Let's take you home." He doesn't sound happy, and I'm not sure if I should take this change as a blessing as I follow him back to his car. I don't want to go home. I don't want to return to the four walls that always feel so tight around me like something is sitting on my chest. The car rocks as Rian drives. He doesn't speak or look at me, and I want to shout at him and tell him I feel nothing. Most times, I feel nothing, but he always seems to bring my emotions to the forefront. I feel drained and emotionally wrecked as he pulls up to the house. I'm ready to get out when Rian stops me with a soft touch to my arm.

"Your phone." He holds out the slick device.

"I don't need it here." I glance at him, and he continues to hold it out. I take it from him.

"I won't send you dirty pictures, so don't panic." The teasing in his voice has me getting out of the car, and I want to slam the door, but I close it gently and refuse to look back at him as I walk up to the house, through the front door where my mother is waiting.

CHAPTER SIX

WILLOW

The air is thin as I try to control my pounding heart. I don't have a second before my mother grips my forearms. I'm aware of the door closing behind me.

"I was so worried."

I'm confused as my mother releases me and gathers herself.

"We heard about the bombing. I rang you." Rian's father speaks directly to Rian. He doesn't have the same level of alarm in his eyes that my mother has. In fact, he's calm.

"We weren't there."

My mother covers her mouth with her hand. Red polished nails surprise me. I'm staring at them even as she moves her hand from her mouth and rests it on her abdomen. "I thought you were working there today?"

"It's a lucky thing I took Willow away. I had to work elsewhere."

"Alone?" My mother sounds outraged.

My gaze darts to my mother. What would she do if she knew we kissed?

"What happened to your clothes?" My mother pulls the cardigan out of my hand.

"Catherine." The warning comes from Henry, but my mother ignores her husband.

"Did you touch her?" Her words are barked at Rian, and I die a little inside.

"In what way?" Rian's answer has my walls crumbling.

"In any way." My mother grips my arm, and I just want this moment to end.

"No. I didn't." Rian's words are ground out between his teeth. My mother releases me, and I take a peek at him. He's angry. I've never seen his face so sharp with tightness. "You sound like you would prefer that she was in the building when it exploded."

My mother's nostrils flare, and she shakes her head in disgust. "She is no longer working there."

I glance at Henry, wanting him to intervene, but he doesn't. Rian takes a step closer to my mother, and I'm tempted to protect her, but I don't move.

"You wanted her to work with us. She knows the location of the black market. She is the first outsider to ever stand in it. She met the men who work there. She could identify so many."

I want to scream that I won't say a thing. I understand how dangerous all this is.

"So, she's in the door now, and there is no way out," Rian confirms.

"Rian." Henry's voice has all of us looking at him.

"Blitz and Fox are waiting for you." I thought he might scold Rian for speaking to my mother in such a way, but now that I think of it, I have never heard him speak to Rian like he was his son. They talk to each other like they are equals.

"Henry!" My mother's word bounces off Henry as he continues to focus on his son.

"They aren't alone." He informs Rian.

Rian still doesn't leave, and I see his hesitation.

"Henry." My mother's voice is louder. She wants him to do something. She wants him to say that I won't ever have to work there again.

"I'll see you tomorrow, Willow." Rian's departing words are the nail in the coffin.

I focus on the tiles as my mother turns her anger on Henry. It's toned down slightly, but it's still there. "How could you let him speak to me like that?" I can hear the upset in her voice, the quiver that she's fighting to hold back.

"Because he's right. You wanted her to be a part of this, and Willow is. Honestly, Cathy, I'm just glad she's in one piece."

I finally look up at Henry, and his eyes hold his truth.

"Come on, Willow." My mother walks past Henry, and I follow her upstairs, where I know she will question me about the time I spent with Rian. My stomach twists as I step into my bedroom. My mother closes the door behind her.

"There's blood on your cardigan." Her voice is hinged with hysteria. I've never seen my mother this out of control, not since she married Henry. She marches into the bathroom, and I hear the water running.

"God damn it, Willow." I jump at her sharp words. She's holding the cardigan; the area that she scrubbed has turned a dark shade of gray. "It won't come out. It's ruined."

"I have nine more of the same cardigan." When my mother bought something she liked on me, she did it in quantities of ten.

"So what, you just abuse your stuff?" She turns on her heel, and I hear the water running again. "Where are you bleeding?" She returns without the cardigan, and she appears calmer. I hold out my hand, so she doesn't start inspecting me.

"Did Rian do this?"

I frown, not sure why she would think Rian would hurt me. He never has. "He took me to a garden, and I caught my hand on a rose thorn."

"A garden? Where?" My mother grips my cut hand, and I soak up the pain.

"I wasn't paying attention," I answer honestly.

She releases me and exhales loudly.

"I don't understand. Why are you so upset?" I'm taking a step into the unknown. I never question my mother, but she's acting strangely. "You wanted me to get a job."

"Yes. Just, I didn't think there would be bombs going off."

"I'm okay, Mother." I try to reassure her as she sits down on my bed. She pats the spot beside her, and I join her.

"What was it like?"

I'm surprised by her question, but I answer her. "It was a large market with lots of stalls. They were selling guns and knives. I even saw a guy with a bazooka."

My mother's face pales as she faces me. "Did he introduce you to anyone?"

"Yes. Margie. She's the woman I work with."

"What did she sell?"

"Jam," I answer and fold my hands in my lap. My mother falls silent, and I look at her to see she has mimicked my movements. I'm curious about the red nail polish that coats her nails. It looks freshly done.

"Did Rian do any business?"

Something uncomfortable worms its way under my skin, and I face my mother, but she doesn't look at me.

"No. Nothing. Well..." I think of him cutting off the thief's hand.

"Well..." My mother prompts when I don't speak.

"A man stole some items, so Rian...hmmm...cut off his hand."

"You witnessed this?" My mother doesn't sound as horrified as she should. Yet, I know there's nothing normal about us.

"Yes," I answer, and we fall into silence.

My mother stands after a moment.

"Come on." When she speaks now, she sounds more like my mother. I stand, and she starts unbuttoning my shirt.

"Do you know when you were five I lost you in the mall?" My mother shoves the blouse down my shoulders and removes it. She's smiling at the memory. She places the shirt in the wash basket before returning to me.

"I was hysterical. I was so convinced someone had taken you." My mother moves behind me, removes my hair from the band, and runs her fingers through it. "You nearly broke my heart in two that day, Willow."

"I'm sorry." My words are automatic and cause my mother to walk around so she can face me.

"You were five, Willow. You don't have to apologize. Sit down on the bed."

I do as my mother instructs, and she removes my shoes. "Anyway, it took three hours before the police arrived, and they shut down the whole mall. Every second that passed dwindled any hope of finding you. Stand up."

I do, and my mother pushes down my trousers until I'm only standing in my underwear. She places her hands on my shoulders and smiles. "This woman, wearing a red bandana of all things, came running towards me." My mother's eyes glaze off with unshed tears. "She describes this little white-haired girl in her pet shop." My mother runs her hands through my hair.

"You were there in the pet store petting a small puppy. You had no idea of the pure panic you had caused." My mother's hands run down my arms, her smile leaving completely. "I didn't go back to that mall for years."

I'm ready to apologize again when my mother's fingers run the whole way down to my wrist. She turns my arms over, and we both stare at the destruction there. Her fingers run across the white raised lines. "My baby." Her voice wobbles, and I want to feel what she feels. But I don't. She releases my wrists, and my arms hang on either side.

"Take a shower and try to rest." She places a kiss on my cheek and leaves me alone.

My own fingers find their way to the raised flesh, and I keep touching them like they might make me feel again, but I don't believe it. I think the day I made these marks, everything in me drained along with all my blood. Removing my bra and underpants, I step into the bathroom and turn on the shower. I remember the burning of my flesh as I ran the blade across it. My stomach tightens at the ecstasy of the feeling. I have no razor blades here. My mother doesn't allow it, even after all this time. We go to the beauty salon once a week, and they tend to all my needs. I've tried to use bobby pins—pulling the rubbery substance off the top and jabbing them into my thighs. The pain was minimal compared to what a blade could do.

I reach out and check the water before stepping into the spray of the shower. The moment the water coats me, I think of Rian. I think of his kiss, and my heart pounds.

I wash quickly, feeling guilty for my impure thoughts. My hand touches my cross. I have no idea what I believe in, but I know I need to pray more if judgment day is real, and I have to face God. My heart won't weigh well against my evil deed.

Wrapping myself in my towel, I hear a noise from my wash basket. It's a slight buzzing sound. Opening it, I remove my trousers and take out the phone that Rian had given me earlier.

My hands tremble, and I take the phone with me to the bed. Opening it, I see a small white envelope bouncing around the screen. I touch it, and it opens.

"If you need me, just ring me, no matter what the hour." My heart crashes in my chest.

My fingers hover over the buttons. I have no idea what to write back. Do I thank him? Do I need him? I hate the sense of loss that courses through my system. I have no idea what I'm searching for. I close the phone and place it on the top of my bedside table. I think twice and place it in the top drawer. Closing it, I get changed into bed-clothes and tidy up my room. I scrub at the blood on my cardigan until my fingers turn a bright shade of pink. I can't get the blood off, no matter how much I scrub.

I return to my bed. It's not bedtime, but I refuse to go back downstairs. I take the phone out of the drawer, open the phone, re-read, and re-read Rian's message.

"Thank you." I quickly send and regret it almost immediately.

I'm staring at the phone and jump when it vibrates in my hand. The little envelope bounces around the screen. I press on it, and I can't stop the swell that erupts in my chest as I read his message.

"Anything for you, Willow."

CHAPTER SEVEN

RIAN

"Anything for you, Willow." I send back and wonder if she understands that I really would do anything for her.

Blitz clears his throat, drawing my attention back to the three men who are tied to the chairs in front of me.

Leaving my phone on the small, round table beside Fox, I walk back to the three men.

"I will take a volunteer. I think it's only fair to allow two of you a chance to reconsider."

"I swear, Rian. I know nothing." The man closest to me cries out.

It didn't take much to discover his name is Peter. I turn to Blitz and grin as I roll up my sleeves. "I knew he would break first."

"I had my money on the skinny one at the end," Blitz says.

I turn to the man on the end and walk towards him. His lanky frame bends with the chair. "No, his eyes hold too much anger. He'll hold out and try to spite us."

Angry eyes glare up at me, and the man tightens his jaw and juts it out in a gesture of pride.

"But, everyone talks eventually." I step away from him and let that sink in.

"Please, Rian," Peter continues to beg. He follows my finger and the tremble in his chin travels all the way to his hands.

"Just tell me any member of the Rat Pack," I point at the door, "and I will let you walk away." He knows nothing. His massive shoulders fall forward in defeat. He's a bad catch, and I should release him.

I step towards him, and his head snaps up to me—fear sparkles in his eyes. My fist smashes into his face; the crunch of bones under my rings is always satisfying.

"You know I'm trained as a boxer." Everyone knows that information about me, but a reminder never hurts anyone. I don't allow Peter to answer. He'll be an example for the other two. Instead, I smash my fist into the same spot and watch his flesh tear. Blood erupts and feeds my thirst.

"Three hits, Peter, and then you have a chance to speak." I grip his head and lift it up; he's ready to protest when I slam my fist into his face again. His cries have fear igniting in the man beside him, the lanky one tugs at his tied arms. The fire in his eyes, I can't wait to extinguish.

"Give me one name, and you can all go." It was a simple request—liquid pools down the side of the chair under Peter.

"He pissed himself." Blitz dances away from the pool of urine. Fox sneers behind me. We all pause as the door opens, and the sound of heavy footfalls sound across the wooden floor. I don't resume my work but wait until my father appears around the partition.

He stands tall in front of the three men. Lanky shows his first sign of fear, and that kind of pisses me off that he's more afraid of my father than me. That is something I will have to fix later.

"Good evening, gentleman."

"Mr. Steele." Fox places his newspaper on the table and sits up straighter at my father's arrival. I grin at him, but he refuses to meet my eyes. He always gets shifty around my father. Most people do, that is, except for Blitz. He sees my father as his father.

"Henry, these men stole from us." Blitz folds his large arms across his chest as he glares at the three men in question. My father already knows who they are, but I don't interrupt Blitz. I pick up Blitz's cigarettes and lighter from the side table and light one up. I'm an occasional smoker, and right now, I know my father will try to scare these men with his words. To me, it's time-consuming, but I'll just take a break.

My father folds his arms behind his back. "Ten million this year." He snaps his fingers, and Peter whimpers. "Gone. Taken by someone who thought they could take from me and get away with it." My father stays mostly close to Peter. He can sense the weakness there. I want to tell him that won't be fruitful for information, but perhaps it might scare the other men into speaking.

"Now, someone has to pay for that. Someone," My father points at each. "As in one of you, either tell us what we need to know, or your lives are gone." He clicks his finger again.

The cigarette burns my throat. Picking up my phone, I read Willow's message again. "Thank you." I can hear her soft voice in my head.

"Edward Riley." My father speaks the name to the ceiling, and Lanky perks up. My father registers the movement too.

"How is your daughter?" My father looks at his wrist. "She'd be leaving her band practice now, waiting for you to pick her up. Or I could send someone to get her."

Edward struggles against his restraint, and I hope we are getting somewhere. I put out the cigarette and move back to Peter, who sinks into the chair. I stand outside his pool of urine. His face is swelling on the left side, his eye almost entirely closed.

"Leave my family alone." Edward barks, and I have to laugh at his fucking stupidity.

His dark eyes swing to me. "Leave my family alone," I repeat his words. "Don't hit Peter," I say before plowing my fist into the right side of his face. The skin snaps and his roar is delicious. "Do you feel stupid, Edward? Shall I explain that to you again? You say leave my family alone, and you also say don't hit Peter."

Peter's nose breaks under the force of my knuckles. I dance back as blood sprays down his top. "Are you understanding me now?"

"Yes!" Edward's angry roar has me wanting to hurt him. He doesn't understand enough for my liking.

"I can make a bomb that will blow his head off his shoulders." Blitz offers up.

"Not yet." My father stops in front of Edward. I move away from Peter, he's a lost cause, and I step in front of man number two. He's kept his head down and his mouth shut. I kneel down in front of him, and slowly, he meets my gaze.

"You want to tell us something?" I ask him. His gaze darts to Edward and I grin. He knows something. "I can kill Peter first, and then you can tell me." I rise, and Peter starts to cry. His cries are muffled through blood and swollen tissue.

"Roger," The middle man offers up.

"Don't!" Edward barks.

And I decide that I want Edward to tell me.

"Don't say anymore." I surprise the second man as his brows draw down in confusion.

"I want Edward to tell me."

The defiance in his eyes has me stepping closer. "I want you to give up Roger."

I glance at my father, and he doesn't look overly impressed. He doesn't stop me, but I know he'd rather have his information and go back to Catherine right now. I want a message to reach everyone. I want them to know that it doesn't matter how strong you think you are, I can break you.

"Peter," I call his name.

Peter cries out, and blood drools from his mouth.

"I need you to pay attention. You will be the one who gets to walk away."

I face Edward, and fear starts to trickle into his eyes. "Tell me all about Roger and do it quickly."

Edward glances away from me, but not before I see more of the fight drain from him. "Roger works." I clap my hands, directing his attention back to me.

The smell of smoke wafts through the air as Blitz lights up a cigarette.

"You look at me, while you sell out your friend."

He clenches his jaw, his nostrils flare. "Roger Smith. He works on stall number eighty-two. He was bragging about working with the Rat Pack. That's all I know."

"That's all you know?" I question. It's enough.

"Yeah." Edward still has some fight in him, and I need it removed.

I slap his face with only a small amount of force. "Thank you, Edward." I grin at him, and more fear makes its way into his features, but it's too late for him.

"We are done here, boys." My father speaks up before placing a hand on my left shoulder. "Good work." I nod at him, and he leaves the room.

"Can I go?" The middle man looks bewildered.

Blitz answers him. "No. You can't."

Fear drips down the line of men.

"Are you watching, Peter?" Peter nods and stares at me with one wild eye open. Fear will make him remember this.

Edward's face is sharp, and it takes a few hits before I hear bones break. It takes a long time before he cries out, and once he does, I'm breathing heavily as I stand back. Blitz doesn't miss a beat as he steps in and finishes Edward off quickly with a knife to his neck. The second man starts to scream, and Blitz shuts him up quickly.

Fox has returned to reading his paper. I walk to him and push it down, leaving a trail of blood all over it. He tries to push me away. "Are you both finished having fun?" Disgust coats his tongue. If Fox had his way, it would be a quick death. Just shoot them. His method wouldn't ignite the fear that Peter's words will say about what happened here.

Blitz carefully helps Peter stand, and I walk back to him.

"You did good, Peter." He's barely upright.

I nod at Blitz, and he removes Peter.

"So, we have a name. Shall I get this Roger Smith?" Fox asks, folding his paper.

"No. Let the word spread first; we might actually get some volunteers to give up someone higher in rank."

"How do you know that Roger isn't?"

I glance at Fox. "He was bragging about being in the Rat Pack. That's not the actions of a high-ranking member."

I remove my rings and start to clean them on the white towel. Picking off a piece of flesh that had gotten lodged in my signet ring, I wipe it in the towel before I clean the blood off the rest of my rings.

"Let Peter's fear infect the rest," I speak as I shine my rings. "Once it does, we shall see what comes out of the woodworks."

Fox stands and gets ready to leave. "Someone has to clean this up and burn the bodies."

"Get Blitz."

"Blitz did a lot of the work already."

Fox isn't happy and I grin at him. "You have to pull your weight, Fox." He has the brains, but that doesn't mean he isn't getting his hands dirty. I always make sure that both my men are as knee-deep in it as I am.

"At least help," Fox asks, and I'm ready to leave him here alone, but he's too weak to be able to get the bodies out of the room.

I pick up my phone and text Blitz.

"When you're done, come back and help Fox clean up." I hit send and push my rings back on.

"Help is on the way." Picking up my jacket, I salute Fox, who isn't impressed, and I leave him to get rid of the two dead bodies.

CHAPTER EIGHT

WILLOW

The next day I'm dressed and ready for work. The black device feels heavy in my pocket. It feels wrong, and each time I hear footsteps on the stairs, I'm afraid it's my mother. I'm worried she'll find the phone and take it from me.

I get off the bed and make my way downstairs. I'm wearing the same outfit as yesterday. Entering the kitchen, I note that only my mother is here. She smiles at me straight away and hands me a cup of green tea. My stomach rebels the moment the liquid pours down my throat.

"How did you sleep?" My mother points to the table where the bowl of fruit awaits me. She's coated it in Greek yogurt. I place my mug beside it and start to eat.

"Good," I answer once I have taken at least three spoonfuls. I'm waiting for Rian to arrive. I'm tempted to glance over my shoulder every two seconds, but my mother is watching me carefully as I finish my breakfast.

"I spoke with Henry last night." My mother walks to the table and sits down. As she moves past me, I inhale the scent of the coffee beans. To distract myself, I pick up my horrible tea and take a sip.

"You don't have work today."

My stomach dips, and I force a smile. "Fantastic."

My mother takes another deep drink before looking up at me. "Something is different about you lately." She tilts her head and assesses me like if she stares at me long enough, she'll see the cracks.

My acting isn't holding up. I know this. I often feel emotions bubble under the surface—fear skitters across my skin at the thought of all my feelings boiling over.

"I think you need a break." My mother nods.

The air is thin as I inhale it. Is she sending me away? Has she had enough of my madness? I've brought so much pain to my mother. I want to beg, but maybe locking me up is for the best.

"Some of the local youth are having a party tonight. Brittany, who is the most popular girl in the area, has given me an invitation for you." My mother's eyes beam with pride.

I'm confused. Why isn't she locking me away?

"I said you'd go. It's time you start to mingle with people your own age. I think you're ready."

I'm not.

The idea of doing something normal is drawing me in, but I'm not normal.

My mother does the oddest thing. She rolls her eyes at me and laughs. "Don't look so frightened, you will be fine." She drinks from her mug before getting up. I can't even pretend to smile. She pauses before she passes and places a kiss on my head.

"You deserve this."

I close my eyes against the onslaught of pain and shame that rises.

No, I don't.

"I'm really happy just being here with you, mother."

I look up and she smiles down at me. Her features have softened, and she touches my face gently. "It will make me very happy if you go and have fun."

I tighten my hands around the mug of tea. The heat is almost burning the tips of my fingers, I find my smile. "Okay."

She pats my head and steps away. "There will be rules." She places her mug in the sink before turning back to me. "This is your first outing, so it might be overwhelming. So no drinking."

"Of course." I think of sniffing the vodka, and my face burns.

"No smoking."

"I won't." I've never tried it, and don't think it would even be something I would ever bother with.

"No, boys." Her words are harsh.

My stomach twists. I shake my head quickly. "Of course."

Guilt swirls in my mother's eyes, and she steps close to me. "It won't be forever, Willow. I promise. It's just that...boys bring too many emotions."

"I'm not ready yet," I reassure her, and her brown eyes soften.

Time passes quickly as my mother drags me from one shop to the next. She selects a simple white knee-length dress. It's comfortable, but I hate the color. White is too pure for my flesh. I don't complain or speak my mind. After we go to the beauty salon, we move onto the hairdresser. It's a day of being pulled and prodded. I flick through magazines, not reading them, but I don't want to have a conversation with anyone. It never goes well. They ask questions I don't want to answer. My mother normally sweeps in and saves the conversation from plummeting to the floor. All day she's spoken for me. I find it easier to pretend I'm engrossed in the fashion magazine on my lap. The phone in my pocket vibrates, and every cell in my body roars to life. I look up and meet the hairdresser's gaze in the mirror. Did she hear it? Will she ask me what it was? I'm being paranoid.

"Is there a toilet I can use?" I ask.

She takes the iron tongs away from my hair. She's nearly finished, but I want to read the message that I know is from Rian. I'm almost giddy as I walk to the toilet. I don't want to walk too fast in case I draw attention to myself, but my feet are begging me to go faster.

I don't have the door locked when I take the phone out of my pocket. The small envelope bounces around the screen, and I eagerly press it.

Where are you?

My heart jumps around in my chest as I stare at the message. Why would he want to know where I am?

My fingers hover over the buttons, and I'm ready to write back when someone knocks on the door.

"Willow."

I nearly drop my phone in my panic to get the phone into my pocket. Once it's safely away, I open the door and step out.

"Are you okay?" My mother runs her hand through her freshly done hair.

"Yeah, fine." I don't ask why. That would seem odd.

"Okay, you go back and get finished so we can go home and get you ready." Her excitement lights up her eyes as she enters the bathroom. I walk back to my seat like I have a bomb in my pocket. I don't lie to my mother, so why am I keeping the phone a secret?

"Remember when you go in, ask for Brittany." My mother stares at the house, and I can see she's unsure now about me going to the party.

I sit and wait for her to tell me that I can go home. I'd gladly leave this behind me. The small handbag I clutch has my card, red lipstick my mother insisted I wear, and my phone. I haven't texted Rian back yet, and haven't seen him, so once I have a moment, I will.

"Okay, go." My mother's words have me trying to prepare myself. My smile is automatic as I climb out of the car. I give her a small wave as I walk up to the house. Every single room has lights on, I can hear the soft thump of music, and the closer I get, the more voices I hear. I glance back, and my mother is still sitting there waiting for me to go in. My finger pushes down on the buzzer, and no one answers. I'm ready to bolt when the door opens. A girl with long blonde hair and black dress answers. She's beautiful as she smiles at me. She glances over my shoulder and waves at my mother.

"Oh my word, you must be Willow."

She's really sweet. "Brittany?"

"That's me." Her smile widens, and she steps back to let me into the house. I take one final look at my mother before Brittany waves at her and closes the door.

"I'm so happy you arrived. Honestly, I didn't think you would." Brittany walks and talks, and all I can do is smile at her as we pass people who gaze at me with curiosity.

The music grows louder as we enter a large sitting room that seems to hold most of the guests. Everyone here is my age, drinking and laughing. As Brittany enters, they all take us in. I don't react but allow Brittany to bring me around the group, and I'm slowly introduced to people. Most are pretty drunk already.

"This is Mandy." Mandy's red flaming hair flows down her back as she whips it behind her shoulder. She's very drunk.

"Aren't you a bible thumper?"

"Jesus, Mandy." Brittany's eyes widen, but Mandy slaps a hand on her hips.

"I go to Bible study, if that's what you mean."

Mandy's gaze narrows in on the silver cross that dangles from my neck. "Bible study." She sneers before taking a drink from her bottle.

"I'm sorry, Willow." Brittany links her arm with mine, and I'm tempted to pull my arm away from her, but I remind myself she's being nice, and once I pass a few hours, I can leave.

"It's okay."

A group of guys bouncing a white ball on a table roar to life when one of them gets it in a red cup. "That's Chad," Brittany says, while drinking from her own cup that she picks up off the counter.

Chad couldn't have heard her, but his gaze zeros in, and he wears a smile like someone who knows their worth and then multiplied it by ten.

His blue eyes jump to me, and his smile widens. He says something to his friends, who follow his movements towards us. He doesn't look away from me.

"Who have we got here?"

"This is Willow."

Chad's eyes light up. "Want to play a game with us boys?" He points at his friends behind him, who all watch with interest. Most people are drinking and talking, some watch us, and I've never felt so out of place.

"No, thank you."

"Let me get you a drink." Brittany steers me around Chad, who turns when we do. I don't like him, he's too cocky, and cocky people are dangerous people.

I take the cup from Brittany and raise the liquid to my lips, I pretend to swallow, and it looks like I do a good job of it as Brittany smiles at me.

"Brittany, Mandy is really drunk. We need you." A short brunette drags Brittany away, and I'm grateful to move around myself. I pour my drink on top of a plant and make sure no one is looking.

I wander through the house. People are friendly. I see Brittany trying to pull Mandy away from some guy as I move past a sitting room. Double doors lead outside, and the atmosphere seems chill in comparison to inside. I take out my phone and decide it's a perfect opportunity to text Rian. A red cup appears in front of me. I follow the arm all the way up to Chad's smiling face.

"I saw you stumbled and spilled your drink all over the plant." His blue eyes sparkle. I glance around for his friends, but he's alone.

"I didn't stumble." I clutch the phone. "So no, thank you." I decline his drink, making it clear I'm not interested.

"Okay, you didn't stumble." He's smiling like this is some private joke between us.

Two of his friends spot us, and I want to end this before they come any closer.

"I'm not interested, Chad." I'm direct, and his smile slowly falls off his face before he slowly forces it back on.

"Willow." He says my name slowly, and I'm ready to walk away. His hand circles my wrist, and I freeze. "You don't have to be rude."

I glance down at his fingers that circle my arm, and he slowly removes them as his friends arrive. I walk off, my heart races a little faster, and when I glance back, Chad and his friends have gone back into the house. A guy strums on a guitar, and I sit down on a lounger and remove my phone.

I'm staring at Rian's message. "Where are you?"

"At a party." I send it quickly before I lose my nerve. I know he meant earlier. Maybe his dad never told him I wasn't working today.

The strum of the guitar is nice, and I sit still as Mandy stumbles into the garden, narrows her eyes, and enters the house again. I check my phone. I've only been here for thirty minutes. Two more hours and I can leave. I think that'll cover it.

CHAPTER NINE

WILLOW

I push down the want to join in. I shove it so far down, that I become numb as I sit on the lounger. I've put the phone away and just watch people come and go. Some of them give me sideways glances. Others don't even see me. I like those people. They are so caught up in their moments that they don't see. I want to be that blind. I want to be so engrossed in someone's story or laugh like the air is growing thin. I'd even settle for the girl who's sobbing on her friend's shoulder.

I'm surrounded by people, and yet I've never felt so lonely. I frown at the emotion and the sense of emptiness that tugs at me. I won't make friends sitting here. I get up and decide to look for Brittany. Maybe I should try to have a normal conversation.

The house is louder, and everyone seems so much drunker. Three people walk into me, but their apologies are quick, and I accept. I see Brittany, who's still nursing Mandy. My bit of hope of maybe having a friend deflates as I turn away from Brittany and nearly walk into Chad. His smile is back on his face.

"A peace offering." He holds out a red cup.

I don't take it, and he leans in. He's a lot taller than me and has to dip his head to whisper in my ear. "It's a 7up. I won't tell anyone."

He takes a step back and holds out the cup that I accept this time.

"Thank you." He's trying, so maybe I should too. "You are welcome, Willow." His eyes dance with alcohol, but he isn't even close to being as drunk as most people here.

"So, why haven't I seen you at a party before?" He leans against the wall, and his confidence and ease at how he holds himself is something to be envied.

His large frame is clad in all denim.

"Maybe I have been at parties before." I take the smallest sip of the 7up, and it tastes normal.

He shakes his head. "Nope. I'd remember someone like you, Willow."

His compliment should have my knees going weak. I see how every girl in the room watches him, but I don't feel it—*because you're not like the rest of the girls, Willow.*

I want to be, at this moment, I want to be normal so badly that I force a smile for Chad, and his eyes light up in victory.

"You want to play a game with a few of us?"

His offer is nice. I take another sip of the 7up. His eyes trail across my lips. "Sure."

Without warning, he takes my hand in his. His warm flesh tightens around my fingers protectively. I'm staring at our hands as he moves us through the crowd. I should feel something, but it's just a lump of warm flesh. Rian flashes in my mind. When he looks at me, he makes me quiver. I frown. I'm not sure that's exactly a good thing. I look up as we move down steps. I'm ready to stop when Chad looks back at me and grins.

"It will be fun."

The noise in the basement isn't as loud as upstairs. I can't see around Chad until we clear the steps. His group of friends from upstairs are here. All playing pool. I'm very aware I'm the only girl. One of his friends slaps another on the back to get his attention.

"What did I say?" Chad tells them, releasing my hand.

They clap his back like he's just won a game of ball or something. I'm tempted to fold my arms at my waist, but I don't want to look out of place.

"So we are playing pool?" I ask, and Chad looks back at me like he forgot I was here.

"Yeah, pool." His grin is different, and fear reaches out and tightens around the base of my spine.

He holds out the cue and I take it. I hate how his friends stand back and watch us.

"There have to be stakes," Chad says to me as he picks up the blue chalk cube and runs it along the tip of his cue.

"Okay." I haven't played pool before, or is this snooker? I have no clue.

"So, ladies first. Name your price."

I shrug and glance around at his friends. One drinks leisurely from a brown bottle. Two of the others are hunched over a table. I see the white powder and refocus on Chad.

"Fifty," I say.

He nods. "Fifty it is. But if I win..." He walks around to me, and every alarm bell is ringing wildly. I clamp down on it.

"I get a blowjob."

I laugh at his arrogance. All his friends are watching, and I know I am a fool for coming down here with him. It is time to leave.

I hand him back the cue; his smile falls from his face. "I'm not playing." I turn on my heel and my foot touches the first step when a hand tightens around my waist.

"I'm only messing with you."

I swing around and he releases me. "I'm still not playing." I try to leave again, and this time, Chad pulls me back down into the room.

"What do you want?"

"Well, since you're offering, I'll take that blowjob now." His smile is gone. I'm waiting for my wild panic to return, but right now, standing in front of Chad and his friends, I can't get a grip on any feeling. I'm not sure if that's a good thing or a bad thing.

"You can have your pick of any girl upstairs. I'm sure they would give you what you want. But I'm not."

I try to leave for the third time, and when his hand tightens painfully around my wrist, I know I'm not walking away from this. I glare up the stairs and think about shouting for help. Would anyone hear me with the loud music?

"No one will hear you," Chad whispers in my ear like he just read my mind. His large hand reaches around, and he squeezes my breast almost painfully. I push back, and he stumbles.

"Don't touch me." My chest tightens, and it's painful, like someone is sitting on my chest.

"You came down here knowing what I wanted. Now you want to tease me." I'm dragged against his chest, and it's like my limbs grow heavy. I'm moving until the base of my spine hits the pool table. Chad's sloppy kisses coat my face, and I try to turn away. His large leg parts mine, and I'm back there at that moment that changed my life. I couldn't take it all in then; I can't take it in now. Chad's hand tugs at my dress, and it's his friends' howls that draw me from my numbness. I push him away and try to fix myself.

"Don't be like that." He laughs and draws me back.

My hand connects with his face, the sound rings out through the room, and his friends hiss before bursting into laughter.

"Don't touch me." I push away from the table and try to walk away. His slap has the power that most men possess. It sends me into a spin. I catch myself on the pool table. The pain rings through my head, and fear starts to claw its way across my body as he spins me around and his hands are heavier, rougher now.

"Stop!" My shouts only encourage him to grow rougher.

"Leave her alone, man." I'm not sure which friend has spoken up, but Chad isn't listening, and I'm not waiting for one of these boys to stop this.

"Chad, you won. You got her." The same friend tries to reason with him. My hand reaches back as Chad's fingers make their way into my panties. I grab two pool balls, and with all my force, I smash them into his head.

There's a moment when he grows still before he stumbles back from me. Blood starts to drip from a wound on the side of his head. He reaches up, and his fingers come away slick with blood. His stunned face turns feral. I swing again and hit him. This time he falls to the ground. I fire the balls at his friends who duck, glass shatters, and I'm taking the stairs two at a time.

I hit a wall and collapsed onto the floor in a tangle of arms and legs.

"Calm down." Brittany's words penetrate my panic.

"Willow. What happened?" Brittany asks, but her gaze is drawn down the steps like she might know.

I'm up and running out of the house.

"Willow, please." Brittany is quick on my heels. "Did Chad do something?"

"Why would you ask that?" I'm making my way back to her.

She shrugs, and guilt shines in her eyes. "I saw how he looked at you."

I'm shaking my head. "Has he tried to force himself on someone before?"

More guilt. "You are as bad as he is."

I turn, and her fingers tighten around my arm. I shove her off and fix my dress. I can't ring my mother. I can't tell her what just happened. I shouldn't have gone down the steps. I take a few controlled breaths and glance back. Brittany hasn't left, but she also doesn't come any closer.

I take the phone out of my bag. My heart slams against my chest as I dial Rian's number, and it rings.

"Willow." The moment I hear Rian's voice, the storm in me settles.

"If you aren't busy, could you pick me up from a party I'm at?"

There is a pause and I feel stupid.

"Give me the address."

I glance at Brittany. "Address."

She rattles it off, and I pass it onto Rian. "I'll be standing outside."

I hang up and run my fingers through my hair.

"Willow, I'm very sorry." Brittany takes a step towards me.

"Go inside. I won't tell anyone."

I know that's all she's worried about.

"I want to make sure you get home okay."

I can still feel Chad's hands on my skin. I feel dirty. My hand tightens around the purse, and I hold my head high. Glancing down at myself, I don't see anything out of place. I appear fine. The black Bentley that comes around the corner has me ready to bolt towards it, but I walk slowly as Rian pulls up. He's ready to get out, and I stop him, catching the door.

"There's no need. We are leaving." I close his door, and he stares at me through the glass as I walk around to the passenger side.

"Thank you for picking me up," I say the moment I'm in. Nerves skitter through me when Rian doesn't speak. I'm afraid to look at him in case he can see something in my eyes.

"I'm tired. I'd like to go home." Brittany is still standing on the lawn like a beacon. What is she waiting for?

"This is going to work two ways. One is that you tell me what happened. Two is I get out of this car and find out myself."

I glance at Rian for the first time. His moss-green eyes are on fire, but otherwise, he appears his usual calm self. His gaze roams across my face, and something savage twists his lips. "Did someone put their hands on you?"

My face still burns from Chad's slap, so I'm not surprised I'm marked. I force a smile. "You should see *their* face." It isn't a lie, but I want to leave.

He reaches for the door handle and I quickly grab his arm, stopping him. "Please, Rian, just take me home."

He pauses and stares up at the house like he might be able to see through the walls and into the house.

"You said you would do anything for me. Well, now all I'm asking is that you take me home. Please." He releases the door handle and starts the engine. He doesn't speak or look at me as we drive past the house. Brittany watches me, her eyes heavy with guilt. I need to distract myself.

"What's the difference between pool and snooker?" I glance at Rian, his jaw is set, but he loosens it and tells me the difference. For a moment I think he might forget. That way I can forget, and things can go back to the way they were before.

CHAPTER TEN

RIAN

I pull up to the house and Willow tenses in her seat.

"Where were you playing pool?"

She's distracted as she stares out the window. "In the basement." Her head snaps around to me like she's made a fatal mistake.

She has.

"Did you win?" I ask.

She swallows before nodding, her gaze bounces between me and the house.

"No," Her whispered word has her clearing her throat. "I'll go in the back door. I can't let my mother see me like this."

I drive slowly around the back of the house. The mark on her face is growing darker with each passing second.

"Please don't say anything." Willow unbuckles her seatbelt and sits up straight before running her shaky hands through her hair.

"To Catherine?"

Willow's brown eyes grow wide briefly, but tonight I've seen more emotion out of her than at any other time. That tells me someone hurt her badly.

"Yeah, my mother would freak."

I cross my heart. "I won't breathe a word."

A ghost of a smile coasts across her face, but it's swallowed with her upheaval. "Thank you." I don't stop her as she climbs out of my car. I sit and watch her slip through the backdoor.

Taking out my phone, I glance up at all the windows. I don't want Willow to get caught sneaking in.

"What's up?"

"I need to hurt some people."

"Will I meet you at your house?" Blitz asks, and this is why we are friends.

"Yeah. Wear dark clothes."

"Why? Are we breaking in?"

I glare at the back door like I might see Willow standing there with the hollowness in her eyes and a mark on her face.

"No. We are going in the front door, but it won't be pretty."

"See you in ten." The humor in Blitz's voice travels through the phone before he hangs up.

My thoughts turn to how I'm going to hurt the person who hurt Willow. Climbing out of the car, I walk around and open the trunk. A shovel, baseball bat, and an iron bar; that's all that sits in the trunk. It's enough to do some serious damage.

"So, are you going to tell me who we are messing up?" Blitz climbs into the car. He's dressed in a black hoodie and slacks.

"Why are you wearing a white shirt?"

I grin as I pull away from the house. "I want to see their blood on my clothes."

Blitz laughs before taking out a pack of smokes and lighting one up. He offers me one, and I take it.

"So, what happened?"

After taking a few pulls, I flick half the cigarette out the window and try not to think about the mark on Willow. I'm too close to snapping. I've never hidden how I feel about Willow, but I don't speak of it either.

"Someone hurt Willow," I say quickly as I turn off and onto the street that I had just picked Willow up from a few minutes ago.

Blitz doesn't say anything else, and when I pull up to the house, he tucks his large frame down and peers at the uptown residential property.

"Just follow my lead." We climb out of the car and my adrenaline starts to bubble with the thoughts of hurting someone.

The girl who had stood on the lawn earlier opens the door—her gaze darts between me and Blitz. I smile, grabbing her attention. I place one arm along the frame of the door. I lean in close enough to her that I see her pupils dilate.

"Show me where the basement is," I say it nicely.

Her brows drag down, and she wavers. Her hand grips the door, and I warn her with a look not to even think of closing it. I stand up straight and lose the smile. She's wise and steps aside, letting Blitz and me in.

Nearly everyone at the party is wasted, which will make this work to our advantage. I keep my head down, and Blitz drags his hood over his face, as the girl leads us to the basement door. She's ready to dart when I grip her arm. Her chest grows red, and the panic in her eyes has them widening. I lean in close.

"You tell anyone I was here, and I'll come visit you in the night." I don't look to her to make sure she understands my words. I don't have to. The tremble in her arm that I still hold, tells me my message was received loud and clear.

I release her and jog down into the basement. A handful of guys are playing pool. The smell of weed is heavy in the air. I smile at the first guy who glares at me and takes a step in my direction. His fingers tighten around the cue stick and his chest puffs out.

"Who the fuck are you?" He chews gum as one of his friends stands to his left. Blitz pushes down his hood beside me. He's big, significantly bigger than them, and I see the uncertainty in their eyes, that is, until the drink and drugs make these clowns brave.

Scanning the area, I see what I'm looking for. I walk around the two guys, and walk over to a brown leather couch.

"What do you want?" This guy holds an ice pack to his face.

"What happened to your face?" I ask, glancing back over my shoulder. All four guys are standing close to each other. Two of them holding the pool cues like weapons. The way they watch the guy on the couch tells me he's in charge.

I turn back to him as he opens his eyes and sits closer to the edge with a smirk on his face. "Who's asking?"

Snickers erupt behind me.

"Are you as dumb as you look? I fucking asked." I kneel close to his face, letting him know he's no threat to me.

Indecision flickers across his eyes. "Do you remember Willow?"

His gaze darts to his friends. I snap my fingers, regaining his attention, and his irritation.

"That mad bitch couldn't take a joke. She fucking attacked me."

I nod and rise to my feet. Chad stands too, and I think that's wise.

"So, this is what's going to happen. You are going to tell me everything you did to Willow."

He pushes the ice pack back up to his face and smirks. "Who the fuck do you think you are?"

I nod and look back at Blitz. "I tried to do this the nice way."

"Chad." A guy with a mop of red curls steps forward. He sways slightly and squints at me. His behavior isn't from drinking. "I know who he is."

I fold my arms across my chest and face the redhead. "Who am I?" I ask him.

"Who the fuck cares!" Chad barks from behind me, and I'm looking forward to hurting him.

The redhead starts to back away from the room, and Blitz blocks his path. "No one is leaving without my say so."

"Listen here, dipshit…" I've had enough of Chad's back talk. Without turning, I drive my elbow into his face and walk towards his four friends as he roars behind me.

"Who wants to sing like a canary first?"

I'm speaking directly to the redhead. He's the weak link. There's always a link weak; you just have to know where to look.

"Chad hurt her. Not me." He sings like I knew he would.

Blitz grabs his shoulders, keeping him in place.

"Shut the fuck up, Derek." Chad is on his feet.

I hold up a finger to Derek. "One second, Derek." I turn and walk back to Chad, who's pushing back his shoulders like he might have a chance against me. His face is a bloody mess. I don't pause as I drive my fist into his nose. The crunch of his nose under my ringed fingers is satisfying along with the spray of blood. He grips his face and spins away. I return to Derek.

"Sorry about that, Derek. So, I'm wondering…" I eye each one of Chad's friends. "…what each one of you was doing while Chad hurt Willow?"

"What… what do you mean?" Derek is sweating, as he should be.

"If you help someone get rid of a body, it makes you as responsible as the person who committed the murder." I smile at Blitz. "Isn't that right?"

Derek glances over his shoulder at Blitz, who squeezes his shoulder painfully. "That's right."

"So, to me, each one of you is as guilty as Chad." I glance at Chad, who's bent at the waist, still nursing his face.

"He wanted a blowjob, and she wouldn't give it. I tried to stop it." I'm staring into a set of terrified blue eyes, and I can't slow down the blood that fuels through my system. I can't stop the darkness that moves along the edge of my vision. Chad subjected my Willow to this.

Blitz's mouth moves. I'm pretty sure he says, "Oh, Shit". Before I lose it.

My rings fall into the sink. I pull off my shirt that's soaking in their blood and let it fall to the floor. My left fist is ripped to the bone and my blood mingles with theirs. Turning on the shower, I step under the spray.

He would have raped her if she hadn't fought back. I spread my torn hand across the tiles of the shower and hiss as the pain runs down my arm. I press harder until blood oozes from the cuts. I stop when the pain becomes unbearable.

Once dressed, I wrap my hand and put my rings back on. They have gotten their blood quota for the year.

Leaving my room, I do something I've never done before. I seek out Willow. I need to make sure she's okay. I need to see the mark on her face. I need to see the horror in her eyes, so I know killing Chad was worth it.

Her bedroom door is open, which isn't something I've seen before. I don't enter but stuff my hands carefully in my pocket as I stand on the threshold. She's sitting on her bed. Her hair is still down, but she's back in her gray cardigan and dark trousers.

"How are you?"

She doesn't startle at my voice. She doesn't look up at me either. "I'm fine, Rian."

She's anything but fine. I'm staring at her floor, I'm tempted to step into her room, but for the first time, I'm unsure. She doesn't need to feel unsafe in her own space. I won't take that from her.

"If you want to talk. I'm here."

She finally looks up at me, and her eyes give me the confirmation I'm seeking. Chad deserved every punch and kick I gave to him.

"Talk about what?"

I won't force her, and she knows it. "Anything, Willow. Anything at all."

Her brown eyes waver, and I think she just might speak to me as she stands up. The mark on her face isn't as stark, and the closer she gets, I can see why. She's covered her face in makeup. "I'm fine, Rian." She repeats her words carefully as she walks towards the door. Her hand grips the wood, and she holds her head higher. She's shutting me out. I want to reach out and stop her from closing the door, but I don't.

"Goodnight." She doesn't meet my eye as she closes her bedroom door.

"Night, Willow." I step away and remove my aching hands from the pockets. My white bandage has turned red again. My head swims with the violence that I had thought left my system but hasn't. I know Chad's friends are alive, and I'm tempted to go back and finish each one of them off.

CHAPTER ELEVEN

WILLOW

I don't sleep that night. I'm haunted by the memory of the flickering lights that the Donald Duck cartoon flashed across the white walls of our sitting room. I was ten, such a young age to most, but I was far beyond my years. My mother used to say that *I was out before*, I saw the world differently. I saw too much darkness and very little light.

Climbing out of the bed, I try to banish the green couch's image with its small buttons. The image alters and twists until blood coats most of the fabric and the white walls. I can still taste the fear that came with the giddiness that day. It was all twisted up in one, and I had laughed.

I straighten my bed now and get dressed before applying another layer of makeup to my face. The red mark looks stark in the morning light, and it takes a few minutes before the worst is covered up. Letting my hair fall in front of my face, I brace myself for what this morning will bring. My mother hadn't come up to my room. I left the door open and waited for her to seek me out, but she didn't. Instead, Rian had. My stomach twists now at the image of him standing at my bedroom door. His hair was still damp from a recent shower, and all I could think about was him naked. The thoughts were wrong, and I had to close him out. Sometimes he was too much, for too many reasons.

Noise in the kitchen has me pausing at the door and adjusting my armor. I smile and step in. My mother smiles back, and that allows me to breathe a little. I'm aware of Rian sitting at the end of the table. His gaze weighs heavily on me, and I want to look at him, but I don't.

"Good morning." I take the cup of green tea from my mother.

"Good night?" My mother's eyes shine with an interest that she hasn't displayed before. I sit down and remind myself that I can do this.

"Yeah, I had fun."

The joy on my mother's face makes the lie worth it.

"I think I may have made a friend."

"Brittany? Rian told me she dropped you home."

That's why she hadn't come looking for me. I glance at Rian, and his eyes roam over my face like he's looking for something.

I nod and look back to my mother before taking a sip of my tea. "Yeah. She's so nice."

My mother pats my arm. "I'm so happy." She goes to the counter, and I focus on the sound of the knife hitting the glass chopping board as she cuts up my breakfast.

I take a peek at Rian. He's still watching me. My stomach tightens. His bottom lip is larger than the top, his tongue flicks out slightly, and my heart jumps. He knows I'm staring at his mouth. I look away as Henry enters the room.

Before he speaks, I see it in his eyes. Something is wrong. Something is very wrong.

"Willow, there is a detective here who wants to speak with you." The tea sloshes over my hand, driving me out of the chair.

"Dear God. Get your hand under the water." My mother takes the mug from me and ushers me to the sink. The surrounding sound is muffled and I pull out of her tight grip. She stares at me, and I know I need to keep it together. I push my hand under the cold stream of water and allow it to ground me.

"Did he say why?" My mother is trying to sound like she has no clue why a detective would be looking for me. I knew this day would come.

Taking my hand out of the stream of water, I turn to Henry.

"He didn't say."

"Where is he?" I try to smile.

"I let him wait in the front sitting-room."

My mother places her hand on my shoulder like she might be able to stop this. "I'm fine, Mother." I step away from her hand and into the hall. There is relief in ending this nightmare, yet fear has my legs wobbling. Heavy footsteps behind me have me turning.

"What are you doing?"

"You're not going in there on your own."

"You're not coming in with me," I say to Rian. A new fear grips me. He's going to know what I am.

He gets distracted and reaches out, touching my hair. "Yes, I am."

I pull away from him, wanting to demand an answer as to why he is doing this, but it is his home. I can't exactly stop him. My feet move and stop outside the sitting-room door. The heat of Rian behind me isn't a comfort. I spin around and push a hand against his chest. His heart beats firmly under my splayed fingers. I focus on my fingers and not on his heavy green eyes.

"Please. Just give me a moment alone." I'm frowning as I try not to cry. I don't want him to know what I am.

When he doesn't answer, I glance up at him. My heart bounces around in my chest. Being this close to Rian has me letting my guard down.

"One minute."

I don't pause, but remove my hand from his chest and step into the sitting room.

The detective rises. He has his blond hair parted down the center and brushed neatly on either side. He walks to me and offers me his hand with a crooked smile on his face. His blue eyes are soft; he doesn't look like a man who works in this line of work. He reminds me of a priest, he has that look that draws you in and makes you feel safe.

"Willow, I'm detective Lacy."

I place my hand in his. His handshake is firm and quick.

He reaches in and takes a small black notepad out of his jacket pocket. I sit down on one of the salmon colored couches across from him.

"You have a beautiful home." His words are kind, and once again, I think of a priest. Maybe that's the vibe he wants to give off, so I will spill all my sins at his feet.

"Thank you." I sit up straight and cross my legs. My heart has returned to a normal rhythm, and the fear I felt only seconds ago is gone.

"Chad Michaels was attacked last night. He's in a coma."

Bile claws its way up my throat. I'd hit him twice with the pool balls. Oh, God, had I damaged his brain? I'm not sure if I'm breathing. "That's terrible," I manage to say, and my voice comes out steady. The door opens, and Rian steps in. He literally gave me one minute.

The detective rises again. Rian holds up his hand. "Sit down."

Lacy does, and it's funny the control Rian has over people.

"Rian, I only need a minute with your sister."

I cringe at the word sister but hope it doesn't show.

"By all means, take as long as you want." Rian sits down beside me, and I want to tell him to leave, but because this isn't about my past, I feel steadier.

"It's okay, Detective Lacy, I don't mind him staying." I don't want this to be dragged out.

Lacy returns to his notepad. "I interviewed a few people at the party, and they said you fought with Chad." The door opens again, and my mother and Henry step in.

Why not?

My mother steps up to Detective Lacy with an outstretched hand, and he rises, taking it.

"What is this about?" My mother's voice sounds distressed.

"One of the party-goers last night was attacked. He's in a coma."

My mother steps away from Detective Lacy. "It was the party your daughter attended."

"My daughter wouldn't hurt a fly."

My chest tightens, and my skin erupts in goosebumps. More lies. When will it stop? "I didn't argue with him. We liked each other." All eyes turn to me, and I force a shy smile.

I give my mother an apologetic look before looking back at Detective Lacy. "Ask anyone who was there. We had a drink, a bit of a talk, and we went down into the basement for a game of pool—you know the rest."

"So, you never fought?" He's watching me intensely, so is everyone in the room.

"Well, initially, I turned him down, that may have looked like a fight. It depends on where you were standing, and how intoxicated you were."

His smile is quick as he closes the notepad. "And you were drinking too?"

"No. I don't drink."

My mother slowly sits down.

"Ever?" Why does it always surprise people that I don't drink?

"I don't see how that is relevant." Rian's voice is filled with irritation.

Detective Lacy raises a brow. "I suppose it isn't. Where were you last night?"

My stomach somersaults.

"With me," Henry speaks up.

"All night?" Detective Lacy asks.

"Yes. He never left my side."

Lacy nods and places the notepad in his pocket. He stands up. "Well, thank you for your time. I'll be in touch." He steps up to me and takes a card from his pocket. His eyes are kind again. Or maybe it's a trick of the light. "If you remember anything else, please ring me."

I take the card and give him a brief smile. "Thank you."

"Let's hope Chad pulls through, and he can tell us who did this horrible crime."

Rian steps close to him like there is a challenge in his words. "Yeah. So you can stop harassing innocent girls."

There is nothing innocent about me. I had hit Chad with the pool balls. I must have caused some kind of brain damage. I try to focus on the rug as I stand. I can't break, not now. Not in front of everyone.

Henry moves past Rian and walks the detective out the door before it gets further heated. I know my mother is glaring at me. One rule, no boys—and I had lied about breaking it. But I need to stick to that lie for now.

"I'm sorry, mother," I say the moment the door closes. Rian is still in the room, but right now, I need to fix this.

"I told you to keep away from boys. Now look what it has brought upon us."

"It was a kiss," I whisper the pained words. A stolen kiss. "I just wanted to fit in and be normal." My voice grows small because a part of that is the truth. I had wanted to fit in so badly that I had gone down into a basement with him.

"How can I trust you?" The look in her eyes tears at me. I've seen that look before and the room starts to spin.

"You can't." My words are only for her. Why would she trust someone like me?

Her anger dissolves like a tablet in water, and I'm in her arms. "Don't say that." Her words are harsh as she presses a kiss to my head.

"It was a kiss," she repeats. "Just one kiss." She kisses my head again, and I need to get out. I'm choking on her panic.

"I'm fine." I wriggle out of her hold as Henry arrives back in.

"Do I need to contact a lawyer?" Henry's words have my stomach twisting.

"Of course not. My daughter isn't..." My mother's angry words trail off—my gaze darts to Rian, who watches me.

"No, Henry, that isn't necessary. Unless kissing a boy is a crime?" I force a smile.

He half laughs. "No, it's not, Willow."

"Are you ready for work?" I'm nearly out the door at Rian's words. I have never wanted to get out of a room as bad as I do right now.

CHAPTER TWELVE

WILLOW

The car is too small. I roll down the window and the air that lifts my hair, refuses to fill my lungs. Closing my eyes, I bite my lip to try to stop the tremble. It's in these moments that I want to be ten again. I want to go back to that time and change it.

The car slows. I can taste the dust as Rian drives along the dirt road and slows down. I know we aren't at work, but I don't care.

The car grows silent under us, and I'm so aware of Rian. His smell circles me, and it's like a window is opened as the air trickles into my lungs, and I take a deep breath. The sound returns, and I open my eyes. Warm hands grip my face, and I'm staring into green eyes.

"Take a breath." His steady words have me taking a lung full of air. I can't stop taking in every single detail of Rian's face. His straight, long nose and heavy eyes are captivating. He's frowning, and I don't want him to. Reaching up, I touch between his brows, and his face relaxes. I want to touch him more. I've never wanted anyone like I want Rian. I know it's wrong. Everything about us is wrong. Taking in another lungful of air, I trail my fingers down his face, and he closes his eyes briefly before opening them again.

His tongue flicks out and wets his large bottom lip. I know what it feels like to kiss him. It's the earth shifting under your feet. It's the tilt of a room before you pass out. It's other-worldly.

That's Rian.

"Take another breath." His fingers tighten on my face, and I'm shifting closer as I inhale him. I feel drunk on the fumes of my past. It's slowly crawling up my legs and I'm waiting for it to suffocate me.

"I hurt that boy." The words explode from my lips. No tears come like I thought might with my confession.

"I hit him twice in the head with the pool balls."

Rian continues to hold my face, his thumbs stroke my temple. My core tightens, and I try to stay in the here and now and not fantasize about Rian's hands on me.

"That's not the worst part."

He doesn't flinch. His head has moved closer. I didn't see him move, but I'm sure his breath is fanning more on my face than before—it's warm and a comfort to me.

I know I need to stop. He's going to see what I am if I continue, but I need to say something. I need to say something real for just once.

"I don't feel bad. I don't have any remorse for hurting him." My heart quickens when Rian doesn't respond. "I'd do it again."

Excitement sends my temperature rising. There, I said it.

"Good."

That isn't the response I expected. "Rian, I put that boy in a coma."

He needs to see who he has his hands on.

He's holding me. His eyes flicker to my lips, and I hold still as his warm mouth presses down on mine.

It's like the edge of a jagged bottle on my soul. I want to pour myself into him. I grip his broad shoulders, and my core tightens. I want to break all the rules. I want to feel. His hands leave my face and the heat of his fingers rolls down my neck.

"Fuck me." I breathe the words into his mouth, and his whole body freezes.

I don't want to open my eyes; I don't want this to end. I don't need to be dragged back down to earth.

Rian's hands move down to my waist, and I open my eyes. His gaze swirls with a want I've never seen before. I feel shy now. I've never done it before, but I want to. I refuse to take my words back.

"If you don't, I'm sure I can find someone else." I'm ready to pull away.

His hands tighten on my waist. "Willow." He growls my name and my panties grow damp. My heart beats wildly, invigorated in the moment.

"Fuck me," I say it louder and slam a hand against his chest. I want him to hear me. I want him to do as I say. "You keep saying you want to fuck me. So here is your chance."

He licks his lips, and I don't know what's holding him back—panic dances at the edge of my vision like a vulture.

I slam my mouth down on his, overwhelmed with the desperation I'm feeling, and Rian responds to my kiss with a force that sends me back in my seat. He's over me, and excitement has my blood bubbling as he adjusts the seat so it's fully back.

He's hovering over me. "You didn't put Chad in a coma. I did. Honestly, I thought I had killed him, but obviously not." This is Rian. He has no remorse.

Just like you. A voice whispers in my head.

"Now, I'm going to fuck you, but I need you to be sure because I don't think I'll ever be satisfied with just one taste of you, Willow." He leans his body closer. His cock pushes against me, and the air catches in my throat. "If I take you, I won't give you up. You're mine."

"You hurt Chad?" That's what comes out of my mouth, yet all I can think about is that I will be his.

"He hurt you. I know what he did. I know how they all stood around as he put his hands on you."

I try to cross my arms over my chest, but Rian's too close. I feel uncomfortable with his words.

"I'm okay." I try to reassure us both.

"You will be once I finish the job I started."

My heart crashes against my chest. "He's in a coma. It's enough." If I was normal, I would be outraged or disgusted. But I'm not.

"He put his hands on you, Willow." Rian's free hand roams along my side, and I'm tempted to close my eyes at his touch.

"When we lose control, we do things that we can regret. But what you are talking about isn't a moment of lost control. It's premeditated." I know too much about that. "That's where you must draw the line." I reach out and touch his face. He doesn't answer me, and I don't mind. I've said my piece.

"That's the offer." My cheeks flame as his cock grows against my stomach. I haven't had sex, and now I'm not sure about my words, but I don't want to talk about Chad.

Rian isn't responding with words, his body pushes closer to me. "I'm also a virgin, so…" I dare him to say anything.

He surprises me when he grins. "I know."

I want to ask him how he knows, but I don't.

"Here is the new deal. I get to touch you now, and I'll take you up on your offer of sex another time."

My stomach clenches with excitement at the thought of Rian's hands on me. Am I actually thinking of crossing the line with him?

His lips touch mine gently, and I can sense how much he is holding back. I don't want him to. I want to feel the savagery that I expect from Rian. But he isn't giving it to me. His tongue plunges into my mouth, and I can't stop the groan that falls from my lips. The car shakes as traffic moves past us. I know it's daylight, but I don't care. I want to leave the here and now, and Rian is that doorway for me.

His hand touches the waistband of my pants and with expert fingers he pops the button. I'm damp and he's going to know how much he turns me on. His large hand slips inside. Too much roars in my system and I inhale deeply. Tasting Rian. My hands grip his shoulders, dragging him closer to me. I want more of him. His kiss turns harsher and that's exactly what I want. My kiss is as frantic as his. I'm grinding against him and I start to beg. It doesn't make sense. I'm begging him for more.

"Please, Rian." I don't finish. My head falls onto his shoulder as he drags my pants down to my knees. I open my eyes and fall into his oasis before he dips his finger inside me. It's invasive, and I freeze briefly. His free hand grips the back of my neck, and his breath fans across my face as he draws his fingers out before moving them back in. His movements quicken, and I'm moving with him. I'm riding his hand while looking into his eyes, and it's terrifying to give him this control, but hope blossoms inside me as his fingers drive deeper inside me. I hope that I'm not as dead inside as I thought I was. My core tightens around his hand, and I'm pushing myself down on him, begging for more. I'm reaching a height that scares me. Rian's hand tightens on my neck. The burn has me pumping faster along with his fingers. I'm ready to give in and shatter on his hand, but he pumps faster, his thumb runs along my clit, and I dig my nails into his shoulders.

My lip trembles as I fall deeper into his moss-green eyes. I've always danced on my own, but being in his arms and feeling this high, cracks the walls around me. I don't think I could ever dance on my own again.

I call out as my body shakes and quivers. I cum on Rian's fingers. I can't catch my breath. The warm air I drag into my lungs tastes of heat, Rian, and my arousal. Rian's movements slow, and I start to come down from my high. I'm waiting for the shame and self-disgust, but it doesn't come.

Rian removes his hand, and I grip him tighter. I don't want him to move. This cocoon I don't want to leave. I drag him closer to me, and his body pushes against mine. His arousal seems even bigger now.

"Tell me lies." My breathing is still unsteady as I grip on to Rian. My lips linger along his neck, and I press a kiss there. His skin is warm, and I kiss it again.

"This won't happen again." His voice is deeper than I have ever heard it.

"That's not a lie," I confirm as I kiss his neck again.

"I don't want to fuck you right now."

My body tightens, and I consider doing it. I want to know what going that high with Rian would feel like.

"Chad will wake up from the Coma."

I stop kissing his neck. "Rian."

"He put his hands on you." Rian presses a kiss against my neck, and he forces me back into the seat. His mouth is warm and moist, and the kiss sends shivers down my body. He's too much.

"I won't let it stand." Rian kisses my collar bone, and I arch my body against him. I'm losing myself, but that's what I wanted.

"I'm telling you to leave it alone."

His laughter is quick and sends shivers racing across my flesh.

He leans out, and his eyes have darkened. "Are you telling me?" He repeats, and I see the challenge in his voice.

"Yes. I'm telling you. You will let Chad live."

Rian smirks, and I'm not feeling so brave now. "What happens when he opens his eyes and tells Detective Lacy what I did?"

"He won't," I whisper the half-truth.

"Are we still lying to each other?"

"I would never lie to you, Rian."

His laughter has me wanting to squeeze my legs together, but he's still laying between them.

He leans in slowly and captures my lips between his. "You're mine now." His words have my heart pounding, and I hate the crushing feeling that's consuming me. Sadness chokes me, and now I realize allowing him to touch me was a huge mistake. A mistake that can never happen again.

CHAPTER THIRTEEN

RIAN

She won't look at me now. She's turned her head away, her hair acting as a shield. My cock is still rock hard, and I can't find the strength to move. I've never wanted anything so bad.

"This can't happen again." She bites her bottom lip.

Anger boils through my system at her words. With Willow, it is two steps forward and ten back. I'm not accepting it.

"You should have thought about that before you asked me to fuck you." My sharp words have her gaze snapping up to mine. If I leaned in, I could kiss her traitorous mouth and stop the words from pouring out.

Her brown eyes grow wide, and I see her darkness. She's ready to snap, and I can't help myself, but I want to push her.

I move quickly and kiss her, she reacts by slamming a hand to my chest. I don't break the kiss until her hand strikes my face. The sting across my cheek has me leaning away from her. I grin as her chest rises and falls rapidly. I want to keep pushing. I want to see what happens. But in the space of a second, she's shutting down. Her vibrant brown eyes fade like dying embers.

"I shouldn't have done that." Her monotone has me getting off her. I climb back into my seat and turn away, giving her a minute to fix her clothes.

"Why?" I take in a slow breath. I'm not pissed that she hit me, I'm pissed that she's shutting me out. I try to think of something other than her, but it's impossible. Her smell has infiltrated my car, and she's all I can smell. I glance at her as she fixes her cardigan.

"Violence solves nothing." She finally looks up at me.

I love how her lips are red and swollen—my cock twitches painfully. "It solves most things for me."

"Rian…" Her voice holds a pleading that I won't ever give into.

"I'll make a deal with you." I turn more so I'm facing her fully.

She shakes her head, sending blonde waves across her shoulder. "No deals. That's it. It's over. I shouldn't have said what I said."

"Which part?"

She wrings her hands on her lap. "You know which part." Her voice is low.

Yeah, I'm going to make her say it. "You said a lot, Willow. So you'll have to be more specific."

Her brown eyes harden, and she gives a curt nod. "Fine. About wanting you to fuck me. I shouldn't have said it."

I shrug. "But you did." I start the car, ending the conversation.

"It was a mistake," Her words are low, but I hear them.

"A mistake is when you do something once, or, in your case, say something once. You didn't just say it once, Willow. So, it wasn't a mistake." I tighten my hands on the steering wheel. "What exactly are you afraid of?" I want to pull over. I want to make her tell me. I want to kiss her. I want *her*.

"I'm not afraid, I don't want you." Her raised voice has me glancing at her. Her cheeks are glowing a soft red.

I laugh. "Do you know why I like you?" I slow down as I make the turn into the airstrip.

She doesn't answer.

"There is a darkness in you that calls to me. You aren't this good girl you pretend to be." I slow down and glance at Willow. She's staring out the window. She might look like she's not listening, but she's twisted her hands so tightly that her knuckles have turned white.

"I'm not pretending."

I pull into the carpark and pull up close to the side door. Willow reaches for her seatbelt, and I grip her hand, making her look at me.

Fear shines in her eyes, and it's all-consuming. I tighten my hold on her hand, and her eyes widen. "Tell me what you're hiding."

Her gaze flickers down to my hand. "Or what? You'll hurt me?"

Her words are worse than the slap she gave me. I release her and sit back. She doesn't waste a second before bolting from the car.

My phone rings as I climb out too. "You want to tell me what you did last night?"

I close the door of the car and start to walk to the building. Willow follows behind, her arms wrapped around her middle like she has a belly ache.

"I was with you."

"Rian." The warning in my father's voice has me opening the door and letting Willow step in first. She won't meet my eye.

"Yeah, it was me."

"You let him live?"

"I didn't mean to. I thought he was dead." The noise of the room has me raising my voice.

"How are you going to fix this? I don't like leaving behind a trail that can be followed."

"I'll sort it," I answer. Willow still has her arms wrapped around her waist as she walks with her head down.

"Okay."

I'm ready to hang up when my father speaks again. "What did he do?"

"He hurt Willow." At her name, Willow's shoulders tense, and she half glances back at me. It's like she wants to look but decides against it.

"Okay, I'll speak with you later."

This time, I hang up and slip the phone into my pocket. I match Willow's steps. She's so small beside me. Her size makes you think she would be easy to break. I grin at that thought. I've never met anyone so resilient. I've never wanted to push someone's buttons so much. The thought of never getting to touch her again has me looking away. After that small taste, I know I'm hooked. I could never let her go.

"I know you'd never hurt me." Her words are spoken while she looks at all the vendors. When I don't respond, she glances up at me. I stop walking, and so does she.

"I shouldn't have said that." She tightens her cardigan around her waist.

"That's a lot of things you shouldn't have said today." I take a step closer, towering over her small frame. "Let's pretend today, you can say anything you want, and it will be erased. What would you say?"

She shrugs. "I don't know, Rian." I don't move, and she shrugs again.

"I've been waiting for you." Fox's voice springs up from my left.

"You'll have to wait a bit longer. I'm taking Willow to Margie." I start to walk again, and Willow looks over her shoulder.

"He's fine." I reassure Willow.

Something must have happened. That is why Fox is waiting for me. I walk Willow over to Margie and I don't get as much as a goodbye. She starts fixing pots that don't need to be fixed.

"If you need me just ring," I say.

"Okay," Willow speaks to the pots, and I hesitantly leave her.

Fox is halfway down the market. I walk through a cloud of cigar smoke and nod at each salute I get.

"Which do you want first? The good news or the bad news?" Fox asks, falling into step beside me. Blitz is walking down the aisle towards us.

"I'll take the good."

I don't think the good will really be good.

"We found Roger Smith."

I pause and glance at Fox. "I thought I told you not to seek him out."

"I didn't. I was tipped off and I moved in."

I stuff my hands in my pockets. My bandaged one still aches. I hadn't noticed it the whole time I was with Willow, but she has a way of making me block out everything around me—except her.

Fox tilts his head as Blitz arrives.

Blitz grins at Fox. "Did he tell you what he did?"

"I'm in the process of telling him. If you could just give me a second." Fox faces me. "He tried to run, so I shot him."

"Is that the bad news?"

"Yes." Relief swims in Fox's eyes.

"What did you find out?"

Blitz sneers. "He was too trigger happy. The guy took two steps and Fox plugged him." Blitz laughs.

"I overstepped; it won't happen again." Fox glares at Blitz.

"Who tipped you off?"

Fox stands straighter. "An informant that I gave his name to."

Fox uses street kids to gather information for him. He pays them pennies, but they are loyal to him. I nod.

"We will have to start over, won't we?"

I start to walk and Blitz pushes up his glasses before falling into step beside me. "You want to hit this place again?"

"That wouldn't be fruitful," Fox answers for me as he tries to keep up. The faster we move, the worse his limp becomes. I grin at Blitz when he notices Fox's struggle. I'm pissed that he went against me, but not pissed enough to do something about it.

We leave through the side door.

"The job we did last night went wrong." I take a cigarette from Blitz and wait for the lighter, as he sparks his up.

He blows smoke into the air.

"He's not dead; he's in a coma."

"Oh, fuck!"

"A job?" Fox moves around us. Blitz offers him a cigarette, and he declines with a curl of his nose.

"It wasn't work-related. It was personal," I say to Fox, before stepping away from them both and looking out at the chain-link fence. I have that feeling of being watched. Parked just outside is a black car that I've seen around the house before. Someone is following me.

"That car is following me," I say without looking away from it.

Blitz stands up beside me, and the car slowly pulls away. The blackout windows keep the driver hidden. I take another drag of the cigarette before crushing it under my boot. Glancing up at the sky, it's cloudless, and nothing moves in my airspace.

"For how long?" Fox asks, stepping up beside us.

"A while," I answer, turning to Blitz. "I need you to go to the hospital and make sure Chad doesn't come out of the coma."

"What do you want me to do? Pull the plug?"

I slap Blitz playfully on the face. "I don't give a shit. Just make sure this time he's dead."

My mind hasn't left Willow, and it should have. I had too much on my plate. The problem with the Rat Pack is it's growing, and now our only lead is dead.

"The next time I tell you not to go after someone, you listen to me." I don't look at Fox as I speak to him.

"I won't." He doesn't like being told what to do. It's not often I have to pull him up, but what he did was sloppy and out of character. I take another look at Fox.

"How long have we been friends?" I ask him.

He misses a beat in his footing before he finds his rhythm again. "Fifteen years. I punched you in the arm for taking my bike and you broke my nose."

"It's still crooked," Blitz says, moving past us.

Blitz enters the building, and I'm ready to follow—only Fox stops me.

"Why do you ask?"

I look down at my friend. "I'm feeling sentimental today."

Fox laughs as we enter the building. I haven't been away from Willow long, but it already feels too long. The market is busier today. I see lots of new faces. Each one has been cleared and noted at the gate. Anyone that comes here is kept in a permanent file.

He's a genius.

"I didn't see the drone out today." I checked the sky once I saw the car.

"No, I had to have the camera replaced. It should be back up in the next hour."

The gap in the front of his teeth always makes him look younger than his actual forty-something years.

"When it's back up, if you notice any cars loitering outside the fence line, especially when I'm here, will you make a note of it?"

"No problem."

I leave Fredrick and continue down to Margie's stall. The minute it comes into view, everything in me stills. Margie is there, but Willow isn't.

CHAPTER FOURTEEN

WILLOW

Bits of the green apple still cling to the side of the building. I'm staring at it like my secrets are falling on the ground for all to see. My legs are moving and I'm frantically picking the apple up off the ground. Emotions rise in me like a wave and I close my eyes, pushing my hands into the asphalt. The sharp, tiny stones dig into my palms, and I relish the pain.

Margie offered me the apple and I stared at it, it was like she was the wicked queen offering me a poisoned piece of fruit.

The green apple sat on top of the red lunchbox. My mother was aware of it as she moved stiffly around the kitchen. She didn't say anything, but she always watched for my reaction. It was his way of saying sorry without saying it. Once, green apples had been my favorite, but he had poisoned it. Ruined the once delicious fruit that I had enjoyed.

I'm aware of a door opening, rushed footsteps that pause. I close my eyes and inhale Rian.

"So, I take it you don't like green apples." His voice doesn't hold the humor that his words are meant to carry.

Bile rises up my throat, and I have to choke it back down. My heart beats madly. I don't want him to see me like this.

His footsteps are heavy until he reaches me. I open my eyes as he kneels down. "You have to talk to me, Willow. Let me help you."

I glance at him, and the adrenaline in me spikes at the idea of sharing my burden with someone—at having a friend.

I'm so alone.

"Maybe you could–just this once–walk away and pretend you don't see me," I say the useless words.

Rian raises both eyebrows. "I always see you, Willow."

The image of the red lunch box fills my mind, and I fear it's going to break it–that is, if my mind isn't broken already.

"Margie gave me a green apple." The words slip from my lips as I rise and dust off my hands. "Her nails were black, the smell of her clothes turned my stomach." I'm staring at the asphalt as I let the image of Margie's dirty hands consume me, until I can't see the red lunch box anymore. The walls that had been slowly closing in finally push back out, allowing me to breathe. "I didn't want to be rude, I didn't want to refuse, so, I took the apple." I glance at Rian and his moss-green eyes are focused on me, drinking up each word I say, so I decide to keep feeding them to him.

"She was watching me, waiting for me to take a bite, and I didn't want to. So I took the apple out here..." I point to the smashed piece of fruit.

A muscle works in Rian's jaw, and I'm ready and waiting for him to call me out on my lie, but he doesn't.

"I'm going to take you home."

Confusion has me rising. "Am I fired?"

I don't want to be. The mere thought of being trapped in the house again has a tremble enter my bones.

"No." Rian rises and holds out his hand for me to take. I don't accept. We walk back to the car. I've never wanted to run away from myself as badly as I do right now. I don't want to be around Rian. He's turning me into a mess, yet the thoughts of being completely alone have me considering asking him to take me to the garden. But I don't. I need this between us to end. I need to find my control. I need the numbness back—the numbness that he stole from me.

I glance at Rian. He appears so massive sitting in the driver's seat. His fingers are long, and I tighten my thighs at the memory of them inside me. One of his hands is bandaged, and I don't ask how it happened. I'm sure the person he went up against is either dead or faring far worse. No one gets the upper hand with Rian.

"Don't you ever get sick of the violence?" I ask.

"Don't you ever get sick of pretending?" His jaw is tight as he speaks.

I'm used to Rian smirking at me, but this irritation, I'm not used to. I don't answer him but stare out the window.

"I like hurting people."

I look back at Rian.

"I'm good at it."

I frown at his words. "I'm sure you're good at other stuff."

His jaw relaxes a fraction. "I'm good at a lot of things." His grin has heat pouring through me.

We don't talk after that. The drive home feels too short and I'm a mixture of sadness and confusion.

Once Rian turns off the engine, I get out of the car. The lights are on in the garage. There are three other cars parked in here. Two are my mother's, and one is Henry's. My mother doesn't let me drive. She doesn't feel I'm ready yet.

Rian gets out and steps into my path, blocking me from entering the kitchen. He towers over me and I have to crane my neck to meet his gaze.

He doesn't speak but takes a step closer. His gaze moves down to my lips, and I know this is dangerous. His hand reaches out and he touches my hair. He rubs it like it's some magical force. His gaze flickers up to mine and my stomach hollows out. Blood rushes to my ears.

Rian's mouth curves into a smile. His gaze flashes over my face before landing on my mouth again. My heart is threatening to leap from my throat when the garage door opens.

"Willow?" My mother's voice has everything in me growing still. Do we look like we are doing anything? He's too close. I step away from Rian and bump into his car.

"Everything okay, Rian?" My mother takes the three steps into the garage. I stand up straight as Rian turns to face my mother. I still can't see her.

"No, it's not." His voice is heavy with an accusation. I step away from the car and around Rian. My mother's skin is growing pale and worry filters through my system.

"What's wrong?" My mother's brown gaze bounces between me and Rian. I want to tell him to stop this, but I can't seem to move from my frozen state.

"I don't like you moving furniture around in the front sitting-room. I like that room just as it is."

Relief swims in my mother's eyes and that scares me more than anything. If I can see it, so can Rian.

"You looked worried there, Catherine. Like I had caught you in some big lie."

"I don't think your father would appreciate your bullying tactics." My mother looks past Rian. "Let's go, Willow."

"She's not a dog, Catherine." Rian's voice is cruel, and I feel like I'm dreaming. He's never spoken like this before, and I don't know what to do.

"Now, Willow!" The bark of my mother's voice has me moving. I don't look at Rian as I pass him.

My mother's spine is rod straight with anger. I follow my mother up to my room.

"Mother..."

"Don't!" She barks as we climb the stairs.

She enters my room and holds the door open for me to come in. I've had the sensation of being under water since my mother stepped into the garage. The muffled sounds erupt back into focus as she closes my bedroom door.

"You're beautiful. I see that now. I see how he looks at you." My mother's words aren't a compliment. "I see how you look at him."

I'm shaking my head. Bile claws up my throat. "He's my step-brother." I can't hold my mother's gaze as disgust has me almost expelling the meager contents of my stomach.

"We can't choose who we fall for." My mother takes my face in her hands, making me look at her. There is a smile on her face that has my lips trembling. "I know that. But what happens when you get too close?

What happens when the cracks start to show?" She releases my face. "What happens when he sees the real you?" She walks over to my nightstand. "Maybe someone like him would accept you." She opens the drawer and removes my phone. "Maybe." She says turning to me. I see the strain around her eyes. "Or maybe he won't." She steps closer to me and I fold my hands in front of me. "I've built a life for us here. I don't ask for much."

The image of my mother wavers and the air dries up in the room.

"Don't cry."

My tears obey and dry up.

"You have a choice to make, Willow."

I open my mouth to tell her I choose her, of course, but she holds up a hand.

"Don't tell me now. Think about it and give me your answer later."

I can't look away from the black device in her hands.

"Do you want this?"

She holds it out and a pain erupts in my belly. It's odd, it's only a phone, but it felt like a doorway to maybe something that could help me. Now I see it's a tool that tells my mother I'm betraying her.

"No."

She nods with a small amount of approval and satisfaction and leaves my room. I'm staring at the mirror across from me and all I see is an evil little girl who terrifies her mother with her secrets.

A scream lodges itself in my throat and I want to release it. Bending at the waist, I grip my knees and try to take in some air.

I need her to know that I'm sorry. I'm spinning, running from the room when I collide with a solid chest.

"What's wrong?" Rian's voice is as heavy as his hands that steady me.

It's all his fault. Taunting me. Always touching me.

I shove him away. "Don't touch me." My voice rises and it startles me. I clamp a hand across my mouth and storm back into my room. I close the door, but his foot stops it from closing and he's forcing his way in.

"Get out!" I try to keep the panic at bay.

"Shhh." He's locking the door.

I can't stop shaking my head. My mother. My mother. My mother.

"Get out." I run and slam both hands into his chest. "Get out, now." My hand connects with his face and he grabs both my arms, pinning them to my side before he drags me against his chest.

I can't move. I can't breathe. "What are you doing?"

I try to break free, but he holds me with a firmer grip. It's his warmth, it's his hard chest. It's his smell. I'm becoming familiar with him. It's all too much. The wall that has held everything in gives way, and the first tear falls. My body shakes, and I crumble into his arms. Rian releases my arms and picks me up off the floor, holding me to his chest as I cry my heart out on his shirt.

CHAPTER FIFTEEN

WILLOW

My chest tightens, and I swear it's going to cave in and crush my soul. No peace comes with the onslaught of tears, and Rian holds me tighter to his chest, making the stream of tears grow faster.

"You have to go." I sob out, and he shushes me.

I struggle against his chest. I need him to put me down. Rian's hold grows heavier, and we move lower as he sits on my bed, holding me against him like I might disappear. His heart thrashes against my ear.

"Tell me what's wrong." Rian's voice is deep, and it brings me to the surface of my pain. This time when I lean out, he gives me some space instead of crushing me to his chest.

"You have to go," I whisper, as salty tears fill my mouth. My tongue flicks out and licks the substance from my lips.

"Did she hurt you?"

My heart deflates at his words, I can't hold Rian's eyes. She's not the monster, I am. I'm shaking my head. A weakness has entered my system and I used the last of my energy to scramble out of Rian's arms. He releases me but still sits on my bed.

"Please leave."

He rises and towers over me. My stomach hollows out and a sharp pain erupts deep in my belly.

"You don't make this easy." He takes a step towards me. I hate how my bones quiver. All I want to do is step closer, but I hold steady as he closes the distance between us.

His large hands grasp my face, and his thumbs rub away all the falling tears before he leans in. His minty breath fans across my face. I close my eyes as Rian's mouth moves over my lips. He pushes his body closer to me and I stand on the tips of my toes, my hands automatically wrapping around his shoulders.

The kiss changes far too quickly and he's devouring me and all my agony. I forgot—for just a moment—how he can make my head spin when he kisses me, and how it feels like I'm levitating. It's never enough. He's too much.

I sink into the bed and my body is rippling with the feel of his on it. His cock prods heavily against me and I automatically spread my legs, allowing him to move closer. I moan into his mouth. His hands still hold my face steady as his tongue frantically enters my mouth, like he might not get to taste me again. His large thigh presses against my pussy, and I don't want to come undone so easily, but the sensation between my legs is almost painful in its intensity.

His hands leave my face and everywhere they touch, I come even more alive. My body throbs for him, and I know why my mother never allowed me to be intimate with anyone. It makes me feel too deeply, and right now I'm knee deep in pain, lust and darkness. I'm scrambling, once again, because of Rian. My heart beats wildly as I scan the room and try to even out my breathing. I'm trying to grasp for control. My armor is placed on my chest with shaky hands, but it liquifies off me and pools around my feet as Rian approaches me. He appears as breathless as I am. I hold up my hands and he stops walking.

"I need you to leave." I swallow and shake my head before looking at him again.

His nostrils flare and he flashes me a warning. "Willow."

"No, Rian. This is lust, that's all. I've never had these interactions with anyone, that's why I want them..." I need to add—with you—but can't.

His moss-green eyes grow darker, and I know I'm being cruel.

"I don't want to be with you. I want you to leave my room, now." I fold my arms across my chest, stopping the impulse that courses through me to step up to him and beg him to ignore me. This pull that I have towards Rian is dangerous, and I need to end it. I need to choose my mother. I bite the inside of my cheek until my mouth fills with a metallic taste.

"It didn't seem like you didn't want to be with me a moment ago." His shoulders tense and his jaw clenches. Fear skitters up my spine. I know he would never hurt me, but that doesn't stop a new fear from taking root and blossoming deep in my belly. I know what Rian is capable of.

He has no idea what you are capable of.

Warmth spreads through my hands and I wipe them along my trousers. "Get. Out," I say each word carefully. I'm falling, and I'm waiting to collide with something that will smash me. Blood roars in my ears as Rian takes another step towards me. His brows are furrowed. He looks terrifyingly dangerous—like a viper ready to strike.

"You still owe me a fuck." His words are delivered with a cruelty that has never been bestowed upon me by him before.

Anger flares inside me, and I wrap my hands behind my back so I don't strike him. "Fuck you."

His laugh is heavy with anger, and some part of me wants to stop this. I'm drawing a battle line with Rian, and it's a war I won't win. I try to soften my features and exhale a shaky breath.

"Please. Rian." I'm not beyond begging.

"Please what?"

I can't hold his gaze, it's too hateful right now. "Fine." I walk away from him and reach for the door handle. Warm and surprisingly gentle hands wrap around my arm. Rian's breath brushes the back of my neck.

"I'll leave this time, but I told you once before..." his voice is a whisper, and I close my eyes against the shiver that erupts across my skin, "You're mine, and I'm not letting you go, Willow." His warmth is gone and the door opens as Rian leaves my room. My knees threaten to buckle. I'm determined to end this agony inside me. I fix my hair and wash my face before leaving my room.

Entering the kitchen, a calmness washes over me. I'm giddy as I check to make sure it's empty. The counters have recently been wiped down. The smell of disinfectant is heavy in the air. The knives rustle in the drawer as I drag it open. Checking over my shoulder to make sure I'm still alone, I take one out and stuff it in the waistband of my trousers. I hiss as it nicks the skin. I don't examine anything but relish in the burn across my flesh, it's like an old friend, one I love and hate.

Leaving the kitchen, I make it to my bedroom without seeing anyone. Locking my door, I remove my cardigan and lay it neatly on the bed before doing the same with my shirt. The knife continues to slice into my flesh. Each burn has me clamping down on the inside of my cheek. Once I'm in my bra, I enter my bathroom. I release the blood that pools in my mouth down the sink. I refuse to meet my eyes in the mirror. It's none of her business, anyway.

Removing the knife, I wrap my hand around the hilt. I have no inclination to end my life. I have no desire for that. Turning my left arm around, so my palm is face-up, I count the ten scars that saved me from losing control. I don't look at them and feel these were my lowest moments. These were my strongest! I did what needed to be done, just like I need to do now. I press the blade heavily on my skin, watch the flesh part, and blood rush down my arm. It's a beautiful kind of pain as I close my eyes and sink to the floor. It's so red, and I love this moment. It's so close to being euphoric. I'm floating and free with bliss. Slowly the pain starts to register, and I drop the knife. My mind starts to speed up with all I need to do. I need to clean and return the knife before it's noticed. No, I'll get rid of the knife. I need to bandage my wound and clean up. I need to find my mother and tell her I choose her. With a new found purpose, I give myself one more moment watching the red liquid flow from my arm. I need to stop it before I grow too weak. Grabbing a towel, I push against the wound and cringe as it turns pink. I'll have to get rid of it.

After wrapping my arm and putting on fresh clothes, I feel more like Willow. The one thing that is bothering me is the towel. I wrap it and the knife in another towel and put it against my back, using my shirt and cardigan as a harness against it. I'm careful with my steps as I leave my room and make my way downstairs. I think about entering Rian's domain and dumping the towel there—I'm sure he has plenty soaked in blood. The idea of his bedroom springs to mind, and I grip my damaged arm and squeeze the thought away.

"Willow." I turn slowly and smile at the man in front of me. His large frame would intimidate anyone. He pushes black glasses up on his nose.

"Have you seen Rian?" He asks, folding huge arms across his chest. The movement strains the dark blue material of his jumper.

"I can't say I have." I let the lie fall from my lips. I have no idea where he is now, and I don't want to bump into him.

"Okay." He hesitates and I see a question on his lips, so I turn away before he can ask me anything else. I walk carefully, making sure the towel doesn't shift. I've packaged it perfectly, I remind myself.

Outside the air is cool against my skin and I dispose of both towels, while moving rubbish on top of them so they are well hidden.

"What are you doing?" The same anger is still in Rian's voice. I close the lid on the trash can before turning to Rian.

"Your friend is looking for you."

Rian glances behind me, and I don't think he's aware that he's taken two steps closer to me. My heart gallops as I think of the contents in the bin.

I move away like I've nothing to hide. I'm expecting him to forget about the bin, but he walks past me.

"I was taking out the rubbish." My voice sounds devoid of any emotion, and I use that to bring my heart rate under control. I hear the lid go back on the bin before I turn to Rian.

Relief swims through me, and with that emotion comes something deeper. Folding my arms behind my back, I squeeze the cut and allow the pain to take over everything else.

"Willow..." Rian stuffs his hands into his trousers pockets. He hunches forward and his eyes hold a vulnerability I've never seen before. It's beautiful and deadly all at once and right now, I need to use it to my advantage.

I exhale and force a smile. "I didn't take you for someone who couldn't take no for an answer."

It's a flick of a switch. He's standing taller, his eyes darker, and he flinches like I've burnt him. He displays a smile of his own, only his sends dread pooling in the pit of my stomach.

I'm aware of the approaching figure, and all I can hope is that it isn't my mother. When I look back towards the house, I see Blitz approach us. I use it as my moment to escape Rian.

CHAPTER SIXTEEN

RIAN

"Go on in. I'll be there in a minute."

Blitz pauses but goes back into the house. I'm staring at the bin. Willow was shaken, and I've never wanted to know so bad what someone is hiding because she is hiding something. She looked pale and shifty. Her smile was too wide, and now I know trying to smash down her walls isn't the answer. I need to peel the layers back slowly. She has no idea how patient I am. She needs to understand that when I said she was mine, I meant it.

Taking the lid off the trash can, I see the edge of a white towel. Pushing aside all the scraps of food and packaging, the towel becomes more visible.

I take it out, and it unravels. I've seen my fair share of blood—I've spilled a lot of it—but the sight of the soaked towel sends something primal racing through me. I want to grab her and examine every inch of her body. I open the towel, and a knife tumbles out onto the ground. The tip is smeared in blood. I have no idea what any of this means. Gathering up the towel and knife, I tuck them under my arm and return to Blitz.

When I enter the room, he eyes the contents in my arms but doesn't question it. I place them on the side table.

"The detective was with Chad. I couldn't do anything."

"So, he's still alive." I turn to Blitz.

He removes his glasses and rubs his eyes like he's been up all night. "I can't do anything when he's being protected."

This is a headache I don't need. "Put someone at his bedside at all times. If he wakes up, we need to know." I'll have to make a personal visit.

Blitz sits down and puts his glasses back on. Leaning against the sideboard, my gaze keeps drifting to the white towel. *What's she up to?*

"So you and Willow?" Blitz grins at me. I don't exactly discuss her, but I won't hide my feelings either.

"She will come around to the idea."

Blitz snorts a laugh. "Brute force can work, but I'm not sure about her."

"Brute force isn't my style." I flick the towel open and remove the knife. Holding it up to the light, I study the blood.

She hit Chad when he attacked her, had someone else hurt her? The thought has me nearly curling my fingers around the blade. Is she panicking right now?

Irritation courses through me. Why didn't she come to me for help?

"Everything alright?" Blitz asks while jutting his chin towards the blood-soaked towel.

"I'm not sure."

I look at Blitz now. I trust him with my life. "Tomorrow at the market, I'm going to put Willow with you."

"I'm searching the floor space."

I nod and push away from the sideboard. "I know, but I can't leave her with Margie." I sit down beside Blitz, still holding the knife.

"I need you to suggest she helps you."

"I'll do it, but why do I have to suggest it? Why don't you?"

I twirl the knife at the tip of my finger before glancing at Blitz. "She'll go against me." My jaw clenches at that thought. She's panicking lately. Her panic is forcing her to push me away. I need to make her trust me—that way, she will finally open up and tell me why she dumped a knife in the bin outside.

I'm sitting in the kitchen as I do every morning. Catherine moves around, making Willow her green tea. I've thought about telling her to make Willow a coffee, but that would only get Willow in trouble. She's watching me with her hateful eyes. The bang of the spoon on the table is meant to get my attention, but she can fuck right off. The way she treats Willow, I have always let slide, but lately, it is getting harder to ignore.

I turn my attention to the doorway as Willow enters. She's wearing trousers and a shirt that's covered by a frumpy cardigan. My hands remember the softness of her skin. She does the same thing. She refuses to look at me as she kisses her mother's cheek and takes her cup of tea. This is the point where she normally sits down and finally looks at me, but this morning she doesn't.

"I was looking for you last night." She stays standing as she speaks to her mother.

"I was out." Catherine glances at me, but Willow makes it appear like I'm not here.

I grin into my coffee as she continues to ignore me.

"I needed to give you my answer."

Once again, I'm aware of how much Catherine stiffens. "Later, we can talk. Now sit and eat your fruit."

Willow hesitates. "Later." Catherine reminds her, and they are doing a piss-poor job at trying to appear that everything is okay.

Was Willow looking for her mother last night to help her with whatever situation called for a knife and a towel drenched in blood?

Willow sits down, and her gaze is drawn to me. I smile at her, and she quickly starts eating her breakfast.

"Oh, I wanted to ask. I'm missing a knife. Has anyone seen it?" Catherine is watching Willow, and so am I. Willow looks up and shakes her head.

"I don't cook. You know me..." She smiles. "I'd burn water." Catherine looks relieved and smiles at her daughter.

Willow is a good liar. "I did."

Willow's gaze shoots up to me, and her skin pales. I hold her terrified gaze and watch as her eyes pool wider. Releasing her, I stand up with my mug of coffee.

"I needed it, and I highly doubt you would want it back."

Catherine curls up her nose at me as I pour the coffee down the sink. "I never knew we were counting the knives—I feel like I'm back in prison."

This topic ruffles Catherine's feathers. It's not public knowledge. My father makes sure to keep it buried.

Willow's spoon rattles against her bowl, and I want to see her reaction to that. "I have work, Catherine, so I'll leave you to count your knives while I take your daughter with me."

Her lips form a thin line of anger, and I wink at her. "Are you ready, Willow?"

I relax when my gaze lands on my beauty. She hasn't looked at me, but that's okay. I'll soon have her alone. She kisses her mother on the cheek and pauses. "I want to talk the moment I come back."

"Okay." Catherine sounds distant, and I really don't give a fuck.

Willow is quiet most of the drive, but I'm aware of how many times she glances at me. "Ask your question. I won't hold you to anything," I say as I signal to turn onto the road towards the airstrip.

"I don't even think asking you why you were in prison is a question. I can think of hundreds of reasons."

I grin at that as we pass the barrier. "Give me one."

"You killed someone." I glance at Willow. She's watching me with wide eyes, but I don't answer her.

"How did you get caught?" I park, and my intrigue with Willow keeps growing to a very dangerous level. I turn off the car and unbuckle my seat.

"That is a very unusual question to ask." Now I turn to Willow, and she tries to hide her gaze from me. Reaching across, I touch her chin, and her whole body tenses.

"It doesn't matter." She drags her face away from me and undoes her belt.

"It's not *how did I* get caught, but *why did I* get caught."

I regain Willow's attention; she gives me a confused look.

"I needed to get inside the prison, so I robbed a liquor store. I made sure it was a mess. I got caught and made sure my lawyer was crap. I got a week behind bars."

"You went to prison on purpose?" Willow shifts closer, and I don't think she's aware of what she is doing.

"Yes. I wanted to send a personal message—no better way than to do it myself."

She's shaking her head in disbelief. My father had been raging over my decision.

"What was it like?"

"Getting my revenge?" I ask.

Willow shakes her head and lets out a shaky breath. "Prison." Fear has her mouth dragging down. I think of the towel and the knife.

"If you hurt someone, I can help you."

Willow jerks back like I slapped her, and I don't want to play this game. If she's in trouble, I can fix it.

"I found the towel and knife. So don't deny it. Just tell me what happened. I'll help you."

"You think I hurt someone?" Why does she sound so fucking pained?

"I think someone hurt you, and you protected yourself."

Her laugh is bitter. "Why? Good old Willow would never hurt someone first?"

"I don't believe you would."

She shakes her head and reaches for the door, but I grip her arm.

"Let me go, Rian."

"I have always let you go when you needed to run, but this time, Willow, I can't." I wrap my hand tighter around her wrist.

My mind won't slow down. "If you're in trouble, I will help you."

"Jesus Christ, Rian. I'm not in any trouble." She glances down at my tightening fingers.

"That's not a fucking answer."

Her eyes widen at my tone, and I hate frightening her. I loosen my grip slightly.

"I want an answer," I say this without growling.

Her heartbeat throbs in her neck, and she holds her head higher. "You won't understand."

Her cheeks redden.

"Try me." I'm not saying try me. I'm saying tell me now.

"You're hurting me." She raises both brows.

My touch isn't hard on her wrist. She glances down, and I release her.

In the most mechanical movements, Willow rolls up her cardigan. "I'll tell you. But this is where it ends. You can't force answers out of me." She's angry as she opens the buttons on her shirt and rolls up the sleeve. She turns her arm around so I can see all the white scars and the one that is bandaged.

It takes a lot to shock me, but this right here does. I'm looking into her dark empty eyes.

"Don't look at me like that. I told you, you wouldn't understand. Now you've seen it." She tries to push the shirt back down, but I reach out and take her wrist in my hand. My fingers run across all the raised skin before I start to pick at the bandage. Willow tries to pull her arm back, and right now, I don't care if I'm hurting her. I need to see it.

"Rian," her voice rises, and I yank her closer. I'm careful as I pull off the bandage. The cut is raised and starts to bleed slightly.

"You're making it bleed."

"This is not okay," I speak to the cut before looking up at Willow. She stops fighting me. "Stop looking at me like that. This is none of your business." This time I allow her to take her arm back. I can't look away as she bandages her wrist.

"Did you do it because of Chad?"

Willow fucking laughs as she fixes her shirt. "I told you, you wouldn't understand."

My fist collides with the steering wheel, the horn blares, and Willow jumps in her seat.

I hate the fear I see on her face. "This isn't funny." I want to grab her, but I don't want to hurt her.

She swallows, her laughter gone. "I wasn't trying to kill myself. It just grounds me."

I rub my forehead. "I have no fucking clue what you are talking about."

Her eyes swim.

"Make me understand this, Willow."

She shrugs like this isn't a big deal. "It just gets my emotions in check and then I'm good."

"For how long? I mean, there are several cuts."

"Eleven." She says quickly.

"Does your mother know?" Willow glances away from me. "That fucking cunt."

Willow swings back around to me, and it's the first time I've seen such a strong emotion on her face. "Don't speak about her like that. She doesn't know. How dare you?" Her face tightens, and I sit back in my seat and try to reign in my anger and confusion.

"I want to go to work." Willow reaches for the door and gets out. I don't stop her.

CHAPTER SEVENTEEN

WILLOW

I stand beside the car, watching Rian as he gets out and shuts the door. My heart rate won't slow. I'm not embarrassed that he saw my marks. I'm afraid of what he will do with that knowledge. He locks the car and stares across at me, and I hate the look I see in his eyes.

He's already regretting ever going near me. I start to walk. Rian can have anyone he wants. I take another peek at his side profile. No one would ever refuse him. His wide shoulders are stiff, and I want to make him look at me. I don't blame him for the disgust I see in his eyes. My mother is right—if he really knew me, he would run. Even a man like Rian doesn't want to be with someone who is a mess like me.

Rian opens the door, and we step into the noisy market. Everyone's gaze shifts to us, and I feel so exposed. My legs don't move, and Rian's warmth penetrates my back. Leaning into him crosses my mind just to see if he would push me away.

This is what you wanted, Willow, I remind myself. I am going to choose my mother. This evening when I go home, I'm going to tell her and ask her to speak to Henry. I can no longer work here. As I start to walk through the market, Rian falls into step beside me, but no matter how many times I look at him, he doesn't return my gaze.

My stomach twists at his rejection. I tug my sleeves down over my arms like my wounds are visible for all to see.

The movement has Rian's eyes on me. "Are you sore?"

I shake my head and look up at him. "No."

He quickly looks away. I clamp down on the inside of my cheek, hating how he can't even look at me.

Blitz, his friend, is approaching us, and maybe it's a good thing that he takes Rian away. He smiles at me, and I force one back.

"I was wondering if Willow could help me today?"

I quickly glance at Rian and shove my hands behind my back. He nods his head. I didn't expect that. He's letting his friend just take me. Hurt races through my system. He can't bear to be around me.

"Could I have a word with you?" I focus on Rian. He nods at me but keeps his gaze over my head.

"I will just be a moment." He tells Blitz, and I follow Rian.

What are you doing? I want to tell my inner voice to shut up as I follow Rian through a steel door along the side of the building. We enter a room that has rows of steel shelves, all stacked with boxes. The lighting here is dim.

"What is it?" Rian's voice makes me regret my decision to want to be alone with him.

I can't bear his rejection. The disgust I keep seeing in his eyes is piercing me. I don't think but act. I step into his space and reach up, pressing a kiss to his bottom lip. Rian doesn't react, and I grip his face, dragging him closer to me. I continue to kiss him, and finally, he responds. I'm airborne, and my legs respond, wrapping themselves around his waist. My back is pressed against a shelf as Rian devours my lips. He still wants me. I'm tugging at his jacket, and he helps me get it off him. I want to touch his skin, his shirt is next, and I take a moment and break the kiss just to stare at him. He's chiseled, and I think to myself, of course he is. My gaze roams across his wide shoulders, and my stomach squirms when I meet his moss-green eyes. My backside rests on a shelf, and I love the feel of Rian's hard cock pushing against my core. He takes my face gently and places the softest kiss on my lips.

"What are we doing?"

I shake my head. "No questions." I lean in, keeping my eyes open and press my lips against his. He responds by capturing my bottom lip. His hands work quickly, pulling off my cardigan. My shirt takes the both of us to get off because I have so many buttons. The air kisses my flushed skin, and I have to sit still as Rian drinks me in. He makes me feel beautiful when I look back into his eyes that swim with pure lust. His lips move across mine, and I push myself harder against him. When he moans into my mouth, it's the best sound I've ever heard. My fingers roam along the band of his trousers. I dip two fingers under and love how his muscles bunch together everywhere my fingers touch. Rian's large hand grips a hand full of my hair as he tilts my neck, giving himself more access to my mouth. His tongue enters and it's my turn to groan. Dampness pools between my legs and I grind myself against his shaft.

His lips leave my mouth and make a burning pathway along my neck. My fingers keep moving along the band of his trousers and finally the want wins out and I unbutton his trousers. Rian is breathless as he grips my face and makes me look at him.

"No questions," I quickly say before he ruins it.

He's breathing heavily as he stares down at me. I'm terrified that he is going to stop and I'll never experience this. I am giving myself this one time with him.

"Rian." His name falls from my lips on a breathless whisper and he's lifting me up and removing my trousers. The steel under my backside is cold. Goosebumps break out across my skin as Rian's gaze touches all of my flesh while he removes his trousers. His thighs are roped with muscles and I swallow at the bulge in his boxers. He pushes them down and his cock springs free. I have a moment of wanting to back away at the sheer size of it. Rian's arms wrap around my waist as he drags me towards him. I meet his gaze and I keep my focus there. I allow my fingers to roam across his chest and shoulders.

"You're so pretty." Looking at him now is hard. I wonder if he knows how breathtaking he is.

"Pretty?" His lip quirks up as he pulls me closer. His fingers pull at my panties and my stomach tightens with fear and anticipation as he drags them down my legs. He stands back, and his gaze slowly and painfully roams across every inch of my flesh. When he steps back, I'm already seeking his warmth. His large cock presses against my opening and I'm bracing myself for the pain I have been told will come.

His kisses are gentle. "You need to relax." I'm waiting for him to enter, but he continues to deepen the kiss, his cock grinding against my clit. I relax as I grow wetter. My body pushes against him, wanting it. He releases my face and repositions himself. I look at him as he places his cock at my entrance. I bite down on the hiss as he enters me. Pain slices through me, but with it comes a pressure that starts to push its way inside me. Rian slams his mouth down on mine as he pushes deeper in. Pain flares, and my eyes water when he's fully in. I feel too stretched and he starts to move out slowly. The muscles on his arms clench and bunch together under my fingers as he tries to pace himself. Opening my eyes, I continue to kiss him as he pushes back in, this time it isn't as gentle, but with the pain comes the pressure that threatens to fill me up. Rian must sense me looking at him and he opens his eyes. His lips press against mine as he withdraws and enters me again. My fingers dig into his arms and I feel myself grow wetter with each time he enters me. My body burns and starts to shake as the pressure keeps climbing inside me. Rian's movements grow faster and his breaths labor against my lips. I grip him tighter as my heart threatens to rip from my chest. I'm staring into his eyes and I have an overwhelming need to cry. Slamming my eyes shut dampens the emotion.

"I want to see you cum."

I open my eyes at Rian's breathless words. He's moving faster and deeper, but his gentleness I never expected. I can feel the high build inside me, just like when he had touched me in his car, only this is ten times more and I'm waiting for it to end. I don't believe it can drag me any higher, and yet it does.

"Rian." His name has him pumping harder, and I hit a high that I never knew existed before. I shatter in his arms. His movements grow frantic before he spills his seed inside me. I feel it all, and it drags my own climax out. It's like my nerve endings are on fire as I slowly come down. I can barely breathe, and now, in the silence, all I can hear is our mingled breathing and the sound of the market somewhere in the distance.

Rian's flesh is sweaty, and I cling to it as I rest my head in the crook of his neck. His cock is still inside me, and I sense it twitching. I'm tightening my hold on him because I can't let him see me cry. This is my way of saying goodbye. I'm not angry. I'm glad I gave him this part of me. I don't think anyone else would have been so gentle. I could sense his need, and he held back and placed me first. I press my lips to his neck. His hands move up and down my back, sending shivers skittering across my flesh.

I press another kiss to his neck before my tongue flicks out, and I capture a falling tear.

"Pretty?" Rian's word makes me laugh, and I finally let him see me. I'm smiling up into his moss-green eyes.

"Very pretty," I say.

He doesn't smile. Instead, his hands grip either side of my face. "You should see yourself right this moment, Willow. You're fucking everything."

My heart skyrockets, and my smile slips. "You could have just called me pretty. No need to go so far."

His laugh has my stomach squirming. "Pretty is for flowers and apparently me." His hands tighten on my face, and his smile leaves those perfect lips. "You aren't pretty. You're disarming, and you're mine." Rian leans in and presses his lips against mine, and I know I should correct him, but I only have this one day with him, and then I will be ready to give him up. I return the kiss with my own want for him. I hold nothing back, and I feel him grow inside me.

"Really?" I'm searching his face.

"Really." He grins before dragging my mouth back to his.

CHAPTER EIGHTEEN

WILLOW

"What?" His face lights up when he smiles, and I can't stop smiling at him. I shrug. Rian's hands still roam along my bare back, and I close my eyes against the delicious shiver that assaults my flesh.

"Nothing." I open my eyes. My breath hitches with how close his mouth is to mine.

It's a distant sound, but it takes a second for my brain to register the noise of the stockroom door opening.

"Oh, shit."

Rian drags me closer, which isn't possible—as he faces Blitz. My cheeks burn, and I bury my face in Rian's neck.

"He's gone." Rian drags me out of the crook of his neck.

Being interrupted is a stark reminder that this is a once time thing. "We better get dressed." I press a kiss to his shoulder because his mouth would undo me again.

"You're cold." Rian slowly detangles himself from me, and I'm ready to jump down when he places a large hand on my thigh. "Stay there."

I nod, not sure why he wants me to stay here. Rian isn't shy about his nakedness as he gathers my clothes off the ground and steps back to me. He holds out the shirt, and I slip one arm in at a time. He's focused on buttoning it up, and I take the moment to remember every little detail of his face. His gaze snaps up to me.

"This shirt is ugly."

A real laugh falls from my lips and rocks my belly. All my clothes are ugly. I know that. But they are muted and understated, just the way they should be.

Once he has the shirt buttoned up, he doesn't move. Instead, he runs his hand across my wrist. The bandage is bulky under the shirt.

"This can't happen again, Willow."

My heart slams against my ribcage. "Of course." I manage to force down my emotions and try to withdraw my hand, but Rian doesn't let my arm go.

He shakes his head. "This can't happen again, Willow." He repeats. When I don't answer him, he continues. "If you want a high or a release, come to me." A sinful grin tugs at his lips. "I'm sure I can help you." He releases my wrist, and I can't look at him.

This is the last time I will allow him to touch me. I nod so he will allow me to finish getting dressed. My cardigan comes next, and then he helps me into my trousers. I can't stop looking at his naked body. He's even more intimidating naked. His body is carved to perfection. I can't find a flaw.

When I'm dressed, Rian pulls on his slacks. I can feel his gaze on me every so often. He picks up his black shirt but doesn't put it on. Instead, he walks back to me and holds out his palm. Right in the center is a white circular scar.

"I was in church."

I can't stop the surprise that spreads across my face. "The church is still standing?" I ask.

His lips tug up, and he leans in, placing a kiss on the side of my mouth.

"Yes, it is. It was Jesus on the crucifix that got my attention. That and one of the choir girls."

Rian grins, and my stomach swirls.

He holds out his hand again. "I wanted to know what it would feel like to have a nail driven through my hand."

My fingers skim across the scar. "You didn't!"

"I did." I can hear the humor in his voice. "It hurt like a motherfucker."

I'm trying to focus on his words and not his chest or the idea that he liked a choir girl. He was drawn to what he perceived as good girls. Cutting this off is the best idea. I am the furthest thing from a good girl.

There is a silence between us as I continue to touch the scar.

"Don't hurt yourself again."

"Don't you ever hurt yourself again either." I finally look up at him.

"It sounds like we have a deal. If I feel the need to drive a nail through my hand again, I will come to you for a high instead."

He stands there staring down at me with a soft smile waiting for my reply. I give him a smile. "Get dressed before anyone else comes in."

Rian doesn't move immediately. He's watching me. I can see the questions swimming in his intelligent eyes, and I don't want to answer them.

He pulls on his shirt, covering up all that tanned skin.

It's odd standing out in the market again. I can't meet anyone's eye. Do they know what we were doing? I'm also very aware of how sore I am. I didn't expect that.

"Can I borrow Willow?" Blitz draws my attention to him.

"We can both help."

Rian's response seems to surprise Blitz, but he recovers quickly, and we all start walking down the middle aisle of the market. I start putting distance between Rian and me and step up beside Blitz. He's huge beside me, and I try to look past the sheer size of him.

"So, what exactly are we doing?"

Blitz stops walking and taps a heavy black boot on a large tile under our feet. He slowly kneels and calls me down with the hook of his finger. I'm tempted to look at Rian, but I don't. I focus on Blitz and kneel too. Blitz knocks on the tile.

"We are looking for blank spaces. This sound..." He knocks again. "Tells me the floor is solid underneath us. We are trying to search for an echo."

"Why?" I ask as we rise.

This time Blitz looks to Rian and he gets the approval as he starts to talk again. "We think a rival gang has found a way onto this property. We discovered that an old drain system runs beneath us. We've found some abandoned tunnels and sealed them up, but with the sheer size of this place, we need to keep checking. Some old tunnels that we had boarded up months ago, were reopened. So it's a constant job."

"Why not move the market, if it is that much trouble?"

"Because this is my land, and I built it up to what it is today. Moving won't solve the problem. We need to find the problem." Rian speaks up and I nod like I understand.

Blitz walks onto the next tile and kneels down, tapping. "What do you think?" He asks me.

"It's solid."

He nods and gets up. "We can work side-by-side today."

I'm glancing around, thinking how many football pitches would fit into this space. It's endless. "Why not get more people on the job?"

"Rian has trust issues." Blitz doesn't look to Rian for approval this time, and I can hear the laughter in his voice.

"I would never have known."

Blitz laughs. "She's funny."

I hide my smile at his words and peer up at Rian. He's grinning at me, and my heart pounds wildly. Why does it feel so normal with him? I quickly get to work and start tapping on the tiles. Blitz watches me for the first few but must finally trust that I can hear the difference. Time moves fast and Rian stays with us the whole time. I keep expecting him to leave, but he doesn't. He doesn't help either. He just walks leisurely with us.

"Earlier, I didn't see anything."

I freeze at Blitz's words, heat rushes to my cheeks. I glare at him.

"I just thought I would put your mind at ease."

"My mind was at ease, but now it's not." I fire quickly.

"Why don't you take a break, Blitz," Rian speaks behind me. I realize I had forgotten he was there.

"I thought I was helping," Blitz says while rising.

"It's fine." I don't want to cause any trouble between these two. Blitz leaves, and Rian takes his place.

"You didn't have to send him away."

"I was saving him the embarrassment." Rian knocks on the tile and moves to the next. I knock on mine and am ready to move on when I knock again.

"Rian." I can't stop the excitement that bubbles up inside me. "I found one."

His smile is instant as he comes back to me. "That's my girl." He grins at me and knocks on the tile. He looks so proud as he rises and leaves me to stand over the tile. I fold my arms across my chest, trying to ward off the tightness that has settled there. He had called me "his girl."

He returns with a hammer and chisel. He starts hitting the grout before dragging the tile up. I look down into a dark hole and feel a sense of disappointment. I'm not sure what I was expecting. Rian leaves again, and when he returns, he clicks on the flashlight. I'm looking down into a deep tunnel. Rian moves the flashlight to the side of the wall, where a ladder is attached. He hands me the flashlight. "Hold that so I can see."

He grips the side of the tile and disappears under the floor.

"Do you think it's safe?" I ask, shining the torch on the top of his head. He looks up and squints against the flashlight that I quickly move away.

"I highly doubt it."

My heart jumps. "Don't go down. Get back up here," I hiss, but my voice bounces off the empty space below us.

"You sound concerned." He's jesting, and I stay quiet until he reaches the ground.

"Catch," I call before letting the flashlight go. Rian catches it, and I turn and lower myself under the floor. "I don't want you coming down here, Willow." All the joking has left Rian's voice.

"Tough. It's my discovery. I want to see."

"You don't get out much." He sings below me.

I don't answer him but keep moving until his strong arm wraps around my waist. "Stay close to me." His words are whispered against my ear, and a shiver assaults me. He helps me the rest of the way down before moving the flashlight from tunnel to tunnel. It parts three different ways. The main thing I notice, is how clean it is and it doesn't smell like I would have expected.

"You pick." Rian bounces his light over each tunnel. I point at the middle one and then realize he can't see me.

"The middle one." He reaches back and twines our fingers together as we start to walk down the middle tunnel. The feel of his hand on mine runs through my system in ripples. No matter how much I try not to focus on his touch and smell, I can't.

A noise like someone dropped a heavy bar bounces up the tunnel, and Rian clicks off the flashlight. He drags me closer to him, and for now, I allow myself to lean into him and enjoy his warmth. My brain is trying to tell me I could be in a very dangerous situation, but I ignore the warning and focus on Rian.

The noise comes again, and it can't be ignored. Rian's fingers tighten on mine. He shifts, and I have no idea what he is doing.

"You stay right behind me," his words are whispered into my ear, and he releases my hand. I reach out and touch his back, bunching the material in my fist as I move down the dark tunnel when he does. I know I should be afraid. Any normal person would be. But I'm with Rian Steele, and I know nothing can hurt me when I'm with him.

CHAPTER NINETEEN

RIAN

Willow's grip loosens on the material of my shirt, as light starts to filter in along with a lot of noise. I have no idea what I really expected, but it wasn't this. I grip the knife before kneeling down. Willow follows my lead.

Below us is another market in full swing. Hundreds of people move around the makeshift market. A market beneath a black market. I'm watching, searching for a familiar face from upstairs, but they all blend together, as I take in the magnitude of what I'm looking at. Willow's fingers wrap around my ankle, and I reach back, touching her hand. We need to leave. This isn't safe for her.

"Move, and I'll cut her."

My gaze is dragged up to some scrawny kid with a knife pointed at Willow.

"I wouldn't do that if I was you." I rise slowly, keeping my own knife tucked at my side.

"Shut the fuck up." He pushes the knife closer to Willow. Only a small portion of her face is illuminated from the distant light, but I can see the fear there.

"Do you know who I am?" I'm standing now, and the kid doesn't even flinch as I step closer.

"Don't move." He glances behind him. More people must be coming. I move quickly. He strikes out as I knew he would, I throw my hand into his dagger and it slices through my old wound easily coming out the other side. I rip my hand back with the knife intact. The boy's face sinks as I swallow the scream while dragging Willow closer to me.

"That was fucking foolish." I take a step towards him. Pain nearly robs me of air, but my hate has me clutching my own knife. He was going to hurt Willow.

"He's only a kid." Willow's panicked voice has me pausing. "Please don't," her whisper has me pulling the knife out of my hand, I swallow the bile that rises. The boy leans against the tunnel wall, his skin pale. I want to inflict a high level of pain on him. I'm tempted to drive the knife into his neck, but I can sense Willow's fear behind me. I tighten my hold on the knife and lodge it into the boy's shoulder. A scream tears from his lips and it's too fucking loud. Slamming my fist into his face, he shuts up and crumbles to the ground. I would have killed him; I should have killed him, but not in front of Willow. Blood rushes from my hand. I transfer my own knife into my injured hand and tighten my good hand around her fingers as I start to move back through the tunnel.

I pause at each small noise, but we don't encounter anyone else. Willow's breathing is heavy. Once we step into complete darkness, I turn on the torch, and we keep going until we step out of the tunnel. The ladder is right in front of us.

"Let me see your hand." Willow's eyes shine with fear.

"Not now. Get up the ladder." I turn my back, keeping a close eye on the tunnels. Willow doesn't move.

"Now, Willow." My voice is harsh and she moves quickly. The light above me disappears and when it reappears she calls down.

"Come on." Worry laces her words and I start to climb. The adrenaline that kept me going, is slowly leaking from my body. The moment I reach the top, I curl my hand in on itself.

"Don't say anything," I say to Willow quickly, as I fully stand on solid ground. I push the tile back in place before standing. Willow keeps looking at me, and I push my injured hand into my trousers pocket.

"Did you find anything?" Blitz asks, stepping up to me. I keep walking. I can feel the blood soaking through my slacks. I reach back and wrap my hand around Willow's fingers. She's shaking, and all I want to do is drag her closer and reassure her that she's safe. That I would never allow anyone to hurt her.

We cut off half way down the aisle and into a side office that Blitz sometimes uses.

The moment we are in, Willow releases my hand and closes the door. She's quick to pull off her cardigan.

"Let me see your hand." She's holding out her hand, and to give her peace, I take my hand out of my pocket. She inhales sharply.

"It looks worse than it is." I half sit on the desk, my body running out of energy. I've lost a lot of blood.

"There's a market under us."

Blitz steps closer, and I try not to cry out as Willow pushes the cardigan against the wound. "We need to get you to a doctor."

"A market? Like what we have up here?" Blitz asks.

"I don't need a doctor." I try to reassure Willow.

"You need stitches." She presses harder on the wound.

I tighten my fist and push it down into the wood.

"Right under us?" Shock laces itself around Blitz's words.

"There were hundreds of people down there."

Blitz juts his chin towards my hand. "They discovered you?"

"No, just some scrawny kid, but they will soon."

"You need a doctor," Willow repeats.

"We need to flush them out, now," I say to Blitz.

"I could make a monster of a bomb."

That isn't wise, it could bring the whole building down.

"You can't kill all those people." The horror in Willow's voice has me pausing this conversation with Blitz, and turning to Willow. She looks too pale.

"Get me some water," I say to Blitz.

"We aren't. Are you okay?" I touch her face with my good hand and she seems to lean into it.

"He was only a boy." She shakes her head and frowns, looking down at her blood-soaked cardigan. "You saved me."

Her gaze travels back up to me and that look in her eyes makes all the pain worth it. "I get to experience the whole nail through the hand thing again."

Willow looks worried as she lifts the cardigan from my wound. Pain races through me and I want to tell her not to move the cardigan, but it's giving her peace that she is doing something. Blitz re-enters with a glass of water and hands it to me. I push it against Willow's lips. "Take a drink." She does as I say.

"Is Fredrick out there?" I ask Blitz.

"Already have him coming."

I curl my hand around the cardigan. "Blitz is going to take you outside for some fresh air." The idea of her being away from me frightens me, but having Willow here while I get stitched up isn't wise, and I have a few things to ask Fredrick.

Willow is shaking her head.

"I'm not asking you, Willow."

She moves slightly back. The door opens, and Fredrick steps in with a small case under his arm.

I push off the table and step up to Willow while softening my voice. "I won't be long." I place a kiss on her lips and sense her relaxing slightly.

I nod at Blitz, and he holds the door for Willow. I watch as they leave before moving behind the desk. Opening the top drawer, I take out a bottle of brandy and slump into the chair.

Fredrick sets up on the table. I unscrew the bottle and drink deeply before pulling off the cardigan. Fredrick takes my hand, turning it both ways. "It went clean through." I drink again as saliva pools in my mouth. Fredrick reaches out for the bottle, I take another swallow before handing it over.

The burn of the alcohol has me gripping the arm of the chair. "You motherfucker!" I'm sure my voice is carrying beyond the room. Fredrick doesn't respond but holds my hand.

"This is going to hurt like a bitch."

I grab the bottle and drink more. "Just do it."

Each stitch is horrific, and several times, I think I might pass out. Once Fredrick stitches both sides, the brandy bottle is empty, but I am alert from the pain. He wraps the wound.

"You look like shit, Rian."

I slide back in the chair. "I was just fucking stabbed." I close my eyes, the alcohol making everything heavy.

"Did you find out anything for me?" I don't open my eyes as I speak. My voice slurs.

The rattle of tablets hitting the table has me opening one eye. "Take three of these." I reach out and empty three into my hand before popping them in my mouth.

"I wouldn't take them with alcohol." Fredrick drifts off as I crunch the tablets. I sit up and push out the chair. Picking up the glass that Willow had drank out of, I down it.

"Every time you're here, so is a black BMW." That gets my attention. I return to my seat. Fredrick reaches into the pocket of his sweat pants and pushes the piece of paper towards me. "The registration. Each time I flew the drone too close to get a look at the driver, he left."

Fredrick gathers up all his tools. "You should rest."

"Thanks, doctor." I'm looking around in the drawer for more alcohol but come up empty. The door opens, and Fox arrives.

"What happened?"

I wait until Fredrick leaves.

"The Rat Pack is operating under our feet."

Fox doesn't sit but stands in front of the desk.

"You don't look so good."

I laugh. "I'm sure I look better than you."

Fox's complexion is nearly transparent. "You need to stop dying your hair."

He curls up his nose at me. "We need to flush them out."

"That's exactly what I said to Blitz."

Fox snorts and finally sits down. "I'm sure he wanted to drop bombs on them."

"You know him so well."

"Let me take a look at some of the old plans. If there is a water system below us, we could literally flush them out."

"Yeah, I'd appreciate that." I slide the piece of paper across to Fox. "While you're doing paperwork, can you find out the owner of this car?"

Fox picks up the white slip of paper and opens it before glancing at me. "Yeah, sure." He folds the paper and places it into his pocket.

"Anything I should be worried about?"

I lean back in the chair and close my eyes. "I'm not sure yet."

I sit up. I need to get to Willow. Standing up, the room tilts, and I wonder how much blood I've lost. Or maybe it's all the alcohol.

"I need us to squash this problem as soon as possible."

Fox stands up too. "You don't look like you should be standing."

I ignore Fox's words. "I want this kept quiet."

Fox nods.

"I mean it." He fucked up the last time when I had told him to leave Rodger Smith, and he had shot him.

"I will." There is a bite in his words, and I don't give a fuck. I don't need this getting out before we have a chance to react. Them finding the boy alive was stupid on my part. If it weren't for Willow being here, I would return and gut him. The boy doesn't know who I am, so I'm hoping that'll give us the time we need to take care of the problem.

CHAPTER TWENTY

WILLOW

Outside, the air is nice, but all I want to do is go back to Rian. Things feel strange, with Blitz walking beside me. Being away from Rian also allows me to clear my head and remember that I need to end things with him. Once I know he's okay, I'll start allowing that to sink into my system.

"So you and Rian?" Blitz asks.

"No, we aren't together."

Blitz nods while stuffing his huge hands in his pockets and extracting a pack of cigarettes. He lights one up and offers one to me. I've never smoked before, and I'm not about to start now.

"No, thanks."

"You sure looked like you were together." Laughter fills Blitz's words.

"I thought you saw nothing," I remind him while folding my arms across my chest.

He shrugs and smokes his cigarette. We walk around the building to the far side. Rian's Bentley comes into view, and we stop near it.

"Should we check on him?" I ask, knowing I sound needy.

Blitz covers up a grin. "Nah, he'll come out here when he's ready."

I take another look at Blitz. "How long have you been working for Rian?" I'm not sure he will answer me, but he surprises me.

"We met when we were kids. I was being bullied, and Rian beat the shit out the kids who hurt me."

"You were bullied?" That is a hard pill to swallow.

"I wasn't always this big. Rian protected me, and he has never stopped."

"You don't look like you need protecting anymore." I'm trying to lighten the mood.

"Rian's protection comes in many forms."

I stop walking. "Like what?"

The door to the side of the building opens, and Rian steps out. His black clothing fits his large frame snuggly. I can't stop the reaction that he sends through me. This isn't good. The moment he steps up to me, he places a kiss on my lips like Blitz isn't standing right beside us. It's like he thinks we are a couple.

"I'm going to take Willow home. Fox is in the office."

Blitz crushes the cigarette under his boot. "See you, Willow."

I give him a tight smile before turning to Rian's car. I need to put some distance between us.

"You need to rest," I tell him the moment I get in and put on my seatbelt.

"I'd offer to drive; only I don't know how."

"You don't drive?" This seems to surprise Rian.

"Never learned." I quickly say before he asks why.

He starts the car, and I can't look at him. He looks pale. "You need to rest."

"Are you going to nurse me back to health?"

My body ignites at the thoughts of getting to see Rian naked again. I stare out the window knowing this isn't going to go smoothly.

"What we did was a one-time thing. It won't be happening again." Silence fills the car, and I take a quick peek at Rian. His white bandage is turning red as he grips the steering wheel too hard.

"Rian, your hand."

He loosens his grip, but he must have reopened the wounds. He doesn't fight me, and I hate the disappointment that courses through me. I had expected some kind of resistance, but I met none. We drive the whole way home in awkward silence. I want to say something else, but the moment he parks in the garage, he gets out of the car.

He opens the door that leads into the kitchen, and I'm waiting for him to leave, but he holds it open for me. I feel horrible as I pass him. He doesn't try to stop me, and the moment I step into the kitchen—I straighten. My mother is sitting at the table, flipping through a magazine; she must be waiting for me.

"Where is your cardigan?" is the first thing she asks.

"I spilled tea on it at work. I left it behind."

"Bring it home tomorrow, and we can wash it."

Rian leaves the kitchen, and I stare after him with a longing that gives me a belly ache.

"Willow?" My mother raises a brow, and I know the decision I have to make. I sit beside her. "I pick you," I tell her.

"Well, don't sound so happy."

I take my mother's hands in mine. "I choose you. You have done so much for me, and I won't disappoint you again."

My mother takes her hands out of mine and touches my face. "There's my daughter."

Her smile is soft, and I sense my heart breaking as my cheeks heat up. I need to be somewhat honest. "I can't be around him, mother. It's too hard. I want you to speak to Henry and get me out of the job."

It's the only way. My mother pulls me into a hug. It's unexpected and most certainly not like her. "There, there, don't fret, you are stronger than you think." She's rubbing my back, but I don't understand what she's saying. "You can't leave your job." I try to move away from my mother, but she holds me still. Her voice has lowered. "I need you to stay close to Rian."

The blood turns cold in my veins.

"Why?" The fine hairs on the back of my neck stand up.

"Just do as your mother asks." My mother finally releases me, and I feel sick.

"I don't understand." I'm shaking my head.

My mother sits back in the chair and glances around her. "Let's go for a walk outside."

I don't want to go for a walk. I want answers.

If I want answers, I know I need to follow my mother out the back. She keeps walking until she is deep in the garden. Apple trees rise on either side of us. The garden is picture perfect, just like our home.

"What are you asking me?" Finally, I can't wait any longer.

"Tell me what happened today?" My mother folds her arms across her chest. The blue pantsuit she wears, fits her tall frame. Blonde hair is swept back from her face. When I don't answer her, she turns her sharp eye on me.

"Nothing, really." The lie is clear to hear.

"You told me you chose me. I'm finding that hard to believe."

I grit my teeth. "I do choose you." She has no idea what I'm giving up. "Rian was stabbed today."

My mother looks shaken, and I hope she will reconsider getting me out of the job.

"He was protecting me."

Now my mother stands even taller. "You were attacked? By whom? How did that happen? Where was Rian?" Her voice grows louder with each question.

"I just told you. He saved me."

My mother turns her back on me, and I stand still as she processes what I am saying. "The person who stabbed him?"

She turns to me. "Rian stabbed him."

"Is he dead?"

Everything about this conversation felt so wrong. "What's this about, mother?"

"Is he dead?" She steps closer to me.

"No. Well, I don't think so."

She turns her back on me again, and I have no idea what is going on. "Mother." The frustration I am feeling comes out in my voice.

My mother turns to me and exhales loudly. She steps closer, and I'm waiting for her to take my face in her hands, but she doesn't. "I know you can't leave your job. I already tried."

"I can't work with him." I start, and my mother stops me.

"You are stronger than some hormonal teenager."

My face blazes. She has no idea this isn't some crush. What Rian makes me feel is so intense that I can barely keep it together around him. Before I can be honest and explain that to my mother, she holds up her hand and smiles. She links her arm with mine and we start to walk back.

"I was talking to Father Cooney." My mother smiles at me. "The Bible group is going on a weekend break."

I swallow the groan.

"I'm going to send you with them. I think the break away from this place will do you good."

I force a smile. "Sounds wonderful."

"Don't pout, Willow." My mother tightens our linked arms. "Luke will be with the group."

My stomach swims with disgust. I can't even look at my mother.

"It may help to get Rian out of your system." She says "Rian," like he is something despicable.

"I thought boys were not allowed?" I'm being careless with my words. My mother stops walking and un-links her arm from mine.

I see the warning in her eyes before she starts to speak with brows raised high. "Boys were not allowed. That was the rule until you broke it, Willow. First Chad, and now Rian. So if you are going to break my rules, I may as well select a worthy partner for my daughter." This time when my mother touches my face, it's gentle. "Have I not always put your interests first?"

"I'm not questioning that."

Surprise filters through my mother's features. The idea that I would question her at all is something new.

"Why are you taking such an interest in Rian?" My mother is walking on dangerous ground.

"I just want to know how careful he is being with my daughter."

I hate that I don't believe her. "He would never let any harm come to me."

"You say that like it's a good thing." Her nose curls up.

"It's not a bad thing, mother." I bite the inside of my cheek.

"It is, Willow. That's what you aren't seeing. Being in Rian's favour isn't a good thing."

Sadly, she shakes her head, and I want her to tell me what she really wants to say.

She faces the house and that sadness fades away. "I'm going to take you to visit Chad."

Every cell in my body pings at once.

"I don't like how that detective was watching you. So I think to throw suspicion off, you should visit him."

My face heats up until it burns the tips of my ears. "I didn't hurt him, mother." My voice is small now. I can't look at my mother. I don't blame her.

She doesn't tell me she believes me, and that crushes me even further.

I get showered and changed numbly. I'm scrambling for my armor that has always worked for me, but it isn't anymore. I'm still sore between my legs, but it's a nice kind of soreness. It's my only reminder of what I gave to Rian.

My mother has changed and is waiting for me in the kitchen. She gives me a nod of approval as she scans me from my beige trousers all the way up to my gray polo neck jumper. My hair is neatly tied back. I stay still as she approaches me and pulls the silver chain so the cross isn't hidden under my jumper.

"Now, you look perfect." She smiles, and I mirror the action.

"Do you ever think of Aran?"

The car swerves, and the oncoming traffic sits on their horns. My mother straightens the car up. "Why would you ask me that?" Her clipped words and reaction make more shame burn through me.

"I'm sorry. I don't know what's wrong with me. I don't know why I just asked you that." I take a quick peek at my mother. Her red nails are wrapped around the steering wheel. That's twice I've noticed her wearing red nail polish.

"I think about him every day."

My heart breaks even further, and even though I just told her I didn't know why I asked her that, I do know. I need to see the hate in her eyes. I need a reminder of all she lost for me. So I continue to pick the scab.

"His birthday is next month."

The car doesn't swerve, but we move faster down the road.

"What, he'll be twenty-six?"

"Stop." My mother's voice is pained.

I need the wound to gape wide open. "Do you wonder if he ever thinks about us?"

This time I meet my mother's eyes, and I see what I am looking for. All the hate in the world rolled up tightly and delivered to me in a bow. "Never mind," I add quickly.

The silence on the drive to the hospital is strained and heavy. This I understand. I face forward, sitting rod straight, and I try not to blink as buildings move past us.

My mother is still rattled as we get out of the car and make our way to see Chad. We stop at one of the small hospital shops, and my mother gets a bunch of flowers. She doesn't say anything as she hands them to me. I take them and pace down the corridor like a bride. The thought makes me giddy. Chad, my poor husband, dying in the hospital bed.

"Why are you smiling?" My mother talks from the side of her mouth, and I quickly lose the smile before I push her too far.

Facing forward, my feet slow down when Blitz and Detective Lacy come into view. This isn't going to be easy.

CHAPTER TWENTY-ONE

WILLOW

"Detective Lacy." My mother takes the detective's outstretched hand.

"Catherine. This is a surprise."

My focus is on Blitz's back as he walks down the corridor. I keep waiting for him to glance back and look at me, but he doesn't.

My mother clears her throat, and my smile is instant. "Detective Lacy." He doesn't offer his hand, and I step around him and my mother and look in through the large pane of glass—my stomach twists. Chad is lying still, his face unrecognizable, a brace circles his neck. He's hooked up to monitors. I'm watching the one that registers his heart move in a consistent rhythm across the screen.

Lacy moves up beside me. "He was a football star. Hoping to play for O'Maghonies next year. If he wakes up, the doctors aren't sure he'll ever walk again."

"It's terrible," I say automatically.

"Willow is devastated and insisted on seeing Chad," My mother whispers the words like I'm not here. Her voice trembles with a heartache that sounds real, and I'm wondering if her mind is still stuck on Aran.

"He made an impression on my daughter."

My stomach twists again. He tried to hurt me. I can't find Chad under the swollen and colored tissue that once showcased a handsome face, but not as handsome as Rian. No one has ever come close to that level. I swallow that thought and the silence of my mother and Lacy registers.

"I liked him," I say before turning to the detective.

"Is it okay to go in?" I'm praying he says no visitors. His kind blue eyes smile at me.

"Of course, Willow."

I'm waiting for my mother to join me, but she doesn't. When I pause at the door for her, she ushers me on with a flick of her long red nails. "Go ahead. I just want to have a word with Detective Lacy." I have the most bizarre moment where I fear she's going to sell me out and tell him what kind of person I am. Fear starts to take root deep in my belly, and I let my eyelids flutter closed, so they don't see it in my eyes.

The room seems quieter now that I'm in it. I don't see a vase, so I place the flowers on a tray at the foot of Chad's bed. I know they are watching me, so I drag a chair up to the top of the bed and sit down. I can't look at him. The fear and anger that he ignited in me that night returns along with a sense of guilt that he's lying here because of what he did to me. I know how messed up all this is.

He had no right putting his hands on me, but that doesn't mean he deserves to be lying here like this. I think if I was ever placed in a coma, I would want my family to let me go. I wouldn't want to wake up and not able to walk—or be like a vegetable.

I sit until it's hard to sit still any longer. Turning my head, my gaze clashes with Detective Lacy's. My mother isn't there anymore, and something in his intelligent eyes makes me face forward.

"Your mother has gone to get a coffee." He pulls up a chair and sits beside me.

I was waiting for the questions to start, and I didn't have to wait long. "How many times had you met Chad?"

"The night of the party was my first time." I focus on Chad like his face is recognizable to me.

"You never bumped into him at a party before?" I hate how he asks the question. It's like he already knows the answer, and he's leading me down a path I don't want to go down.

"I don't go to parties."

"A girl who doesn't drink and party? It's unusual for your age."

I glance at Detective Lacy and force a smile. "I'm shy."

"That night, there were several conflicting reports about you and Chad."

"Alcohol can really alter everyone's point of view, so I'm not surprised there were conflicting reports." I lean forward, and my heart pounds as I spot the indent of a ring along Chad's jaw. There is no way they haven't spotted that.

Rian's fingers coated in rings spring to mind; surely I'm not the only one putting this all together.

This time when I glance at Detective Lacy, he's smiling at me, and I don't like it one bit. Coming here was a very bad idea.

"Your mother tells me you are in Bible school, and sometimes you do readings in the church."

My mother has clearly been telling him a lot. "Yes."

"Reading in front of hundreds of people would be frightening, even nerve-wracking for a shy girl."

My stomach clenches. "I'm spreading the word of God, so I don't mind. I get shy when it's about me."

He nods like he understands.

"Do you want me to give you time with Chad?" I ask, rising, wondering what the hell he's doing here, anyway.

He holds up a hand, stopping me from leaving, and stands. "No. We have someone stationed here all day. We got a tip that his life is still at risk. So I'm covering the shift today."

My heart pounds as I slowly descend back into the chair.

"Coffee, Detective Lacy?" My mother arrives into the room, and the smell of her perfume pollutes the space. After she hands Lacy his coffee, she drinks her own. None for me. She doesn't look at me but stands at the foot of Chad's bed, and the smile on her face terrifies me. Bringing up Aran was foolish. What if I have pushed her so far that I can't pull her back?

"He's someone's son. That's the hard part." She sips her coffee.

"How many children do you have, Catherine?"

My heart is telling me that my mother walked into that one on purpose.

"Two. Willow and Aran."

The air catches in my chest.

"I haven't met Aran."

"He's off living his life." My mother hasn't taken her eyes off Chad. "Unlike this poor soul." My mother turns to Lacy now. "Any updates on the person who committed this terrible crime?"

This time I do look at Detective Lacy. Once again, those soft blue eyes are focused on me. "He had no enemies. He was truly loved by all. A star football player with a bright future. We have a few leads but nothing concrete yet." He says the 'yet' with determination in his voice. I need to calm down and remember I didn't do this to Chad.

I rise slowly, and my mother's sharp eye swings in my direction. With raised eyebrows, she's asking me what I'm doing.

"Excuse me while I go to the bathroom."

"You want me to show you where it is?"

"No, thank you, Detective Lacy. I'm sure I can find it." I leave the room and slowly let the air filter back into my lungs. Each door I pass, I'm wondering who's fighting for their lives behind it. Some doors are open, and I glance into an empty room.

It's easy to find the bathrooms. The whole hospital is sign posted. The toilets are located beside the coffee dock. I'm tempted to go in and get a coffee. The smell is enticing. Turning back to the bathrooms, I enter the small two stall space. No one else is here, so I relieve myself and spend a bit longer washing my hands than necessary. I don't want to go back upstairs. I don't want to go with the Bible group.

I want to run away from all this, run until my memory starts to fade, and maybe I can start over. If I could be anyone, I would be that girl that has crinkles around her eyes from laughing, the one whose eyes always shine, like she is on the brink of bursting out in laughter. Yeah, I want to be that girl. I meet my muddy brown eyes, and I look...dead. I feel dead inside. My fingers push down on my bandaged wrist, and the pain races up my arm.

The door to the bathroom opens and I walk away from the mirror and dry my hands. I meet the gaze of the elderly woman and give her a smile. She smiles back and disappears into one of the stalls.

"Blitz." I pause outside the bathroom. It looks like he was waiting for someone. He could have been waiting for me.

"Willow." He pushes his dark glasses up on his broad nose. He slightly resembles Clark Kent. Maybe the glasses were a look and not a necessity.

"Does Rian know you're here?" The question is delivered with hostility.

I wait until a couple walks past us and step up to Blitz. "I don't work for Rian, so my whereabouts are none of his business."

The smile that tugs at Blitz's lips isn't friendly.

"I'm here at my mother's request to visit Chad. I don't want to be here." I lower my voice as I speak.

"Take care, Willow." Blitz walks away, and a panic has me wanting to race after him and demand that he tell me what he means by taking care. Is it a threat?

I don't linger but return to the hospital room. I've ended up coming down the corridor in the opposite direction. The glass mirror comes into view, and my mother is sitting in my seat beside Detective Lacy. They are both facing forward, but it's in the small movements that I can tell they are speaking to each other.

My heart is telling me to stay put or knock against the glass so they know I'm here, but my head has me stepping closer to the open door, making sure I'm as light as possible on my feet.

"The hand?" My mother's voice holds humor. "That I can't deliver."

"We will have to come up with some alternative." Detective Lacy has the words out of his mouth when his head snaps in my direction. Both he and my mother turn in my direction, and I have no idea what I have stumbled upon, but everything in me hollows out.

Detective Lacy rises slowly and throws his coffee cup into the bin.

"I'll give you both some time with Chad."

I can't look at my mother. My heart drums too heavily in my chest. Lacy leaves, and I close the door after him before I sit down in the seat he just vacated.

"You want to tell me what that was about?"

I glance at my mother, and she still sips her coffee. "What?"

I want to bark at her not to lie to me, but her eyes still hold the hate that I had placed there.

"What you were talking about with Detective Lacy."

"What is it exactly that you think you heard?" My mother raises a brow, and I see the challenge in her stare.

Was she selling me out? "A hand." My voice is so low I'm surprised she heard me, but her paling face and the alarm in her eyes tells me she heard me.

"Whatever you think you heard, you didn't." My mother reaches for me; her nails dig painfully into my hands. "Willow, you heard nothing."

I'm nodding because the fear on my mother's face is leaping off her and spreading through my system. "I heard nothing." I want to reassure her, but I can't unhear it, previous conversations start to rise, and I'm getting a horrible sinking feeling.

"Please tell me this hasn't got to do with Rian."

Her nails sink further into my hand and my mother looks around us. "Are you trying to get me in trouble?" She frowns like she can't believe I would say such a thing. "If he thought for one second... I would be dead,

Willow. Dead." She releases my aching hands. She sits back and closes her eyes. "Maybe that's what you want. Maybe you would be happy then."

I'm reaching across to my mother. "I would never. Don't ever say that. I chose you."

The panic that claws inside me has my voice rising, and my mother sits forward. Her face has softened, and she takes my hand gently in hers.

"Let's pretend this conversation never took place. We can pretend, can't we?" I hear the words she doesn't say. *Like we pretend every day.*

I try to swallow the bitterness. "I'm good at pretending," I say, and she lets me go.

CHAPTER TWENTY-TWO

RIAN

"Where is Catherine?"

My father pours out a glass of brandy. The glass top has a tassel on it, and it bounces around as he places it back on the bottle. That's not my father's taste; it's Catherine's. Her touches are everywhere throughout the house. It has never bothered me before, but lately, the woman has managed to find herself on my radar, and that's not always a good thing.

"Helping out with a fundraiser for the church." My father sounds proud. Proud that she's spending his money and believing she can buy her way into heaven.

"Anything I can help with, Son? You looked troubled."

Willow has avoided me for a full day. Now I can't find her. Blitz said she had been visiting Chad at her mother's request. My father loves Catherine; I have no doubt about that. I love my father, so I'll give a level of respect here that I don't truly feel is owed.

"It's actually Willow."

My father takes a drink before sitting down. "I should have gotten some ice," he says holding the glass up.

"She seems withdrawn." I sit down in one of the brown leather armchairs. Its cold material takes some of the burn out of my system. My hand throbs, and the idea of it being infected, crosses my mind more than once.

"She isn't chatty." My father smiles. "But I agree, lately she seems quieter." He drinks, and I try to keep my irritation at bay. I really need to know why my Willow was cutting herself, and everything in me points directly at Catherine. Talking to my father is already proving to be fruitless.

"No worries. I'll ask Catherine later." I'm ready to leave. I've missed a call from Fox. I hope he has found the water pipes so we can flush out the rats beneath our feet.

"I'd prefer if you didn't."

My father's words are careful, and I sit back down.

"This isn't my place, but your concern for Willow means a lot." He pauses and crosses his legs. His silver suit sits perfectly on his frame. My father keeps watching me, and I don't blink. He should know that once I have something in my sights, I get it—with or without him. He must come to that conclusion because he speaks.

"Catherine's husband took his life when Willow was only ten. It might be close to the anniversary."

Does that mean that Willow has some part of her father in her since she was cutting herself? She told me it wasn't about ending her life. *Jesus.* I run a hand across my face.

My father uncrosses his legs and sits forward. His next words are heavy on his lips. "Willow found him."

I'm picturing a small Willow, with billowing white hair, finding her father dead.

"How did he do it?" Some weird part of me doesn't want it to be him cutting himself.

"He shot himself." Relief is brief when I think of Willow finding her father like that.

"She's never been..." My father once again is being careful with his words. "Stable since then. Catherine said she has episodes."

"Why didn't she get her daughter help?" Anger starts to bubble through my veins.

"She did, Rian. Willow is fragile."

That's bullshit to me. She isn't fragile. She is brimming for release under all that control. She is fucking drowning. Why hadn't she told me?

"So, you see why I don't want you questioning Catherine. She blames herself."

So she should. I want to ask where she was when Willow found her father. My question isn't justified, but anger is making me want to blame someone.

"Didn't you think I had a right to know?" I'm feeling pissed at my father.

My father isn't taken by my anger. He rotates the glass in his hands. "Honestly, Rian, you never showed an interest. I could never have imagined you would. But it's nice that you are now."

I can't stop the grin that tugs at my lips. My interest is not for the reasons he thinks. I'm looking into my father's eyes, wondering what he would say if he knew I had slept with her. I don't give a fuck. It won't stop me, but for the first time, I wonder how he would react.

"Thanks for telling me." I get up as my phone buzzes in my pocket again.

"I think we finally have a grip on the Rat Pack," I speak while taking my phone out. It's Fox again.

"Good."

I glance at my father, and he raises his glass before taking a drink.

Driving back to the market, all I can think about is Willow. I can't get the image out of my head of her bare feet, stepping into a room where her father lay. Did she step into a pool of his blood? Did she try to save him? How long had she stayed with her father until she understood he was dead? I quickly dial her phone. She hasn't been answering me all day.

"What is it, Rian?" I'm surprised when Catherine answers. I wasn't expecting that, but now it made sense.

"You took her phone?"

"My daughter doesn't need a phone." Her words are sharp, and I know the woman can't stand me.

"It's a work phone, Catherine."

"I wouldn't agree from the messages I've read."

"Where is Willow? She has work today."

"She's at Bible study."

"Where?"

Catherine releases a heavy breath down the phone. "What is it that you want?"

I want to call her a cunt because that's all I see when I look at her. I end the call before I disrespect her. I do it for Willow and my father.

Once the barrier is lifted, I drive into the compound and park. I'm considering asking Fredrick to fly the drone and find Willow for me. I laugh at the madness of my suggestion. I had people who could find people. If I didn't get to talk to Willow this evening, I could make the call. She had thought that it was over with us. I had told her that once I tasted her, she was mine. I get out of the car, my mind still on Willow. She had tasted perfect. My body hums with a want for her flesh. I had been gentle with her. But the next time, I didn't have to hold back.

The market is busy again today. Blitz is the first to see me. He puts down the two guns he had been playing with.

"Are you planning on shooting someone?" I ask.

"I'm always planning on shooting someone. Fox is in the office."

Blitz and I make our way there. Fox is bent over a set of maps. His finger running along the center. He doesn't look up as we enter.

"I don't know if this will work."

I join Fox and glance down at the blueprints. I have no clue what I'm looking at.

"This is where you found the market." He glances at me, and I nod. "You see the red lines? Those are the main water pipes They stop on the border of the market."

"They set it up like that on purpose?" Blitz asks what I'm thinking.

Fox shrugs. "I mean, it could just be a coincidence."

"I don't believe in coincidences," I speak while dragging my attention across the map. "Let's say it's intentional. That would mean they had to get the maps." Now I look up at Fox.

"They would. There would be no other way of knowing."

"Can we find out if anyone was inquiring?"

Fox shrugs again. "We could, but it could be a dead end. They could get these maps in the records county department, the library. It's not a secret."

"But it's my land. Should that knowledge not be just for me?" I have no idea how this works.

"You don't own the underground system. It's the council's property. It must have been an old water system that's not used anymore."

I sit down in the chair.

"You look like shit." Blitz frowns down at me.

"I think my hand's infected." That scrawny little fucker could have anything. I highly doubt he kept his knife clean.

"After this, I'm going to the hospital. I'll be admitted for a few hours. You'll come visit me." I speak to Blitz, and he stares at me like I lost my mind. "I'll need you there the whole time, Blitz. Like a witness."

"Let me guess. You're going to the Lourdes hospital." Fox says while folding up the blueprints.

"Exactly." I have to tie up the loose end that is Chad. Being admitted and hospitalized with Blitz and nurses as my witness...it will be a bulletproof alibi.

"So, what do you want to do about the market?" Fox folds up the blueprints.

"Turn the water on. See if we can destroy any of it."

"It won't reach that part, Rian. I think we have the upper hand, and we would be giving away our position."

"Then what do you suggest?" This is starting to get frustrating.

"I think we should load up and go down and take them all out." Blitz grins at me.

"You want to commit mass murder?" Fox growls like Blitz is an idiot, and in this case I agree with Fox. That isn't something I'll do. The water being turned on wouldn't fall back on us. There's illegal activity in the sewers, and a burst pipe that's old and dormant could easily happen.

My head throbs and I can't think straight right now.

"Let me think about it and I'll see what I come up with."

I nod at Fox as he takes the blueprints and leaves the room.

"You can come with me." I get out of the chair, and the noise in the market sends waves of sweat across my body. I was starting to think I might be worse than I had thought.

"You really look like shit," Blitz tells me again like I need to fucking hear it.

CHAPTER TWENTY-THREE

WILLOW

My mother pulls up at a row of cars parked on the church grounds. I'm struggling to stay still. I don't want to go. My mother's conversation with Detective Lacy still spins in my head. I glance down at my hand, the half-moon marks are still visible from when she dug her nails into my hand.

"Luke is coming." The smile in my mother's voice has my head snapping up.

Luke smiles at me, and I force one back. He's a decent soul, and he's always there to listen and help everyone. Maybe that's the problem. He's decent, and I don't do decent. No, I need them to be more messed up than me.

I climb out of the car.

"Hi, Luke." I dip my head in the shy way they are used to from me.

"You look really pretty." My mother joins us and so does Father Cooney.

"Everyone is here."

Maria, Casey, and her sister Laura, along with Josh, and Barb stand huddled together. Their laughter is loud, and I can tell it's genuine. These are the happiest bunch of people you will ever meet. They do drag some hidden happiness out of me, especially Barb, who spots me. Her red curly hair bounces as she comes over and joins us.

"Yay, you're coming." She sings, and I can see she's holding back in front of my mother.

"Mrs. Steele." She bobs her head at my mother.

"Barbara. How is your mother?"

"Very well. She's excited about the upcoming fundraiser." Barb's smile is genuine. I can sense eyes on me and glance at Luke.

I have the urge to roll my eyes, but my body responds correctly by smiling back.

"Okay. Are we all ready?" Maria, Casey, and Laura join us.

Everyone is excited, and I want to reach out and take some. It's like watching someone eating pink cotton candy. "Barb and Willow can ride in my car." Luke offers up.

"Josh, you are with us." Maria smiles at Josh.

"How long are we going for?" I ask and hate the nerves I hear in my voice.

"Two days. Now, if you need me, just ring. You kids have fun." My mother places a hand on my face like I'm a child prodigy and not a nightmare from hell. Guilt swells up inside me, and I want to tell her I'm sorry for provoking her today. I'm sorry that she lost her son because of me. I'm sorry that she lost her husband. I'm sorry.

"Go." She releases my face and walks back to the car. Opening the trunk, she takes out a large suitcase that she packed for me. Father Cooney takes it from her, and like the gentleman that he is, he places it in the trunk of Luke's car.

My mother climbs in and waves at us before driving off. I feel abandoned with people who don't know me. I've been with this group for three years now. They see what I want them to see, not the real me. If they did, I'm sure they would be dousing me in holy water and not holding open the door of the car.

I climb in and Luke closes the door. Barb is already in the back. "Lord, he has the hots for you." She's excited, and I try to focus on her excitement.

"He's like a puppy," she quickly says as he climbs in. I can't stop the smile that spreads across my face.

"What, have you got in your suitcase, a body?" Luke asks.

"What?" My stomach falls into my shoes, and the car grows too small.

"The weight. You must have packed for two weeks." He's half laughing, half looking at me with concern. "Are you okay?"

"Yeah." I shake my head and try to clear it. "I just had a late night."

Barb pulls herself forward, and the car takes off. "I heard you are working with Rian." The way Barb says his name, it's like it's a sin.

I keep facing forward. "Yes."

"I'm surprised your mother allowed that." Luke perks up beside me.

"Why is that, Luke?" the edge to my voice has him flickering a glance in my direction.

"Isn't he like, dangerous?"

"Cars are dangerous. We could crash at any second. The world is dangerous." I glance out the window.

"You know what he means." Barb squeezes my shoulder, and I hate how uptight I feel.

"He's not dangerous to me," I finally say.

"Well, all I'm saying is, he's hot."

I have to glance at Barb. She's smiling with a brow cocked up in the air.

"He's hardly marriage material," Luke says drily.

"Who said anything about marriage?" Barb's word has me smiling internally. I've never been outside Bible study with her, so I've never seen this side. Maybe this *will* be a bit of fun.

"Let's pick some music." Luke definitely doesn't want to talk about Rian, and I'm honestly okay with that. Just the thought of my final words to him causes my stomach to ache.

Country music rolls through the car at a medium level.

"I'm just saying, I think he would be fun." Barb isn't letting her notions of Rian go. "Just, you know, you could introduce us."

I cringe internally.

"I don't think your mother would approve, Barbara."

Barbara rolls her eyes at me and sits back. Luke is four years older than us, and I'm sure everything we speak of will get back to Father Cooney. I can see why my mother would pick him. He's good looking and well groomed. He comes from a wealthy background and never misses Bible study. He wouldn't break a rule, and I'm sure he would tell my mother every little detail of this weekend.

Barbara sings to every song that plays. I can sense Luke's agitation. I'm sure he had wished he didn't have to bring her with us. He turns the music down and clears his throat.

"Your mother tells me you have a love for painting."

"Kind of." I want to exhale loudly, but I keep it in.

"Oh, she made it sound like you really love it."

"I did once. I don't paint anymore."

Barb is back up between us, and I'm surprised that Luke hasn't commented on her not wearing her seat belt. "Why stop if you were so good?"

I glance at Barb. "It makes me sad." Her eyes widen; that wasn't the answer she was expecting.

"My brother taught me." Now I wish I hadn't spoken. Aran was a genius with a paintbrush. He was always a bit odd. My mother used to say he had my father's darkness, but I never saw it in Aran, not even at the end.

"My brother is a dickhead," Barb says, surprising me again. Luke gives her a look of disapproval in the rear-view mirror. "I honestly can't bear him, and he's as dumb as two stones. He has no talents."

I'm suppressing a laugh at her words. Barbara sits back after that, and Luke turns up the music.

We arrive at a beautiful log cabin where we will be spending the next two days. I get out as two more cars pull up behind us. Maria's white BMW is first, and then after her is Father Cooney's sedan.

"Does it have a pool?" Laura blows her bangs out of her eyes as she stares up at the cabin.

"It does not," Father Cooney answers. "But, it does have running water."

"Yippie," Barbs speaks towards me, and low enough that only I can hear.

Luke insists on carrying my suitcase into the foyer. Father Cooney waits until we are all inside before laying down the law. I think his words aren't necessary. Not one of them would break a rule.

"Okay, so I'm not staying here. I'll be visiting the monks a few miles away." Barb squeezes my arm while Marie looks alarmed. She has dark hair just like her two sisters—only she doesn't have bangs like they do.

"We are going to be alone?"

"You are never alone, Maria. There are seven of you here. I will return for our daily prayers, but I trust you all." Father Cooney glances at us one by one. "I've never had a reason not to." Why the hell was he looking at me? Oh yeah. I've never gone with them before.

"Any problems, and Luke has my number. Go pick your rooms and get settled in."

There is a yelp of excitement, and I reach for my suitcase, not feeling any enthusiasm. I don't get to it before Luke wraps his fingers around the handle.

"I got it." I try to take it from him.

"No, I'll bring it for you." His smile is quick.

The three sisters barge in front of us. Josh lounges on one of the large chairs. His blond hair is swept back neatly. He looks like a choir boy.

"We have to have rooms beside each other." Barb bustles past Luke. The hall is tight, and he has to wedge himself up against the wall. She finds a room and dashes out, opening the next door. "This one is Willow's. You can leave her case in here." She points with her finger, and Luke does as she says. His jaw is clenched. I follow him into the basic room. The patched quilt on the bed looks like something your grandma would knit. Not that mine ever did, but it's what I would imagine a grandma doing.

Barb plops down on my bed, and Luke stands awkwardly. "Thank you," I say and pull my suitcase over towards the bed. It weighs a ton. Luke's arms move around me, and I have no idea what he is doing until he removes my luggage and places it on the bed.

Barb widens her eyes at him.

"Thanks."

He gives me a smile before leaving.

"Jesus, he's full-on."

I don't know what to make of Barb. I've always liked her, but, right now, she's full-on, and I want to be alone with my thoughts of Rian and the mess I've made in my life.

When she climbs off the bed, I'm glad that she felt the vibes from me without me saying anything.

She closes the door and comes back. "So, I brought some liquor." She's grinning like a Cheshire cat.

"I don't drink." I keep my hands on my suitcase without opening it.

"Never?" She lets her mouth hang open.

"Never," I answer quickly.

"Okay. Now it is my mission to see that Willow tastes alcohol."

I don't want to make this weird. "Maybe." I give up. I hope she leaves. I'm surprised this time when she gets off the bed.

"Okay, I'll let you unpack." She walks back out of my room, and I finally breathe when she leaves. My mind goes straight to mother again, and that snippet of a conversation I had heard between her and Detective Lacy.

He had said, 'the hand'. I'm thinking of my mother questioning me about what happened with Rian on my first day of work. She couldn't have been talking about that hand? What other hand is there, Willow?

I sit on the bed as another hand springs to mind. I can still see it so clearly. My father's large hands, his knuckles, had some hair on them. His hand was open, palm up. The gold band on his finger shone so brightly, and I knew it was all a lie. He didn't love her. He didn't love us.

My heart gallops at the ringing phone. I'm staring at my suitcase in absolute confusion as the phone continues to ring, and I quickly zip it open, flinging the lid back. There sitting on the top of all my clothes is the phone Rian gave me.

My throat and nose burn. I have no idea why she gave it back, but it can't be good. Picking up the phone, it stops ringing. I swallow the pain. I can't help but want to read our messages. She would never know that I read them. My heart sinks. The phone has been cleared. My heart leaps again as the phone rings. Rian's name flashes across the screen. What if it's a trick? What if it's my mother seeing if I answer it?

My finger hovers across the green button, and I'm pressing it while raising the phone to my ear. "Hello."

"Are you okay?"

My legs grow weak at his voice, and I sink to the floor. "You shouldn't be calling."

His laughter sends shivers racing through me. "Why did you answer?"

I can't answer that. "I'm fine. You sound strange." He sounds drunk, but I don't take Rian as a daytime drinker.

"Where are you?" He ignores my question.

I draw my knees up to my chest. "Why?"

"You didn't turn up to work, and I was worried."

I bit my lip, wanting to tell him I want to see him. I miss him. I rub my forehead. "I'm sorry, Rian. I'm with my Bible group."

"Where is that?"

That's twice that he's asked me where I am. "Why?"

"Just trying to make sure you're okay, Willow." He doesn't sound angry, his voice is soft, and that doesn't feel right after our last conversation.

"I have to go."

"Wait..." There is a long pause.

"Rian?" I'm wondering if he is still there.

"I'll call you later," He finally says.

"Don't." I hang up and throw the phone on the floor like it burnt me.

Why did she do it? Why did she give it back to me? I don't believe I will ever truly understand my mother's motives, but I have to trust her.

CHAPTER TWENTY-FOUR

WILLOW

A knock at my door I'd gladly ignore, but I know if I stay here, I'll end up turning the phone back on.

"Would you like to go for a walk?" Luke smiles down at me.

I slip out of my room and close the door behind me, forcing Luke to take a few steps back.

"I'm going to be really honest with you."

Luke scrubs his chin. "Okay."

"I know my mother is encouraging this, but I'm not ready."

His smile widens and I'm not sure how to feel about his response. "We can always go for a walk as friends."

Friends.

What does that mean? Someone you share your secrets with, someone who makes you laugh, someone who holds you when you cry.

"I don't think I'd be a very good friend, Luke." I don't want to hurt him, so I'm letting him down gently.

He stuffs his hands in his royal blue jacket. "Let me be the judge of that."

He's staring at me, and I don't know what more I can say right now.

I can pretend. I have to remind myself—I've done it my whole life. I let my smile form on my lips. "Friends could work."

He smiles in victory and widens his hand in front of him. "Ladies first."

I move down the hall and pass through the main seating area. Josh still lounges on the armchair. His eyes are closed, but I can tell he isn't asleep.

"Josh. Willow and I are going for a walk."

I cringe at how loud Luke is. Did he have to announce it so loud like it was more than what it was?

I don't wait to hear Josh's response but go outside. It's cold, and I like the bite in the air. It pierces through my light cardigan.

Luke rubs his hand together before his gaze roams across me. He starts to unzip his jacket.

"No, don't. I'm not cold."

He pauses. "It's pretty cold."

"I like the cold."

He slowly zips his jacket back up. "If you change your mind..."

I nod and step out on the gravel that surrounds the cabin.

"We don't get to see you much outside of Bible study."

The fields around us are covered in tall grass. There is nothing around us, only flat ground. To the left, I see the outline of distant mountains.

"I keep to myself." I'm careful where I step. The ground sinks under my feet from the recent downpour.

"It's nice that you are with us."

My stomach tightens. "It's nice being here." That is true. I feel almost at peace in this moment, standing knee-deep in grass, with nothing around me. It would be nicer if I were alone. What would Rian think of this place? Butterflies erupt just thinking about those moss-green eyes and the way his hands felt on my skin. I shiver.

"You are cold."

I have to stop Luke again from removing his jacket. He's more reluctant this time and doesn't zip it back up but keeps it on.

"You said painting made you sad because your brother taught you. Is he still with us?"

"Yeah." A pain in my chest feels so physical that I rub it.

"I just assumed he wasn't with us."

I glance at Luke for the first time since leaving. His gaze is heavy on me, and I don't want him to look at me like that.

"I told you I wouldn't make a good friend. I don't like talking about myself. I think we should go back."

"No. I'm sorry. Let's walk. Just walk." He forces a smile and starts to walk but stops after two steps to see if I am following him.

I do and when he stops talking, I actually enjoy the silence that the outside offers. It's different from the silence of a room.

"My father died when I was three."

"I'm sorry for your loss," I say automatically.

Luke laughs. "I didn't know him, but he sounded like a great guy."

I don't want to ask questions but feel I should. "What happened?"

"He fell asleep behind the wheel of his jeep coming home from a twelve-hour shift."

"I'm sorry," I say again with no idea what to say now. He's broken the silence and I've lost the moment of peace that I had found here briefly.

He goes silent, but I can sense him glancing at me. He's sharing. He wants to share.

"Willow!" Barb is running across the field with her red curly hair bouncing behind her. She looks like something from an old film.

"I told Josh we were going for a walk." Luke takes large steps back towards Barb, and he isn't hiding his impatience.

"Josh is asleep. Can I join?" She's smiling, and I can sense the devilment in her.

"Why don't you finish the walk with Luke? I need to use the bathroom anyway."

Both of them start to protest.

"I'll catch up." I fold my arms across my chest and make my way back to the cabin. When I reach the main door, I finally look back to see Luke and Barb walking deeper into the fields.

Josh is still pretending to be asleep on the chair as I pass him. The phone is bothering me too much. Going to my room, I rummage through my bag and take it out again. Why did my mother give it back to me? I can't figure out her motives, but her conversation with Lacy and her asking questions about Rian—all feels wrong to me.

I turn on the phone and immediately place it on silent. I stare at it for a few moments and when no missed call comes up, I stuff it under my pillow and return to the main room.

Laura, Maria, and Casey are in the kitchen making food. Their laughter slowly filters through the cabin, and I envy them.

"Come on in." Laura is the first to notice me, and I step into the kitchen with my hands folded behind my back.

"We are making supper. Father Cooney will be back for prayers, and then he's gone for the night." Laura mixes up the salad in a bowl as she speaks.

Maria grabs some place mats and knives and forks. She pauses when she's nearly past me. "It's really nice to have you here, Willow."

"Thanks." I dig my nails into my wrist, and the pain has me releasing my arm.

"I love your name." Casey glances at me over her shoulder as she flips a steak on the pan.

"Thanks." Her words have me stepping further into the room.

Let's pretend.

I force a smile, and I'm someone else. "So, what can I do to help?"

"You could cut up some onions," Casey answers me.

I move around Laura and grab a large onion and knife. "You know the trick is to breathe through your nose," I say as I slice the onion six times before turning it and doing the same. I don't cut the whole way down. Turning it on its side, I chop and small squares of onion filter onto the chopping board.

After three onions, my eyes start to water, and I step away. "Or not," I say, wiping tears from my eyes. Laura, beside me, laughs and blows her bangs out of her eyes. She blinks and tears fall. "Jesus, they are nasty onions."

The front door opens, and I can hear Barb before I even see her. She bounces into the kitchen full of life, and her eyes widen in surprise to see me helping.

"Someone give me a job, so I don't attack Luke." Her voice is good-humoured, but I wonder what happened.

"I thought I told you that Willow and I were going for a walk?" Luke's voice carries clearly into the kitchen.

"Yeah, I fell asleep." Josh doesn't sound sleepy at all and makes me aware that I don't know these people at all or their dynamics with each other.

"What happened?" Casey steps away from the pan and hands Barb a bowl full of mushrooms. "Chop them."

She returns to the stove.

"I mean, he'd bore anyone to death." Barb starts, and I realize I like the sound of her voice. I smile a lot internally at her description of Luke. "I really think I'd rather watch paint dry than have another conversation with him."

Laura laughs and bumps her hip with Barb. "Don't be mean. He isn't that bad."

"Besides, he can hear you," Maria says, as she passes us with glasses.

"I really don't care. I'm not one to hide my feelings." Barb chops the mushrooms like she's ready to hurt someone. We work well together, and the meal is set by the time Father Cooney arrives.

Everyone eats, chats, and laughs. I've never been part of something like this before, and I think if I could stay here and pretend, I could really like it.

After food, we sit down and pray for a while. Once Father Cooney closes our prayer, Barb bounces around, waiting for him to leave. He sits back in one of the large armchairs, and he doesn't look like he's going anywhere. I leave them and return to my room to check my phone. I have no more missed calls.

"Are you okay?" Luke knocks on the frame of my door and stands in the threshold, blocking the doorway.

"Yes." I tuck the phone back under my pillow and face him.

"I heard Barb going on about me."

His smile tells me he isn't offended. "I don't blame her," he says, lingering at the door. I think he is waiting for me to invite him in, but I'm not going to. It's like a really odd standoff or something.

"I'm going to be honest. I didn't want to spend time with Barb today. I had really hoped that we could spend time together."

I'm ready to reinforce my earlier words; as I take a step towards Luke, he moves two feet back as I stand on the door threshold.

"Oh, my God! I call dibs." Barb's breathy words disrupt my thoughts.

"What are you doing here?" Father Cooney asks, and both Luke and I move up the hall. I don't get far when Rian comes into view. His moss-green eyes soften when they land on me, but a savagery enters them when they land on Luke. As he walks towards us, I'm shaking my head.

"Rian, you can't be here." Father Cooney calls, and I'm frozen in place because this can't be happening. Why is he here? I snap out of my frozen stance as Father Cooney appears, and everyone else is behind him. Barb's eyes are alight like a movie star just entered. Everyone else is just watching. I step in front of Luke, and Rian looks at me.

"What are you doing?" My voice is low, but everyone is packed too tightly into the hallway, and I know they all hear me.

"What are you doing?" His words are sharp, and my heart starts to rage in my chest.

I force a smile and look at Father Cooney. "It's okay, Father. If I could just have a moment?" The tremble in my voice has me swallowing back the anxiety that is building inside me. I'm praying to God that he agrees, and my legs threaten to buckle when he finally gives his approval.

"Come on, everyone." Father Cooney ushers everyone back into the sitting room. I glance at Rian, and he's staring at me like he's ready to crack at any second.

"Go on, Luke. I'll only be a moment." I speak without looking away from Rian.

When Luke doesn't move, I quickly glance at him over my shoulder. "Luke." His gaze moves to me, and he exhales loudly.

"I can stay." His words are gentle.

Rian's laughter has me cringing. "Do stay," Rian tells him.

"Rian, I want to talk to you alone." I step closer to Rian and die a little inside from how this might look to Luke. No one can know. I don't need any more people judging me.

"Luke, please. I want a moment with my step-brother."

Rian's lips tug up into a sneer, and he nods like he knows I'm embarrassed. I want to slap him. This is his fault; he has no right to be here.

Luke steps around me, and I reach out and place a hand on Rian's chest, begging him not to move.

CHAPTER TWENTY-FIVE

WILLOW

"What are you doing here?" I remove my hand from his chest. His heart is pounding against my palm, and I can almost taste the want for violence that is emanating off him.

"I told you before that you are mine." He steps closer.

I can't let anyone see this. "We can talk outside."

His sneer grows, and I swallow the saliva that pools in my mouth.

I take a step around him, and I am surprised when he follows. Everyone grows silent in the sitting room.

"Father, I'm just stepping outside. I won't be long." I force a smile and refuse to meet anyone else's gaze.

"I don't think that's wise." Luke steps forward.

"You want to come out and join us?" Rian steps up beside me, and I want to curl up and let the ground take me.

"Father, I don't think Willow going with Rian is wise."

"Luke. What I do is none of your business." My words are louder than I intend, but I didn't want someone else hurt because of me.

"Willow, Luke is correct."

Father Cooney folds his gentle hands in front of him. "Rian, I think it's best that you leave."

Luke smirks and looks at Rian smugly. Rian stiffens, and I feel his energy change a second before he lunges at Luke.

Everyone is screaming as he grabs Luke. I'm frozen when his fist smashes into Luke's face. Blood seems to explode everywhere. Father Cooney and Josh try to drag Rian away. They get thrown back like pins being knocked over by a bowling ball.

Casey's cries snap me out of my frozen state, and I'm running towards Rian and Luke. I grip Rian's arm, trying to stop him.

"Stop it!" He pauses and shakes me off, his fist hitting Luke's face again. All I see is Chad's face unrecognizable in the bed.

I grab Rian's arm again. "Please!" My scream has the whole room falling silent. Father Cooney stands up, his face red with anger.

"Let him go." I refuse to release Rian's arm. He opens his fingers, and Luke tumbles to the ground.

"Get out." I slam both hands into Rian's chest. Tears leak from my eyes that I can't control. What he just did was barbaric.

"I said, get out." I slam my fists into his chest this time, and I don't want to stop. I want him to hurt as much as I do right now.

His jaw clenches, and I think he's going to leave until he reaches out and grabs my arm.

"Let me go." I try to pull away from him, but his grip is like iron.

"Rian, you let Willow go." Father Cooney steps in our way, and I can't bear to see anyone else get hurt.

I stop fighting. "It's okay, Father. I'll only be a moment." I swallow tears. Father Cooney doesn't look happy, and I'm sure the moment we leave, he'll either ring the cops or my mother.

The moment we get outside, Rian releases my arm. He won't look at me, and I can see it's taking a lot of control for him to stay still right now.

"That boy did nothing wrong." My lip trembles as I speak.

Rian wheels on me, and I take two quick steps back as his anger grows with his steps. "You are mine. Not his."

His words have me glancing back at the house.

"Are you afraid of them hearing?" Rian's lips tug up into a cruel smile as he takes another step towards me and grips my chin painfully. "Are you afraid of them knowing that you wanted me to fuck you?"

I rip my face out of his hand and start to walk fast. "I told you, this is over," I bark out into the night air. "Why won't you listen to me?"

"I took you for a lot of things," Rian's voice is lowered. "But not a coward."

"You have no idea who I am!" I shout. How dare he judge me.

His face softens. "I think I do."

Curtains move on the cabin window. "You should go." I fold my arms across my chest.

"You think I'm going to leave you here with Luke?" The cruelty returns to his voice.

"What exactly do you think I'm doing here? Fucking Luke? Is that it?"

"Don't push me, Willow." Rian's words are barely controlled, and I know pushing him won't get me anywhere.

"He likes me, I told him I'm not interested. So we agreed to be friends."

Rian doesn't move.

"You need to leave. I'm sure the police are on their way."

Rian sneers. "I don't run, Willow. You should know that by now."

"How did you find me?"

"I tracked your phone." Rian takes a step towards me, and I don't want him near me. I start to walk. The night is cold, but I don't want anyone watching us.

Rian walks beside me, and I'm thinking about walking this field with Luke, how different it feels with Rian. I glance at him, and he's watching me with his hauntingly beautiful eyes.

"I'm sorry about your father."

The world tilts, and my stomach rebels. The ground shifts, and my legs buckle.

"Jesus, Willow." Rian is beside me, gripping me. "Talk to me about it."

The air grows thinner by the second, and I'm picturing him so clearly. His brains splattered against the wall—blood streaming down his chest. The cushions splattered around him.

"When I found out he took his life, all I could think about was you cutting yourself."

It's like someone slapped me across the face. "Took his life?" The words tumble from my lips, and Rian's large hands grip either side of my face.

"It must have been terrifying at ten to have found him. I can't get that image of you out of my head."

I'm sinking further into the ground. A sob tears from my lips and transforms itself into a cry of pain before it evolves into laughter. "Who told you that?" I blink and tears spill.

"My father. Willow, I'm here." He's still gripping my face, forcing me to look him in the eyes. More laughter bubbles up, and I can't stop it. My body temperature spikes, and I'm sobbing again. Rian drags me against his chest, and I give in, sinking into him. The fight for me to get away from my past is slipping hard and fast, and I am starting to feel like I'm drunk or what I would imagine drunk to be.

I push away from Rian. He jolts back and my hand collides with his face. The sound is loud in the dead of night and I strike him again. He doesn't stop me and I hate him for that. I hate him for allowing me this. My mouth crashes down on his, and he responds instantly to my lips. Pushing him back roughly, I climb on top of him. His cock is rock hard already, and when I bend over him, he grabs my face stopping me.

"You never have to hide from me."

I didn't need his comfort right now. I want to hurt him so badly. "Shut up, Rian." I slam my mouth on his. He doesn't return my kiss, refusing me what I need. Ready to break, I grind my pussy against his cock. With a growl, he rolls me onto my back and starts tearing at my clothes.

"Fuck me hard," I pant between breaths, begging him to take me away from this moment.

"No more running from me." His eyes flash with a warning.

"Get off me." I push him away, but he doesn't move.

"Get off me, Rian."

His hands leave my face and grip my wrists, dragging my arms above my head. "You're not running this time."

"Why the fuck do you care?!" I'm screaming. No one has ever cared. Why him?

"Because I love you, Willow."

My body tenses, and I'm not sure I heard him right. I'm shaking my head. "You don't even know me." Tears leak from the corners of my eyes.

"I might not know your past, but I know you. I know when you're pretending or lying. I know how I feel."

My heart threatens to rip from my chest as his moss-green eyes devour me.

"Willow." Father Cooney's voice is like a splash of cold water across my burning soul.

"I have to go back in. I have to make this right," I whisper to Rian.

He gets off me and helps me stand. I have no idea what is going to happen. I'm expecting Rian to demand I come with him. "Should I come with you?"

I run a shaky hand across my face. "I don't think so, Rian. You should go home."

He's already shaking his head.

"What do you expect me to do?"

"Go in and say your piece. Pack your bags, and let me take you home."

"Willow." Father Cooney calls again.

"I'll just be a moment, Father." I try to keep the bite out of my words.

"This isn't going to work." How could he not see that? What we are doing is wrong.

"Willow, you just don't get it. I'm not giving you up."

"You don't get it. I can't do this." I pronounce each word, and for the first time, I think I'm getting through to Rian.

He runs his hands across his face. His bandaged hand makes me think of him saving me.

"Rian..." I want to explain, but I don't know how. I care for him, it's more than care, but I can't allow all those emotions to filter through me.

"This ends now." Shivers assault me, and I'm not sure if it's from his hardened gaze or the damp grass that has penetrated through my clothes. I glance back at the house. Father Cooney is still waiting. "If you care about me, you'll leave." I don't look to Rian as guilt gnaws at me, but fold my arms across my chest and start walking back to the house.

The cabin is quiet when I step in, and each second that ticks by, I'm waiting for Rian to bust through the door and drag me out, but it doesn't happen. The door opens and closes behind me, and I can't stop myself from looking just to be sure. Father Cooney's normally soft eyes are narrowed as he glares at me like this is my fault.

I push that thought aside and move over to Luke.

"Are you okay?"

"What the hell do you think?" Maria surprises me with the level of anger she directs towards me.

Luke groans as he tries to sit up. His face is a bloody mess.

"I'm sorry." My voice is low.

"I think it's best you leave." Maria rises from beside Luke.

"That's very fucking forgiving of you." Everyone inhales sharply at my language. I hold up my hands before she can respond and leave the room. Father Cooney doesn't stop me as I go into my room and pack. I'm dying a little inside as I pick up the black phone. I'm staring at it even as Barb steps into the room.

"I don't blame you," she says.

"It doesn't matter. Everyone else does."

"You can't control what other people do. They know that. I think everyone is just in shock. It was crazy, but don't go."

My finger hovers over Rian's number. I had just told him to leave, but could I really stay here?

CHAPTER TWENTY-SIX

RIAN

I flex my fist several times before glancing back up at the cabin. The small windows are lit up. I'm not finished yet. My blood still roars. I still hunger for violence. The door opens, and Willow appears with luggage that's nearly the same size as her. A red-haired girl steps out after her, I can't hear what they are saying, but it looks like she's trying to encourage Willow to go back inside. Willow smiles, and it's fake, before waving a black phone at the girl. She steps out onto the gravel, and I watch her as she drags her suitcase behind her hunched frame. I let her walk out onto the road before I start the car and slowly drive behind her.

She glances back and blinks from the severity of my lights. I hate how unafraid she is—a girl alone on a dark road. The priest would have had a lot to answer for if anything had happened to her. I put my foot on the pedal and drive past Willow. Stopping, I get out and open the trunk. She doesn't stop walking as I approach her and take the luggage from her hand. She's still holding the phone tightly as she climbs into the front seat. I feel more settled with her beside me as I continue to drive. The violence that raged inside me slowly fades away.

"I can't go home." Her words are spoken to the night sky.

I had no intention of taking her back to her mother.

Each time she glances at me, there is a deadness in her eyes that scares me. I want to apologize for ruining her weekend, but I'm not sorry. The thought of Luke anywhere near her is enough to reignite the violence in me.

I pull up at the gates and Willow glances at me, her brows dragged down. "The garden center?"

"It's my garden." I grin as I climb out and unlock the chain around the gates. The car idles behind me as I push them open. Once we are through, I relock them. Willow glances behind her at the fading gates in the red tail light as I drive through the gardens and to my home.

"I'm still renovating," I say once we pull up.

Willow ducks her head down to look up at the large two-story home. She can't see much in the darkness.

I get out and get her luggage out of the trunk. She's beside me as I open the door and step into my home. I've never brought anyone here. Turning on the lights, I turn as Willow steps into my home. Her gaze is filled with awe as she looks around the entryway, and I have a sudden desire to see my home through her eyes. My hall has its original mosaic flooring. The white slide and sash windows are also original—I had the doors and high skirting boards restored.

I close the heavy red door behind her, and she continues to look around. "This is your home?" Her voice bounces around the empty hallway.

"I'm still renovating."

She glances at me from over her shoulder, and I can't help but think she looks perfect in my home. I don't want to take from her right now. I want her to give herself to me freely. Her cheeks darken. My intentions, I don't hide. I want Willow. I always have, but having her in my home, alone, with no-one to interrupt us, is making this moment harder than I could have ever imagined.

She looks away, but I see the broken look in her eyes. It's there under her curiosity, and I'm sure she will cave at any second from all her pain. Her movements are gentle as she leans in and flicks on the light to the main sitting room. It's a shell, with only its original fireplace. The rest of it has been stripped back. Lights are set up in the middle of the floor, along with all my tools.

"Are you doing it yourself?" She turns but keeps her back to the doorframe, her hands are tucked behind her back.

"Yes. It clears my mind. When I'm here working on the house, I'm just working."

Her eyes smile at me. "Does your father know?"

"No. No one knows."

Her eyes widen.

"Come on." I reach out my hand for her, and she bites her lip. She places her small hand in mine where it belongs.

"I haven't done much. I've been stripping it back and allowing the original features to breathe." I take her through an empty dining room and down a hall. We enter another room that I might have as another sitting area. Double doors that were made from wrought iron open out onto my favorite part of the house. I turn on the lights in the indoor greenhouse, and they come to life.

Willow's hand leaves mine, and I want to reach out and take it back, but instead, I focus on her face as she takes in all the large plants that had no one to tame them. The room is like a jungle, and I know I will leave it this way. I've hung lights from trees and have some randomly placed in the clay of the flower beds. She keeps walking with a look of pure wonder on her face. She stops in the center where a small white table and chairs sit. I've been working on stripping back all the layers of paint to try to get to the original.

"Wow." She smiles, and I know it's real. Her eyes are still puffy from crying earlier. She still looks haunted, like someone who just stepped out of a war zone.

"Yeah, this is my sanctuary."

"You are so lucky to have all this." She glances around the room. It's hers too. She just doesn't know it yet.

"There is a lot of work to be done. I could always use some help."

She won't meet my eye now as she starts to leave the room. "I don't think so, Rian." I follow her, wanting to make her stop, but something tells me not to touch her.

We are back in the hallway again, and she's staring at the front door. Picking up her suitcase, I carry it upstairs. The winding stairs have been sanded back, the wood of the banister under my hand is soft. Her light footsteps on the stairs make me grin. My intentions for getting her upstairs are the furthest from pure. I pass several rooms and enter the only one that is decorated.

My bedroom.

I flip on the light and drag her suitcase in. This is where she belongs. I turn to face her as she steps in. Her gaze bounces from me to the red bedding. It's for her.

"Red?"

I grin. "You noticed."

Her wild brown eyes focus on me, and she frowns, but it slowly disappears as I take a step towards her.

"You can stay here with me tonight." I reach out and touch her face. She leans into my touch, and she has no idea how happy her response makes me.

"Rian…" She's ready to protest, but with her lids closed, I know it won't take much to bend her to my will.

"I want you to stay with me tonight." She continues to lean into my touch, and I press my lips against her swollen ones. My body stills hums, remembering what she feels like.

Her lips move slowly undermine. Tonight, I don't want to go slow. I want to give us both what we need. My lips push harder against her, and she sucks in a sharp breath. She stops kissing and leans away before snapping back towards me. Her mouth is hungry, and I'm all for feeding her.

Lifting her towards the bed, she's already tugging at her cardigan. The heat of her skin under my hands has me touching every piece of available skin as she removes her shirt. She's breathing heavy when my mouth leaves her, and I run my lips across her neck. Her pulse pulses against my lips—my cock is painfully hard. I reach back and unclip her bra, letting her breasts bounce free. She's flushed when I look up at her. There is a moment's hesitation in her eyes. Taking a nipple in my mouth, she cries out. I know I've won as I suck and nip at the sensitive area while my hand forces her legs open, and I rub her damp pussy through her trousers. I wanted this angel on all fours, and I wanted to fuck her hard. I release her breast and pull my shirt off over my head before returning to her other nipple. She cries out again, and it makes me work faster. Pulling at her trousers, the button gives way, and I yank them down along with her panties. Her wild eyes are glazed over as she stares up at me.

"You want me to fuck you hard?" I ask her, spreading her legs wide.

"Yes," her wild eyes match her hungry voice. I move down between her legs and plunge my tongue into her pussy. Her back arches as she cries out. Pushing a hand down on her abdomen, I continue sucking her clit. She's squirming under me, and my cock is pushing against my trousers painfully. I push a finger into her tight pussy. It's soaking, and my finger enters easily. Her panting is growing faster, and she's squirming more. I don't want her to come. I slow down and lean back, removing the rest of my clothes.

Rising up, I move in between her legs. I place the tip of my cock at her opening and ease in slowly. Her gaze is on me, and the wonderment and lust that swirls in her dark eyes has me wanting to fuck her hard. It takes so much effort to move slowly. She's wider this time and wetter. Once my cock is fully in, I pound faster, her head rolls from side to side and she's too close to coming. Removing myself from her, I turn her around.

"Get on all fours." She does and cocks her ass in the air like she's done this before. I want to punish her, but remind myself this is her first time in this position. Gripping her hips, I position myself at her opening, knowing there's no holding back this time. I rock my hips forward and bury my cock in her pussy. Her cries rush from her lips as I fuck her like I've always wanted to.

Her cries rise, and I don't want her to come yet, but I can't stop fucking her perfect pussy. I feel the rush of her juices across my cock and move faster inside. She slumps slightly, and I grip her hips, yanking her back to me as

I bury myself fully inside. She's still grunting as I lose myself in Willow. I'm close to coming, and when she calls my name, it's all it takes for me to empty myself into her sweet swollen pussy that was made just for me.

CHAPTER TWENTY-SEVEN

WILLOW

I've been awake for a while now, and my heart won't calm. I'm in Rian's bed. A stupid smile tugs at my lips as I run my hands across the quilt cover. I was allowing myself to believe that the red was picked for me. One large arm is thrown across my waist, pinning me in place against him. His body is rock hard, but I still want to move closer to his warmth. I turn slowly, and my heart pounds a bit heavier.

He's asleep. His face looks gentle, and I have the urge to touch it, so I do. I try not to think about what today will bring. I try not to think of the hurt that has come before this moment. My chest feels tight, and I've never wanted to tell someone what happened on that day. I've never felt the need to share my deed with someone else, but right now, I want to share it with Rian. The tips of my fingers trace his face and a muscle tenses in his jaw, alerting me. He's awake. I don't stop touching him. I give myself this moment with him. Moss green eyes send my heart rate skyrocketing, and I don't stop the smile that tugs at my lips.

"Good morning."

"I'd like to wake up like this every morning." His hand tightens around my waist, and I don't stop him as he drags me until our bodies are flush. His cock grows hard, and my smile melts away. I kiss him first, my body humming with a want that can't seem to be satisfied.

A ringing phone has me stopping. I'm looking for mine but can't remember where I put it.

"It's my phone." Rian climbs out of bed naked, and I lie back down and drink him in. He picks up his phone from somewhere on the ground.

"It's your mother." He doesn't turn to me as he holds the ringing phone.

"She must be worried. Answer it."

He glances at me now. "What will I tell her?" There is a bite to his words.

"That I'll be home soon."

Rian turns away, and I slip out of the bed as he answers the phone. "Yes, Catherine."

I grin as I can imagine how pissed off that makes her. The way he says her name showcases his dislike for her.

"She's here. Safe and sound."

Rian watches me as I start to pull on my clothes.

"I'll have her ....Yes, I did."

The button on my trousers is missing. I consider getting a fresh pair, but when I see the snarl on Rian's lips, I tug my shirt on.

"You told me she was with him to provoke me. Consider your work done, Catherine."

I stop getting dressed. My mother had told Rian that I was with Luke? What was she doing?

"He's lucky to be alive. I'll have her back soon."

Rian takes the phone away from his ear. So much swirls in his eyes. He's angry, but whatever words he has against my mother, he keeps them to himself.

"I should go back." I button up my cardigan. Rian tugs on his trousers, and each motion is angry. I fold my arms across my chest.

"I'll wait downstairs," I say, and he doesn't look at me, just nods.

I run my hands through my hair as I arrive downstairs. I glance back up to see if Rian is coming, but he's still banging around. I want to see the greenhouse one more time before I leave. I slip down the small hall; everything looks so different in the light of day. It's perfect. This house calls to me, I think it calls to my soul. I need someone to strip me back and let me breathe. I wonder who I am under all the fake smiles and controlled emotions. It's been nearly ten years.

My throat burns when I think of that little girl. Stepping into the greenhouse, it takes my breath away, just like it did last night. I walk through it and let my hands touch the wildness of the plants. One grows so high that it bends from the glass on the roof.

There is a wildness here that I want to become a part of.

His footsteps are heavy as he enters the space, and I don't stop until I find the center of the room.

"It's absolutely beautiful, Rian," I say, without looking up at him.

My heart pounds initially with the thought of what I want to do, but it settles quickly, and soon there is that moment knowing that it's time to shed my skin.

I glance at him, and his moss-green eyes have softened. "More beautiful now that you are standing in it."

His words warm my heart. He has no idea how he turns me inside out. I want to kiss him—but if I start—I won't ever tell him what I need to say.

"There was this girl who spent most of her childhood holding ice packs to her mother's swollen face, cleaning up broken plates and glasses. She held her mother as she cried with the pain from broken bones. Around and around it went, there was no end in sight."

I take a breath and look up at Rian. He's as still as a statue. I take another breath and continue.

"One night, as her father filled his gut with beer, the little girl waited until he finally fell asleep on the couch. Her mother was in the bath, holding a cold face-cloth to her bruised chest." My voice wobbles, and I swallow quickly. Rian moves, and I hold a hand up until he stops.

"She left her father asleep on the couch and walked calmly into his room. She knew where he kept his gun. She picked it up with both hands. It was heavier than she had thought it would be, but still, she carried it back to the sitting room. The TV flickered across his face, he was fast asleep. He looked almost like a father who might hug his wife on occasion or leave his daughter green apples, but underneath the small gestures, there was nothing redeemable."

My vision blurs, and I blink. Salty tears make a pathway down my face and into my mouth. "The little girl raised that gun and smiled. She knew she could end all the suffering. For once, she wasn't going to be a coward."

I lick my lips and look Rian in the eyes. "She pulled that trigger. Her aim was perfect. The noise was deafening, and she dropped the gun. There was so much blood." I can still see him so clearly, and I remember feeling giddy. But my happiness only lasted for a moment. Her screams were like nothing I had heard before. She had raced from the bath, wrapped in a white towel. Initially, my gaze wouldn't move up but focused on the pools of water around her feet. Slowly, I had looked up at my mother.

"The worst part of it all was when her mother entered the room." I reach out now and grip the white chair because a crushing sensation has me closing my eyes.

"At times when the mother had taken a beating, and the little girl had cleaned her face, her eyes would be alive with hate that never died. She wore this look after the beatings, the look of someone knowing one day they would get their revenge."

More tears pour, and I swallow them. "She had this ball of pain and anger…" I can't explain the look she wore after my father beat her.

"But that day…" More pain crushes me, and I exhale loudly on a sob. "She had looked at me like I was a monster. My own mother was afraid of me." I cover my face now with both hands, not wanting Rian to see this kind of pain.

I cry into my hands, and when I feel more under control, I look up at him. He hasn't moved. I have no idea what he is thinking, but I don't stop.

"We buried him in the back garden, and from that day on, I did everything she said because I couldn't bear the way she looked at me. Sometimes she still does, and I hate myself for bringing so much pain into her life."

Rian doesn't speak, and my heart crashes around in my chest with the thought that telling him was a mistake.

"I had to do it," I cry.

Rian moves for the first time; his steps are slow. "You did what she should have done." He holds his head high, and for the first time, I see the pride shine in his eyes. "You protected your family." He reaches for me.

"You did what was necessary." His hands touch my face, and I'm ready to sink.

"You are so brave." He leans in, and my eyes flutter closed as he places a kiss on each eyelid before pressing a final one to my forehead.

"I just wish you didn't have to suffer for it."

I open my eyes, and this is the part that scares me the most. I shake my head that's still in his hands. "I didn't suffer, Rian. If I went back, I'd still pull that trigger. I have no regrets." A sob cuts off my word.

"I just hate that I have no regrets. It's not normal. I'm not normal, and I scare my own mother. I didn't just lose a father that night—I lost my mother, too." Tears stream down into my mouth.

"She hates me," I say, drawing back my pain.

"She doesn't understand what you did for her." Rian holds my face tighter, making me focus on his green eyes again. "Thank you for telling me."

"You make me feel safe, and okay to be *not* normal."

His smile reaches his eyes. "Normal is boring. I don't like boring."

He leans in and kisses the tip of my nose. "I don't ever want to see smiles and just the parts of you that you are proud of. I always want to see the parts you aren't proud of. They are always the parts that are the most interesting."

"I feel so invisible at times." I drop his gaze as I let all the insecurities out.

"I see you, Willow. I always have." Shivers assault my body at his words. "I love you." I don't think I'll ever get used to those three words.

Rian's phone rings loudly in his pocket. He doesn't release my face.

"Answer it," I tell him, because from this moment forward, I have no idea what happens next.

CHAPTER TWENTY-EIGHT

WILLOW

We return to the main house. Rian's father said it was important for both of us to return immediately. The whole drive, Rian, holds my hand, and I let his warmth and the sense of happiness lull me into a false sense of safety that really doesn't exist in my world. So many questions swim at the edge of my consciousness, like loose change in your pocket. It keeps rattling, and the only way to stop it is to wrap your fingers around the coins. Right now, I don't want to touch those thoughts. They are too dark.

I sit up straight the moment we pull up to the house. I recognise the car in the drive—Detective Lacy's.

"Maybe we shouldn't go in." My fear of him seeing that my hands aren't clean assaults my system. I'm too raw right now, too open. I have no control over my emotions.

Rian's laughter has me turning to him. "Don't worry about Detective Lacy. I think he's smart enough not to step on my toes."

Rian pulls into the garage and turns off the ignition.

"And if he does step on your toes?" I ask.

"I'll deal with him." Rian turns to me and takes my face in his hands. I already fear everyone's reaction seeing Rian and me together. I want to say something, but he does first.

"You and I can remain quiet until you're ready, Willow. But if you want to walk in there holding my hand, I'm ready."

I'm not.

Guilt churns in my stomach as I speak. "I think it best we see what Detective Lacy wants."

I can see the disappointment in Rian's gaze. "If that's what you want."

The garage door opens and my mother appears. Anger tightens her gaze and straightens her lips. I pull my face out of Rian's hands. He easily lets me go.

I don't have a second before she pulls my door open. "Get out."

I don't move, I don't know if it's the sense of the army at my back or my confession to Rian, but I don't feel like taking orders right now.

"I've had a really tough day, so I'm asking you nicely to not bark at me."

My mother's eyes widen, and she leans in and glares at Rian. "This is your doing."

I feel exhausted already.

"I'd like to think so." I can hear the humor in Rian's voice.

"Detective Lacy is here for both of you." She's glaring at us as the garage door opens, and Henry walks in. I know it's bad when I see the set of his jaw.

Rian gets out of the car and I follow suite. I can't hold my mother's hardened gaze. It cuts too deep.

"Chad Michaels is dead," Henry speaks calmly. "Detective Lacy is here to question both of you again."

"He can talk to me." Rian closes the car door. "Willow is tired and won't be up for talking."

Henry nods his head like the Detective would just accept it. I'm ready to argue when my mother grips my arm painfully. I'm ready to shake it off, but I give her this bit of control over me for now. I'm too tired to keep arguing.

We enter through the kitchen, and my mother directs me upstairs. I take a final glance at Rian as he enters the sitting room with Henry. He pauses and meets my eyes. Rian winks at me before stepping into the room and disappearing. I feel like I should be going in there with him, too. This was mostly my fault. Chad would never have been on Rian's radar if I hadn't put him there.

"Come on, Willow." My mother sounds drained as she marches to my room.

"What is it?" I ask. The moment we are in, I pull off my cardigan and undo the two top buttons of my shirt.

"What is it? I get a call from Father Cooney saying Rian attacked Luke, and you left."

I take a step towards my mother and stop when something close to fear flares across her face. "You told Rian I was gone away with Luke."

"Yes, so he would see you had moved on. I thought I was helping."

"You weren't, Mother. He was in a rage when he arrived at the cabin."

My mother half laughs. "You almost sound like you're blaming me."

"I am. Why did you put the phone in my bag?"

My mother drops my gaze.

"What are you playing at?" I take another step.

Anger has her head snapping up to me. "How dare you question me when all I've ever done is keep you safe?"

"Safe?" I repeat the word.

"Yes, Willow. Safe. But right now." She raises her hand up and down towards me. "I don't recognize this person."

A sadness is almost crushing my chest. "I do." It's the first time I recognize myself. My words are real. My feelings are real, and it feels like it's time that I get to live too, not just exist in this vicious circle of uncertainty and fear.

"I don't want to be afraid anymore." I plead with my words for her to understand.

"No one will find out." Her voice has softened as she takes a step towards me. "As long as you keep all those emotions at bay."

I shake my head. "I'm not afraid of someone finding out, Mother. I'm afraid of what keeping it in is doing to me. I can't breathe. I always feel numb. I don't feel human or alive most of the time. I never feel safe. I always feel like I'm on the brink of screaming." I'm pleading with her to understand.

"You are so ungrateful. I gave up my life, my son, my husband, to protect—*you*! I built this life for *you*. I gave up sending you to prom. I never got to take my daughter shopping. I never got to listen to your romances, all to keep you safe. I never got to be a mother. I never got to have a daughter. I had to always have my guard up with you." She's brimming with anger at each sentence.

I can't breathe with her anger. I didn't know she harbored this much resentment towards me. I want to scream at her that I didn't get to experience any of that either. Prom was something that only happened in movies. The thought that it was real, and I could have been participating in this life opens a hollowness inside me.

A knock at the door has both of us jumping apart. The door opens before I get to answer it. Rian's gaze roams across me as if he is making sure I'm in one piece.

"Are you okay?" His voice is soft, and my stomach tightens when I see the love in his eyes. He has given me a form of peace and I can't waste it this time.

"Yes." I try to smile my gratitude at him.

"Get out." My mother marches past me and grips the door. "I don't want you near my daughter."

"Why? Are you afraid that I might find out about the lies you fed my father?"

My heart drops into my shoes. I can't see my mother's face, but her hands shake behind the door. "What are you talking about?"

Rian looks at me, and I plead with my eyes. He leans into my mother. "Hurt her anymore and I'll go straight to my father. You understand?"

"Hurt her?" My mother's laughter is filled with bitterness. Whatever fear she had passes quickly as she grips the door before she slams it in Rian's face.

I jump as the door bangs loudly. I've never seen her so angry.

"Tell me, Willow. Are you happy?" Her words are growled. "I hope you are. At least one of us would be." Tears fill her eyes.

"I'm sorry." I need to take back the pain I'm causing. "I'm just tired and emotional." I try to grip her arm.

She stands away from me. "I always felt I had to save you. So I let everything else go to do that." Pain wraps itself around her words. She blinks and tears spill. "Your brother found your father's body."

The bed hits the back of my legs before I crumble onto it. "What?" I couldn't have heard her right.

My mother wipes at her face roughly. "Of course, he rang it in. I had told him your father left us, so you can imagine his pain when he came across his body."

I'm shaking my head. "When was this?"

"Two weeks ago. The cops have opened a murder case. Your brother was beside himself."

I can't stop shaking my head. I want to peel off my skin.

"I told him, Willow." My mother's voice is low. "I told him what you did."

A scream that's been building inside me lodges itself in my throat.

My mother comes closer to me. "I wish you weren't such a silly, selfish little girl. I had to make an arrangement with Detective Lacy in order to keep you out of prison."

I move past my mother, my brain not fully taking in what she is saying. The toilet lid is up, and I empty the contents of my stomach in it. I'm still retching when my mother's heels click loudly on the tiled floor.

"If I can prove Rian guilty of a crime, you get to walk away, and it will be put down as a suicide."

My retching turns to sobs before laughter takes over. She was handing over Rian to try to save me.

"What a fucking mess." I can't stop laughing. My mother doesn't join in as I release the toilet and sit on the floor, wiping vomit from the corner of my mouth.

"Get up." Her growl has my laughter stopping. "Stop being so selfish and play your part in this."

I'm standing on shaky legs. "What do you expect me to do?"

I'm searching my mother's face for some compassion in all this.

"Catch Rian in the act, prove it, and you get to walk free."

"I love him," I admit for the first time.

I don't expect my mother to strike me—the burn sears across my face.

"Love me. Love your brother." She's breathing heavy with anger.

"I do," I say, holding my face.

"Prove it."

"I thought I already had."

My mother sneers, but the pain is evident on her face. "By murdering your father?"

I can't hold her gaze. "I did it to protect you." My lip trembles and I'm a child again.

"You could have picked up the phone and called the police; you could have told your brother. You could have done so many things. What ten-year-old gets a gun and shoots her father in the head?"

I shrug. "A ten-year-old that had too much." I blink the tears out of my eyes.

My mother covers her mouth with her hand while shaking her head. "If you don't catch Rian killing someone, you won't just go down for murder, Willow. So will I."

"No. You didn't do anything."

She's laughing now before she snaps back at me. "I buried my husband and helped my daughter cover up a murder that we got away with for ten years. That's not *nothing*."

"I'll take the blame."

My mother's hands grip my shoulders. "Listen to me. It won't matter. I will get the chair."

My mother releases me, and the look in her eyes makes me think she's going to strike me again, but she doesn't. She leaves my room.

She expects me to hand Rian over. I splash water on my face. If I do nothing, I go to jail, and she gets the electric chair. My stomach rebels again, but I manage to keep it down.

What would Rian do if he knew my mother and Detective Lacy were conspiring against him? What would he do now that I'm involved? I stare at myself in the mirror. One thing I know for sure is that I will not let my mother fry in a chair.

Put Rian behind bars? Could I do that? He had been there before and survived. I push away from the sink. There must be another way. I could plead my case to make Detective Lacy understand. That's what I could do. I have nothing to lose this way, only my freedom. I honestly don't believe I've had that since I was ten, anyway.

CHAPTER TWENTY-NINE

RIAN

She's been avoiding me for three days. Each time I see Catherine in the house, she looks at me with hatred. I hadn't realized we had hit such a low. Me fucking her daughter must be really pissing her off.

"Where is Willow?" Catherine's moving around the kitchen this morning, and I don't see any fruit being cut up. That's her normal routine.

"She's going to church and then to work." Catherine doesn't turn as she makes herself a coffee.

"Oh, she's returning to work?"

Catherine turns, holding the mug tightly. "Yes. She just needed some time away. What happened over the weekend seems to have taken a huge toll on my daughter's mental health."

She's glaring at me, and I'm wondering which lie I'm meant to be scooping up right now. Is it the one where Willow's father committed suicide?

"I'm sorry about your husband, Catherine. I didn't know."

She stiffens, her knuckles turning white as she grips the mug. "It's not public knowledge. But it's hard on Willow. She's fragile."

Catherine is a masterful liar. If I didn't know the truth, I'd believe her. No wonder she has my father eating out of her hand. I want to call her out on her lie, but for now, I'll play along and see how far she goes.

"I'd like to take some flowers to the grave." I stand, and don't hold her gaze, to give her a moment to gather her lies. When I look back at her she's half smiling.

"The grave is far away. With his family."

"Still. I would like to visit it as a mark of respect."

She gives me a tight smile, and I'm wondering if she is as good at detecting a lie as she is handing them out. "Of course. St. Colmcille's Cemetery. Monalty."

I walk right up to her and notice the nervous flicker in her eyes. "I never got his name." I frown like I'm trying to think of it.

"Mark."

I place the cup in the sink.

"Mark Forks." She finishes.

"You didn't keep his name?" I say while rinsing the mug.

"No." Her words are sharp. "I better get Willow ready for church."

"Are you going to pray, too?"

She jerks her gaze at me and fights not to narrow her eyes. "No, I have a beauty appointment this morning."

She had rehearsed that lie. The more I am around Catherine, the more I can see through her bullshit. She must have fed that one to my father this morning, as it has a ring to it, like this isn't her first time telling it. Once she leaves the kitchen, I think of lingering until Willow comes down, but I have a better idea. I'll see her in church. She can't avoid me there. I'll make sure of it.

"I've been standing out here for a few minutes. Didn't want you to think I was a nosy bastard but... have you got a minute?"

"I do think you're a nosy bastard," I say to Blitz as I refill a fresh mug of coffee. "You want one?"

"Nah." He's not in his usual white shirt and slacks. Today he's sporting a hoodie and no glasses. Something's up. He seems almost nervous.

With my coffee in hand, I make my way to the room we use for business.

"This is going to sound fucked up; I've been debating saying something, but fuck it, if I don't, I'll regret it."

Blitz has my full and undivided attention. I lean against the sideboard, and he looks antsy.

"Sit the fuck down, Blitz. You're making me uncomfortable."

He does immediately, and that's more worrying. He touches his face as if his glasses are still there but pauses when he realizes they aren't.

"You remember that boy, Roger Smith? The one the Rat Pack gave up?"

I nod. "Yeah. The one that Fox shot?" The coffee grows sour in the pit of my stomach, and I place the cup on the sideboard.

Blitz rubs his jaw. "Yeah. It was weird that day. That guy was terrified of Fox. I mean, like, I've never seen fear like it. It may as well have been you in front of him." He frowns. "When he got up, he had run two feet before Fox shot him in the back of the head."

It's been bothering me too. But I don't speak my mind. "What are you trying to say to me?" I push off the sideboard.

"Look, Rian, I'm just telling you what I saw." He takes a box of cigarettes and a lighter out of his pocket but doesn't light one up. Instead, He taps the box repeatedly with the lighter.

"The guy's fear was crazy."

"Are you jealous he wasn't more afraid of you?"

"No. Something isn't right. I don't know what, but ..." He trails off.

If what he is saying is true, then I agree. Fox shooting someone is out of character. People don't fear him normally, but that doesn't mean that some kid wouldn't fear him.

"Look. I appreciate you telling me. But I trust Fox with my actual life. He and that kid must have had their reasons."

Blitz takes out a cigarette and places it behind his ear before rising. "Yeah. I'm sure you're right." Blitz doesn't think so. It's as plain as day on his face.

"I've got to go to church."

Blitz smirks at that. "You, at church?"

"Yeah."

"Don't touch the holy water." The lightness in Blitz's voice has me settling a bit. I didn't want him to be suspicious of Fox, yet he had voiced my own uncertainty about what actually happened.

"A reading from the first letter of Paul to the Corinthians," Willow says, glancing up at the packed church. Her gaze skims across the top of their heads. Her confidence shines through her dark eyes. She glances back down at the scripture in front of her. I dip my finger into the holy water just to test it; nothing happens, and I step into the church. I don't go to church. I have no belief in God. So many people believe in all this, but I don't think shit happens because of God. Shit happens because we make it happen.

"Be ambitious for the higher gifts." Willow's voice carries across the church and I keep taking steps up the middle aisle. Murmurs grow with each step I take. Willow glances up, and her voice halts when her gaze meets mine. I smile at my beauty.

"And I am going to show you a way that is better than any of them." She's speaking slowly while still looking at me. "If I have all the eloquence of men or of angels, but speak without love—" Her gentle voice makes me want to listen to what she is saying. She's glancing from the scripture to me and I can see she's clearly rattled. "I am simply a gong booming or a cymbal clashing." She exhales loudly. "A reading from the first letter of Paul to the Corinthians." She takes the slip of paper and is ready to come off the stand.

I start to clap because that was fucking beautiful, even if I didn't understand a word she said. My claps ring out, and I don't give a shit as everyone stares at me. The only one that consumes me is a startled looking Willow, and then she smiles. I glance at the people around me.

"Applaud. Her reading was fantastic." Claps start slowly but soon spread across the church. Willow's cheeks darken as she steps off the altar. Father Cooney follows heavy on her heels.

"You can't disrupt my mass."

"I'm not."

"Sit down, Rian." His words are growled, and his white collar doesn't mean shit to me.

"I'd rather stand." Willow reaches us, and her gaze wavers. The clapping is dying out, but not completely. I glance at everyone, and they pick up the tempo.

"Aren't you going to applaud Willow on her reading?"

"Rian." Willow steps closer. Her voice is low, but I don't miss the note of pleading in it.

"I want you out of my church." Father Cooney can't hide his distaste.

"Not very holy of you, Father." I smirk.

"Get out, now." He's trying to keep all that anger at bay. He needs to get laid.

I reach out, and I'm surprised when Willow doesn't stop me from wrapping my fingers around hers. She doesn't say anything as I walk down the middle aisle with her hand in mine. Each time I glance over at her, she appears dazed and unsure. Each step is filled with hesitation and then it leaves her eyes.

When we reach the double doors, I glance back to see the whole church watching. "Do continue, Father."

I grin as I take Willow away from the hypocrite that Father Cooney is.

I'm waiting for Willow to say something about me interrupting her at church, but she doesn't. "As much as I like this obedient and unfearful Willow, I'm confused." I stop walking and release Willow's hand.

"Maybe I'm sick of hiding." She tucks her hands behind her back.

I'm watching her like I might watch Catherine. I don't like this switch. "You've been hiding from me the last few days."

"I needed space." She shrugs, and her hands reappear. "I had a lot to think about."

I don't think she's lying, but something isn't sitting right with me. I reach out and take her hand again and we continue our walk to the car.

"So, what do you want to do?" I ask.

"Are we not going to work?"

I pause at the door. "Do you want to go to work?"

She won't meet my eyes. Something is definitely up. I will find out—she can't hide anything from me.

"Okay." She climbs in, and I grin at the crown of her head.

Oh, Willow. You have no idea how easily I can read you.

"Thanks for not telling my mother I told you the truth about ..." She shrugs. "You know...my dad."

"No problem. We were actually talking in the kitchen this morning." I glance at Willow and she shifts nervously as I drive out of the car park.

She doesn't ask me what about, and I'm wondering how long it will take her to ask me. I continue driving.

"Anything interesting?" She's trying to sound like it doesn't really matter, and now I know it does.

"Nothing, really. Just small talk."

More silence falls around us, and it feels heavy for the first time. I just want her to be honest with me.

"Did you kill Chad?"

Her question has me relaxing. That's what's on her mind. "Yes, I did." I answer honestly as I take a left down the road towards the airstrip. "I couldn't have him waking up and identifying me."

The barrier is lifted, and we enter the car park.

"How did you do it?" Willow sounds like she doesn't want to know, so I have no idea why she's asking. I stop the car close to the side door.

"Why?" I ask her. I'm just curious why she wants to know. I turn to her, but she stares out the windshield.

"I don't know. It doesn't really matter." She unbuckles her belt.

"I smothered him."

Her head snaps up to me like I've said something barbaric.

She nods. "But how? Wasn't Detective Lacy watching?"

"I had Blitz distract him while I did it. I had myself admitted with an infection." My hand is still bandaged and I did have an infection from the cut.

She's staring at me. Her pulse flickers in her neck.

"Why are you so curious?"

Someone moving outside the building catches my attention. It's Fox, he starts limping his way over to my car.

"Don't know, really," Willow says and gets out.

Fox smiles at Willow, but it looks manic on his pale face. I can't stop thinking about Blitz's doubts when I see Fox. He reaches in and takes a piece of paper out of his pocket.

"I was able to get you a name and address from that registration."

I take the slip of paper from Fox but don't open it. Willow stands close, and she's leaning in trying to see. I glance at her, and she quickly looks away. Her behavior is strange.

"Any more news on the Rat Pack?"

Fox nods and glances at Willow.

"She knows about them, so speak freely."

Fox stands a little straighter. "Do you want the good news or the bad news?"

I laugh at that. "Why do you always have both?"

He grins. "I'm all about choices."

We start to walk to the door.

"The good news first."

"The market under our feet has gone."

I pause. "Gone?"

"I sent down two scouts, and it's all been packed up."

"Who told you to send down scouts?" I take a step closer to Fox, but he doesn't shy away from me.

"You were in the hospital; I had to make a decision. I make them all the time."

I stare at him and his stare back doesn't falter. "The bad news?"

"Fredrick is missing."

"I was talking to him the other day."

"Well, he's a no show, so once again, I sent scouts to his house."

Fox reaches the door and opens it. He pauses and turns to me. "His house was empty. I think he's skipped out on us."

CHAPTER THIRTY

WILLOW

I'm hearing their words over my racing heart. Rian arriving at the church was everything. The way he had looked at me up on the altar like I was an angel. At first, I had wanted him to stop, but his claps lifted me ten feet into the air. I feel so stupid.

I had left with him because somehow he gives me peace, but I also need him to save my family. My heart feels heavy as he continues to talk to Fox while glancing at me.

"I need to use the bathroom."

"Are you okay to go by yourself?" He asks. Fox's lips thin out with impatience. I get the feeling he doesn't like me, but I don't like him either. He gives me the creeps.

"Yeah, I'm fine." I give a quick smile before he sees through my act, which I think I'm doing poorly. The recorder in my pocket feels like a grenade, and I think how stupid it was of me to bring it into a black market that had the most dangerous people here.

I push the bathroom door open and dash into one of the cubicles. My hands tremble as I take the recorder out of my pocket and stop it. Closing my eyes, I try to control my breathing. The noise of the bathroom door opening has me holding my breath. I wait until whoever it is turns on a tap and I slowly lift the lid off the top of the toilet. Placing the recorder in the water, I pause as it starts to sink.

The person turns off the tap, and I can't put the lid on. What if someone finds the recorder? I pull it out as quietly as possible. Sweat has started to gather along my brows. Opening the recorder, I take out the wet, small tape before dropping the recorder back in the water. Once I have the lid on, I flush the toilet. The door closes as the person leaves. Taking the small tape, I tuck it into my sock.

Two days before...

"I want to speak to Detective Lacy."

"Who can I say is asking for him?" The female cop is more interested in what she is writing on a yellow sheet of paper than me.

"Willow." I glance around me, feeling almost dirty in a place like this.

"Second name?" She glances up with a bored expression on her face.

"Steele," I say and her eyes widen as she pushes back her chair. "Wait here."

I'm not going anywhere. It doesn't take long for Lacy to open the door and let me in the back of the cop station.

"Willow." His smile is nice and his eyes soft. I'm hoping he will hear me out. Maybe I'll get lucky with him.

"Thank you for seeing me," I say the moment we sit down in his office.

"What can I help you with?" He's sitting back in his seat, and I'm not sure where to start.

"I know the deal you have with my mother."

His chair creaks as he sits forward.

"I want to make my own."

He raises a brow for me to continue.

"My father beat my mother daily. I was only ten when I shot him." Sweat trickles down my back, saying these words makes my crime even more real to me.

"I will sign a confession. I buried him. I killed him. It's my crime."

He smiles sadly and sits back in his chair. Joining his hands together at the tips of his fingers, it's like he's thinking over my words.

"You were ten, only a child. A child driven by a need to protect her mother."

I nod. He's understanding what I am saying.

"That could hold up in court. But your mother was the adult who covered it up and buried your father in the back garden."

"I'll say I did it."

"No one would ever believe that."

My heart pounds.

"I will ask for the chair for your mother and a life sentence for you if you don't deliver Rian to me." So much for having soft eyes.

"What happens to Rian?"

"Do you know how many people he has killed?"

I shake my head and look away. This isn't going well.

"Hundreds, we think. He's a mass murderer and deserves to be behind bars. You, on the other hand...."

His voice has softened trying to lull me into his version of my story.

"An innocent child. Your mother, a victim of domestic violence. I don't want to have to put you both away, Willow. My hands are tied on this one."

"You are so full of shit," I say, leaning forward.

He smiles. "Your mother has seventy-two hours to deliver Rian to me, or I start the proceedings against you. If you deliver Rian, your father's case will be a suicide."

"What? My father shot himself and dug his own grave? Dragged his own corpse out back? I'd love to see that stick."

Detective Lacy smiles. "I can make anything stick, Willow. Get me him confessing to a crime or bring me something and I will bury this for you."

"What about Fox or Blitz?" My heart pounds as I say their names. I'm sure Rian would kill me for handing them over, but maybe he would understand.

"The only person I want is Rian. Fox and Blitz are foot soldiers. I want Rian."

The door to the bathroom opens again and the feel of the tape in my sock is like a bomb. What am I thinking? Rian would kill me if he knew. I don't think us sleeping together would save me. He had suffocated Chad as he lay in the hospital in case he identified him. I reach down and touch the tape and I have his confession. That is if it isn't watered damaged now.

"Willow." Rian's voice is right outside the door. My heart slams against my ribcage and I can't speak. This sense of betrayal is too much for me to bear right now. It is upsetting my system.

"Willow, I know you're in there." A shadow cast at the base of the door.

"I'm nearly done." My voice shakes too much.

The shadow moves away. "I'll be outside."

My stomach roils and I swallow the bile that threatens to spill. Tears burn my throat when I think of hurting him. Tears sting my eyes, and I flush the toilet again. I need to keep it together. I can do this. I have to give up something I love to make my sin go away. I will save my family. That thought has me gathering some courage and stepping out of the bathroom. A scream rips from my throat.

Rian is still here.

"Jesus, Rian." I place my hand on my heart, attempting to keep it in my chest.

He doesn't smile, and now all I can think of is that he knows, and this is the moment he's going to kill me. He takes controlled steps towards me. I'm waiting for the blow. I'm waiting for the accusation that I deserve. Instead, his lips crash down on mine, and he lifts me off the ground. My body responds to his touch, and I wrap my legs around his waist. We are moving until I'm sitting on the sink counter. Pushing me back, I collide with the mirror. Rian's kisses are almost panicked, and I can't breathe, yet I don't want him to stop. His hand runs along my leg, and I freeze, thinking only seconds ago I had the recorder in my pocket. The tape feels too heavy in my sock.

"What's wrong?" He places a kiss on my neck.

"What if someone comes in?" I try to take the fear out of my voice.

"I'll tell them to get the fuck out." He's reaching for my blouse and I stop him. My core has tightened, and I'm already damp with a want for Rian, but I can't sleep with him when I'm ready to sell him out. I take his face in my hands and kiss him softly. I hope he can taste the apology in my kiss.

"Later." I smile into his moss-green eyes.

"I'll hold you to it." His smiling lips touch mine, and my heart cracks.

"If you ever need to tell me anything, you know I'm here. Right?"

Oh, God. More guilt swirls inside me. "Yeah." I try to scoot off the counter, but Rian's heavy hands clamp down on my thighs.

"You know I can fix any problem. If anyone is bothering you, I can remove them."

He would kill me if he found out. Fear has my tongue heavy in my mouth.

Rian removes his left hand and reaches up, touching my face. "I'd do anything for you."

"I know." I can't hear my words over the blood that roars in my ears.

He holds me in place and I am holding my breath when I start to get dizzy. He leans out and helps me off the counter. I glance at him but he isn't looking at me. There is a sense of disappointment showing with how heavy his shoulders are.

We go back out, and I spend the rest of the day shadowing Rian. My stomach rolls every time I think of the tape in my sock. Fox is around a lot and I don't know if I'm being paranoid, but he keeps looking at me.

"Did the name on the paper ring a bell?" He asks Rian.

"Maybe." Rian's voice is distant, like he's stuck someplace else. The betrayal I feel is like slow falling teardrops that just might overflow. I place my hands behind my back and squeeze my damaged wrist. The pain is too minimal and panic sets in. It's like hitting the buzzer for more morphine—only the drip is empty.

"Are you okay?" I snap my attention to Rian. He has stopped walking, and so has Fox. Both of them are watching me.

"Yes. Did you ask me something?" My heart crashes in my chest.

"I wanted to take you for lunch."

The idea of food has me feeling sick.

Rian takes a step closer to me. "Willow, you seriously don't look well."

"Yeah, I think I have a stomach ache." It isn't a lie. The pain is manifesting itself, and it is growing with each guilty second.

"I'll take you home." I nod as he reaches for my hand. I allow him to take my fingers in his.

"Don't you want to go over our plan?" Fox's face tenses.

"I'm taking Willow home." Rian starts to walk.

"I can get a taxi," I say, but my words fall on deaf ears like I knew they would.

"Rian." I try to stop him but he keeps walking.

"I'm taking you home, Willow. I can call a doctor. You seriously don't look well." I hate the worry in his eyes.

I pull my hand from his as we approach the car. I move faster. "I just need sleep." I climb into his Bentley and strap on my seatbelt. Shifting forward, my trousers have risen. Panic tears through me at the thoughts of him seeing the tape. I can't look at him; fear has me staring at the floor.

"What are you hiding?" Rian's voice has my spine snapping straight, and the fear of God enters my body.

I've been caught.

CHAPTER THIRTY-ONE

WILLOW

Rian didn't see the tape, but he knew something's wrong with me.

I just need to rest. I think it's a stomach bug. That was the excuse I used. By the time I got home, I had an actual headache and stomach ache. I didn't pause as I raced to my room. I couldn't be around Rian for one more second. He had followed me and knocked several times on my room door. With my back firmly against the door, I closed my eyes and waited until he left.

Pacing, my hands feel itchy, and I've never felt more like a trapped animal than I do now. The tape in my hand has my vision blurring. I uncurl my hands and look at the small piece of plastic that could do so much.

I re-wrap my fingers around it and leave my room. Entering the sitting room, I walk with a purpose to Henry's small bar. Taking a bottle of vodka off the shelf, I take it with me as I slip out the backdoor. I've always liked the smell of vodka, and now for the first time, I'll allow myself to taste it. I need all these feelings to go away. Isn't that why people drink, to bury things?

I keep walking until I hit the fence line at the back of the house. The mature garden with its swooping trees makes me feel like I found a secret location that shelters only me. Sitting on the damp grass, I open the cap on the vodka. I wonder what demons my father was running from when he drank every night. I squeeze my eyes when I picture him dead on the couch.

The liquid burns as it slides down my throat. I take a deep breath. The vodka is sharper than I thought it would be.

You can do this, Willow, I tell myself as I take another drink. Each one is less impactful. Opening my hand again, I glare at the tape. I have to hand it over. I still haven't called Detective Lacy. His card and my phone feels heavy in my pocket. I look away from the tape and lie back on the grass. The sky is darkening with a promise of rain.

I could always bow out. I laugh. I already know I won't. I'm a coward, and I want to stay. I don't want to die.

No, instead, you will destroy everyone else.

I drink more, wondering why it isn't numbing me. Anger bubbles under the surface.

"I had to do it," I speak to the sky as tears make a pathway down the side of my face.

"What choice did I have?" I shout at the trees before drinking as much as I can from the bottle. It isn't working. It isn't numbing me.

Laughter rips from me. "I'm broken." That's why it isn't working. I'm not normal.

Pushing the tape into my pocket, I get up off the damp grass and start back to the house. The world tilts and I reach out for the tree beside me. I close my eyes until the dizziness passes before opening my eyes again. I don't want to go back.

You don't have to.

I listen to the voice in my head and leave the garden through the side gate that leads out onto the street, and I just walk and drink. The sky darkens, and for the first time, I think the alcohol is working because as the rain spills, I feel happy.

What's wrong with you?

My mother's voice has me spinning around. The world spins with me and it takes a moment before the buildings stop moving. My mother isn't here. I'm narrowing my eyes into the sheet of rain, but I'm alone. I lift the bottle to my lips to realize it's empty. Throwing it across the street, the glass shatters and the noise has me grinning. I stumble further down the road. I have no idea where I am going. I need more alcohol. It was just starting to work when I ran out.

I stop and cling to a lamp post as I look around me for a liquor store. A light shines across the street, I can't make out the structure as the world shifts again. Closing my eyes, I try to find my focus. His head lay back at an odd angle, blood still oozed down his chest. He had no idea that it would all end. He never saw it coming. My legs grow numb and water soaks into my trousers. Opening my eyes, I look up at the black sky. The rain has stopped, I have no idea when that happened. A phone rings in the distance and I look around me. Reaching in, I take the phone that Rian gave me out of my pocket. I squint but can't make out the name on the front. A shiver assaults me as I become aware of the cold.

I'm pressing the green button before I hold the phone up to my ear. It continues to ring. I keep jabbing and when the ringing stops, I try to speak.

"Hello" My tongue is swollen, my voice is weird. Panic jolts through my system.

"Where are you?"

I smile at Rian's voice. "Where are you?" I lie back down but quickly get up as cold liquid soaks my back. I need to get up.

"Willow, tell me where you are."

I grip the lamp post and try to pull myself up. "On the ground right now." I laugh as I drag myself up the pole.

"Where?"

"Why are you shouting?" I don't like when he does that. "Don't shout at me."

I grip the pole tighter and the phone slips from my fingers. I'm back on the ground trying to pick it up. "Hello." The line is dead. Stuffing the phone in my pocket, I manage to stand. I'm soaked through. Peeling off my cardigan takes a lot of effort, and I can't answer the phone as my cardigan has wrapped itself around one of my arms and won't come off. Standing on the other sleeve, I manage to rip it off. I smile as I stomp on the cardigan. I always hated it. A car engine hums close by, and I glance over my shoulder. A black vehicle slows down across the road until it comes to a stop. I hang onto the lamp post as I stare at the tinted windows. Waving, I'm thinking that I could get a lift. I have no idea where I am. I release the lamp post and take a step out onto the road. The driver slowly rolls down his window. I'm nearly there. Brown eyes stare back at me and I stumble in the middle of the road. I'm staring at a ghost. I close my eyes before opening them again.

"Aran?" His name falls from my lips and I'm shaking my head.

His gaze is hardened with anger and I'm taking a step away from the car. Every alarm in my system is screaming at me to run.

"I'm sorry." My vision blurs as my brother continues to stare at me. The click of his door opening has my heart tripping over itself.

"I'm so sorry."

The judgement on my brother's face is too much, and I start running down the middle of the street. I can hear the squeal of his tires as he turns the car and races after me.

My legs pump hard and fast as I push my body until my lungs burn. Glancing over my shoulder, I skip off the road and onto the sidewalk, as my brother nearly mows me down. I'm not sure what I expected—but him trying to kill me isn't something I ever envisioned. I jump into someone's garden as his tires squeal, and he's turning back around.

My fist beats the door rapidly. "Help me!"

Lights come on inside the house, but no one answers as I continue to bang on the door. Aran has driven back, and now that I know his intentions, I can't stop. I hop the fence into the next garden. The engine screams and my heart nearly rips from my chest as I dash down a pathway and into someone else's back garden. A small shed at the back becomes my focus. The door isn't locked and I slip in. My breathing is too loud.

A scream lodges in my throat as my phone rings. I can't answer it quickly enough. I hunker down with the phone.

"Hello."

"Willow, don't hang up."

"Rian." I hear a car engine close by. I cover my mouth with my hand.

"Where are you?"

I can't answer him. I rise slowly and try to see out of one of the small windows, but it's clouded over with dirt. I move deeper into the shed as the car abruptly stops.

"I'm hiding," I whisper, but I'm not sure he can hear me.

"Where?" His word is growled, I can hear the car engine roar in the background.

"In someone's shed." I close my eyes and try to will my heart to slow down.

"Who are you hiding from?"

I hear the footsteps. He found me. I hold my breath as Rian continues to ask me where I am. I don't hang up because I can't afford to have him ring me back. Maybe this is what I deserved. This is my fate. The door rattles and I tighten my hold on the phone.

"Jesus, Willow, answer me. Are you okay?"

Rian's voice is the only thing keeping me sane as the door opens. I'm ready to dash, when an elderly man looks in at me.

"Are you in trouble?" His voice is gentle. He reaches in and flicks on the light in the shed.

"Yes." I manage to squeeze out.

"Come on inside. We'll get you dried."

"Don't go anywhere with him." Rian's voice is loud in the phone and I bring it to my ear.

"I'm sorry, Rian." I hang up and switch off the phone.

I get up and follow the old man into his house. He gives me a towel and I start to dry myself off. Taking the Detective's card out of my pocket, I can barely make out the number.

"Can I use your phone?"

The old man glances at my pocket, where I stuffed my phone. "It has no credit." I explain.

"In the hall." I walk into the hall with the towel in hand, and the card. I swallow the saliva as it pools in my mouth. I could prolong this, but I'd be no further on. Picking up the phone, I dial Detective Lacy's number. He answers on the second ring.

"It's me. I have the evidence you wanted."

"What is it you have?"

Guilt churns in my stomach and I glance at the old man who stands in the doorway watching me. Maybe he's worried about his bill.

"A recording."

"Of what, Willow?"

"His confession to killing Chad," I say.

"I can meet you at nine thirty at your house. I'll just do a routine questioning."

My chest grows heavy and my eyes burn as I close them. I can't do this.

"Willow." Lacy's voice sounds louder and I open my eyes. Wiping away falling tears, I glance once again at the doorway, but the old man is no longer there.

Mail on the side table beside the phone has me feeling stupid. I'm on the same street as our house. I hadn't gone far before falling down.

"Willow." Detective Lacy calls again.

"Yes, I'll see you in an hour." I hang up and place the towel on the last step of the stairs before walking out the front door and into the night to sell my soul to the devil. I think it always belonged to him, anyway.

CHAPTER THIRTY-TWO

RIAN

She turned off the phone and normally I would ring Fredrick, but that's not possible now. I have no idea where to look. She sounded drunk or high. I try not to let fear take root as I drive back home slowly. I spotted that black car again, and now that I know who the driver is, I know he hasn't been following me—but Willow. Aran Forks is her brother. I'm frustrated with how much she keeps hidden from me.

A flash of blonde hair has my heart pounding. Pulling over, I jump out and Willow freezes when her puffy red eyes land on me. I step in puddles before wrapping her in my arms. She doesn't respond initially, but eventually relaxes into my touch. My mind won't slow.

"What happened?" My heart races too fast when her small fists tighten onto my shirt and she shakes with silent sobs.

"You have to tell me." I'm pushing her back, making her look at me.

"I... I..." Tears stream down her face and the smell of alcohol on her breath frightens me.

"I got drunk." She continues on, and I've never seen her look so broken. "I thought someone was chasing me." She shakes her head. "Some old man helped me get dry and let me use his phone." She sniffles and buries her head back into my chest.

All I know is that she didn't call me. "Who did you call?"

"What?"

"You said you used the man's phone."

"I tried to ring my mother, but she didn't answer." The lie has me leading her to the car. I have no idea what's going on, but her avoidance of the truth is getting harder to deal with. I get in and start the car, but I don't move.

"I love you, Willow." I turn to her and she's curled up in a ball like she went through hell. "You have to tell me what's going on."

"I'm just a mess." She finally looks at me. "I'm not a good person."

"Who said that?" I'm ready to tear the person down.

She gives a short laugh. "I did." There is no humor in her laugh, it's filled with so much sadness.

"Aran Forks?"

Her face pales further as she stares at me. I hate how much she trembles, and how damp her clothes are. I want to know what she just went through.

She shakes her head and continues to stare at me. I tighten my hands into fists so as not to reach out and shake her. I want the truth.

"Your brother," I bark since she isn't forthcoming. "Why is he following you?"

When Fox had given me the name and address of the person that Fredrick had gotten for me, I would never have put two and two together. The conversation I had with Catherine in regards to her husband told me exactly what I needed to know.

My hands collide with the steering wheel and she jumps like I might strike her.

"Give me something, Willow." I try to control my temper.

"Yes, he's my brother. None of this matters." Her voice sounds dead.

I reach across and grip her shoulders, dragging her to face me. "Everything matters." I search her beautiful face. "You matter to me." So fucking much. "What aren't you telling me? Did you ring him?"

She closes her eyes and tuts while shaking her head. "Have you ever felt like you've been backed into a corner?"

I'm frustrated, but I take a moment to answer. "No. There is no such thing. There is always a way out."

She starts to shiver more and I release her and turn up the heat. Rummaging in the back of the car, I find one of my jackets. She takes it and wraps it around her shoulders. I love when she leans her face in and inhales.

"Why did you or your mother never mention your brother?"

"He's older. He took dad's disappearance badly."

"Disappearance? So he didn't know what happened?"

Willow shakes her head and looks away from me. "No." Her lip tugs down and I want to grab her again and force her to give me more than one-word answers.

"Why is he looking for you?"

Willow's hands are wrapped in front of her, she's pushing her nails into her wrists. I'm not sure if she is aware of what she is doing. I reach across and her eyes snap open.

"I don't know." Her lie fucking hurts.

I lean back and put the car into gear. She's silent as I drive down the street, but once we get close to the house she seems to sit up straighter. I keep glancing at her, hoping she will tell me what's going on, but she's shut down. Driving up the drive, I notice the car. The last time we had arrived home together, she asked me to drive away when she saw Detective Lacy's vehicle. This time she says nothing.

"That's Detective Lacy's car," I say.

"Yeah," she answers numbly.

I pull into the garage and I'm not ready to let her go. So instead of questioning her, I confide in her.

"I think someone close to me has betrayed me."

Her head snaps up to me.

"I know. I didn't think someone close to me would do it. I have no idea how to handle it. Normally I would kill them, but this time it's different." I think of Fox, all we have been through. After Blitz's doubts, I didn't ignore my own instincts too. I had Fredrick keep an eye on him. I paid the price with Fredrick's life. Fredrick had confronted him over his visits to the sewers below us. He must have been tipping off the Rat Pack all this time. Fredrick should have left it to me. I still don't understand his full involvement with the Rat Pack. All I know is that he had some involvement with them.

Willow's eyes water and she looks like she's caving in. Now I think maybe I shouldn't burden her with my problems. I reach across and take her hand in mine. She's so cold. "You need to get dried, you're freezing."

"Rian..." She wavers, and I'm holding her tighter.

The door to the garage opens and it's my father. He nods, and Willow pulls her hands from me and quickly unbuckles her belt.

The moment I step out of the car, she's out too.

"Detective Lacy is here. He would like a word." I glance at Willow, her chest rises and falls rapidly.

"Willow, you don't have to. Go have a shower. I'll get rid of him."

Willow drags her lip in-between her teeth and stares at me. She's moving around the car.

"No. I'll be with him in a moment, Henry." Willow reaches me, and I have no idea what's going through her mind. She reaches me and takes my face in her hands.

"I love you, Rian Steele. Don't ever forget that." Her words are fierce and undo me as she places a soft kiss on my lips and then she's gone.

I'm stunned and smiling until I look up at my father. His brows furrowed. "You and Willow?"

"I love her, too," I say.

My father nods. "If you're happy, son."

"When I'm with her, I am," I admit.

I want to go in and make sure she's okay, but Catherine is like security on the fucking sitting room door. I can't wait to see her face when she hears that Willow loves me.

I linger across from Catherine in the hallway. I can't hear what is going on in the sitting room. Each room is insulated well for exactly that reason. Dad knew we would be conducting business from our home.

"Every time my daughter is with you, she comes back in a state, but that will all be ending soon." She has a smugness to her voice that I haven't heard before.

"I don't think it's going to end Catherine. I think it's only beginning."

She fights a smile. "We shall see."

My father is watching me from further down the hall. I think he's still in shock over me and Willow.

I move across the hall, closer to Catherine. She looks at me wearily. "How is Aran?"

She inhales a sharp breath.

"He's been following Willow around." I don't ease up. "I don't like anyone following her around. It makes me antsy."

"Don't you dare touch my son!" Her words are hissed.

I grin and move back across the hall. "Does my father know he married a liar?"

"Leave Henry out of this. I love him." She looks up at the man in question and gives him a smile. He can't hear us, but he smiles back.

"You're going to break his fucking heart and when you do..." I grin again. "I'll be there helping you pack."

The door opens, and Detective Lacy steps out. He doesn't look happy and his gaze shoots from me to Catherine.

"I'll be back in twenty-four hours to collect your daughter."

"What do you mean?" I'm blocking him from leaving.

"I don't have to answer you."

Willow is sitting on the edge of the couch and she looks devastated. I react and grip Lacy, slamming him against the wall. Catherine squeals, but I don't take my eyes off him.

"What do you mean collect Willow?"

"She's a murderer."

"Stop, Rian." Willow touches my arm and I can't let Lacy go, but I don't look away from Willow.

"Did you sign anything?"

"Rian, it doesn't matter."

"It does to me." My voice rises.

"Let me go now or I'll press charges for assault."

I slam Lacy against the wall. "Shut the fuck up." Before turning back to Willow.

"Did you sign anything?"

"No." Her hand flutters to her throat.

I let Lacy go. "Get the fuck out of my house."

"I'll take you down one way or another." He's scrambling as he leaves.

"That was stupid." My father's voice is calm but I'm not.

"I want to go to my room." Willow won't look at me.

"Tell me what happened?"

"It doesn't matter." Why is she so calm? I tighten my fists and her mother shifts closer to her. I'm ready to curse Catherine, but remember she had a husband who beat her. I take a step back but still don't let Willow go.

"You're not leaving this hall until you tell me."

Willow's smile is empty. "I made a deal with Detective Lacy."

"Willow, stop." Catherine grips her arm.

"What deal?"

Willow reaches in and takes a small tape out of her pocket and holds it out to me. "I'm so sorry." Her lips twist and she fights tears. "I'll never forgive myself for even having the thought." She steps over to me and takes my hand in hers. Turning it over, she places the small tape into the center of my palm.

"What is this?"

She won't answer me.

"What deal did you make with him and why?"

"Catherine, if you know something, tell us." My father sounds as frustrated as I do.

Catherine shakes her head. "I have no idea what's going on."

"You're a fucking Liar," I bark at Catherine, and Willow tries to move past me. I grip her arm and close my eyes, trying to control every instinct I have to pin her against the wall and force her to tell me the truth.

"Don't walk away from me." She glances at me sideways. "You said you loved me in that garage. If you do, tell me what's going on."

Willow's lip tugs down. "I'm doing this because I love you, Rian. I killed my father. I've admitted to the crime and now I will pay the price."

"Your father took his life." My dad sounds confused.

"Oh, Henry." Catherine whines and I don't give a fuck about her or my father, I only care about Willow, who pulls away from me and walks up the stairs.

"What is going on?" My father's bark would terrify anyone, but right now, I've never felt so defeated.

CHAPTER THIRTY-THREE

WILLOW

"What have you done?" I've been sitting on the bed waiting for my mother to arrive. The drink has worn off, but for the first time, I really feel like I've shed my armor, and maybe, just maybe, I'll be okay.

"The right thing."

"The right thing?" My mother marches over to me without closing the door. I know what she has lost in all of this, what she will lose now. "You decide to do the right thing now? You couldn't do it when you were ten years old. Why now?!" Her face reddens with rage, but for the first time I don't feel fear.

"Because I've had enough. You won't be punished..."

She cuts me off. "Punished. What do you think will happen to my life here when Henry finds out?" My mother covers her mouth with a trembling hand.

"I'll explain it to him."

"Don't." My mother's nose curls up in disgust. "You've done enough."

"I've handed myself over so you don't have to go to prison." I'm rising off the bed. "I was expecting a bit of gratitude."

My mother looks ready to combust, and a scream of anguish has me flinching.

"All we had to do was hand Rian over and our lives would be perfect." She sobs through her hands.

"I love him." My words sound so weak against her anguish.

"What about me?" She turns her back on me, but I see her face in the mirror. "You still have time. You can still change your mind."

"No." I stand up, knowing that I can't do that. "I won't do that to him."

"You know what they will do to you in prison?" She's facing me again.

My stomach twists painfully, I've been trying so hard not to think of that part or I'll run.

"Beat you and maybe even rape you. Someone like you will be handed around like loose change. Easily attained but a throwaway at the end." She's shaking her head with pure temper and fear.

I quickly grab my mother and hug her.

"Get off me."

I don't let her go but hold her tighter. Her pain wasn't this moment. There were so many of them built on each other. She stops fighting, and I let each bruise, all the swollen flesh, and broken bones, flitter through my mind.

"I love you," I say into her ear.

My mother's sobs take over every part of her and she lets me hold her like I did when I was a child. It's a comfortable place for me, as I spent far too many hours doing this, and it is my small way of taking away some of her pain. This feels normal.

My attention is dragged to Henry, who stands at the door. I have no idea where this leaves them, but I hope he understands why she lied.

"Can I have one more moment with her?" I ask Henry. My mother stiffens in my arms. Henry nods and walks away from the door. Releasing my mother, I close it.

"I need you to listen to me. Don't mention your deal with Lacy. It's on me. Henry will forgive you for not telling him what I did. But if he thinks you were even considering handing Rian over, he never will."

My mother is too lost in her own pain, I'm not sure if she is also remembering all the beatings and me holding her after.

"Mother." I snap my fingers and she looks up at me.

"You have got to listen to me."

She nods and pushes me aside as she half stumbles from the room. I'm alone once again, and even though I know I made the right choice, my heart still hurts at the thought of leaving Rian. I've been waiting for him to follow me or ask more questions. Down in the hall I was terrified of his reaction when he discovered what I was going to do, but now I want nothing more than to see him. It might be my last time. I leave my room and search for him.

I push open the set of wooden double doors that's always driven fear into my heart—they do now, too, but for different reasons. I'm afraid of him not being here—of not seeing him again. I have no idea what I want to say. I enter the room, and I'm waiting for Rian to step out from behind the partition, but he doesn't. Stepping around it, I'm met with empty space.

My stomach twists with the thoughts of not seeing him again. The click of a button has me freezing before my voice fills the room.

"How did you do it?"

My voice sounds shaky.

"Why?" Rian's voice is filled with curiosity.

"I don't know. It doesn't really matter."

"I smothered him."

The click of the tape stops our conversation.

"So tell me, Willow, what were you going to do with the tape?" I hate the pain I hear in Rian's voice.

I can't turn and look at him. "Give it to Detective Lacy. He was meeting me here tonight at 9.30, and I was handing the tape over."

"Hmmm." Rian's voice is behind me, and I shiver at how close he is. "What were you getting in return?"

"My freedom. My brother discovered my father's body and rang it in. Detective Lacy made a deal with me; if I handed you over I would be free, and his death would be noted as a suicide."

"How long have you been playing me?" Rian appears in front of me, and I want to run. His face is tight with anger. I don't blame him, but my words won't make this any better.

"A few days." My heart beats rapidly in my chest, and I want nothing more than to touch his face. "I'm so sorry."

"Don't." He shakes his head. "I should have known." Rian runs his hands through his hair and steps away from me. "How much did you report to him?"

I shake my head. "Nothing. I didn't."

"More lies." Rian holds up his hand, and I see the struggle on his face.

"I love you, Rian." I take a step towards him, and his eyes snap open. The moss-green is so dark, and I hate the fury I see in them.

He clears the rest of the space between us, his hand grips my neck, and the blood roars in my ears. He would kill anyone for this, I didn't really think I was an exception. He's pushing me backward, his rage tightening his hand around my throat.

"You betrayed me."

My vision blurs. I blink when my back hits the wall, and tears spill. "I didn't," I whisper, keeping my eyes closed. I can't bear to see the hate in him. Not for me.

"You did." His roar has me turning my face away from his. His fingers tighten further around my neck. The pain flashes down my body.

"Just do it!" I can't look at him as I shout. "Just end it."

His hand is gone, and I open my eyes.

"You think I'm going to kill you?"

"You said that's what you do to people who betray you." He had said that in the car.

He takes a step back to me, and a whimper falls from my lips. I won't beg.

His gaze flickers to my neck before they travel up to my eyes. I want to ask him not to look at me like that. I turn my face away from him, but he touches my chin and brings my gaze back to his. His touch is a contradiction from the rage I see on his face.

A muscle works in his jaw before his lips slam down on mine—my body sighs against his. His touch is rough as he tugs down my trousers. His belt rattles as he unbuckles it. His large hands grip my thighs painfully as he pulls me up. I wrap my legs around his waist, and his kiss turns savage. His erection sits at my opening, and he doesn't pause as he slams it in. There is a moment my system is stunned with the severity of his movements, but he slams into me again, and pain mingles with a want for Rian. He fucks me hard against the wall. All his anger is in each severe pump of his cock.

His lips leave my mouth, and he buries his head in my neck as he pumps so fast I think he's lost in a frenzy. I join him and call out his name as my own body reaches a peak, and I'm crashing as he pours himself inside me. His movements slow down, and I'm coming back to reality. I'm waiting for Rian to remove himself from me and walk away, but he doesn't. His head is still buried in my neck. His heavy breaths fan out along the sensitive skin that burns now from the recent abuse. He's still inside me, but his hands are gentler on my thighs.

I don't want to leave his arms. I inhale the smell of him and hope I can remember it. My hands tighten around his neck, and I don't allow myself to cry but try to find comfort in his arms.

"You should have come to me." His words are so heavy.

It doesn't matter now. I don't say those words, but it doesn't. Maybe if I had gone to him, things would have been different, but I hadn't.

He removes himself from me, and slowly lowers me to the floor. I'm not ready to let him go, but now I have to. He leans down and pulls up my trousers first before his own.

More guilt churns in my stomach that I had even considered handing him over.

The anger isn't as severe in his eyes when he looks at me. His jaw tightens as his gaze moves down to my neck. My heart pounds as he leans in and places a kiss on my burning neck.

"From this moment on, you are going to do exactly what I say." He places another kiss against my neck. "You are going to ring Detective Lacy, tell him you changed your mind. That you were frightened."

I'm ready to push Rian away. His head snaps up, and his eyes are on fire, pinning me in place.

"Don't question me, Willow. You tell him you want to meet up tomorrow just outside the airstrip. Where you work, it's the safest place to meet. "

Rian reaches into his pocket and takes out a small handheld recorder. "You will play a bit of this for him across the phone to show him you're serious. Tell him you want your father's death written up as a suicide, and you want the paperwork before you hand this over. That's the trade."

I'm shaking my head. He doesn't get it. "I'm not handing you over."

"I need you to trust me. Just do as I say, Willow." He presses a kiss to my lips and the recorder into my hand.

"Now, make the call."

The image of Rian wavers, and I shake my head. "I'm not handing you over."

He exhales loudly with annoyance. "You're so stubborn. I won't be going anywhere."

"You will if I hand this over."

Rian grips my face again. "I need you to trust me. I'm not asking for much, Willow."

My heart trips over itself, and I know that I trust him wholeheartedly. "Okay."

Rian presses a kiss to my lips. "That's my girl." He takes a phone out of his pocket. "Make the call."

I take the phone and hesitate briefly as I see Detective Lacy's number already programmed in. I meet Rian's gaze, and I want to tell him this isn't right.

"Trust me." Rian reminds me.

PITCHBLACK

I glance at the screen and hit the dial button.

CHAPTER THIRTY-FOUR

RIAN

"I'm calling in that favor, Dean."

"When?" His irritation is obvious in his voice, and I grin.

I had gotten a punch or two in when we had met. He's one of the best snipers, but he shot a woman, and this is the price he would pay for it now, he owes me—a life for a life.

"Today. I'll text you the address and your target."

"Today?"

"Did I stutter?"

I can almost see him growl before he answers. "Okay."

"It's important that no matter what, don't let the target get away. I don't care what you have to do to make that happen. Just make it happen."

"I never miss," he says smugly.

"I remember the last time you shot the wrong person."

"That will never happen again."

"Good because there will be a girl present with blonde hair, she's important to me. If anything happens to her, I'll hunt you down and kill you myself."

I don't wait for his answer before ending the call. I would kill him no matter what he said if anything happened to Willow. I text him the location and the target's details before ringing Blitz.

"I need you to be at the airstrip today at two thirty. Be close to the fence line but out of sight."

"No problem." His willingness never surprised me.

"Tonight, I want you and Fox to come over for drinks."

This time he pauses before answering. "Do I have to be there?"

"Yes. You do."

"What do you want me to do at the fence line? What am I looking for?"

"I'll be there too, so I'll tell you then."

"Okay."

I hang up and return to my room. Willow is still asleep in my bed. Her bare back faces me, blonde hair fanned out along the pillow. She's like an angel—the light to my dark.

I sit down on the side of bed, and she stirs. Her hands reach up and the blankets slip down, revealing her pink nipples. My cock grows hard in my pants.

"Good morning."

She opens her eyes, and I'm waiting for her to withdraw like she normally does. Instead, she rolls on her side so she's facing me, tucking the blankets around her small frame. I love the blush in her cheeks as she smiles sweetly at me.

"Good morning." She rises. Her long blonde hair wraps itself around her shoulder. Her gaze searches my face before she kisses me. She has no idea the effect she has on me as her tongue slips into my mouth. It's impossible to keep my hands off her.

"Get back in." She speaks in-between kisses.

A knock at my door has me pulling away, and my father enters. The moment he sees Willow, he glances away but still stays in the room.

"I want a word with Willow."

"You'll have to give her a moment so she can get dressed." I let her wrap the blanket around herself before getting off the bed. My father glances at me before his gaze falls on Willow.

"I need to understand what happened."

"Of course. I'll tell you whatever you want to know." Willow's voice has softened, and her respect for my father makes me love her more.

My father nods. "I'll let you get dressed. Maybe you could meet me in the conservatory?"

"I'll just get dressed." Willow tightens her hands on the blanket, and my cock remembers that she is naked under there. I'll have to wait until later.

My father leaves, and Willow falls back on the bed. "I hope my answers help." She gets up and swings her legs over the edge. She keeps the sheeting around her waist as she gathers up her clothes.

"I can go with you."

She pauses and walks over to me on the tip of her toes before planting a kiss on my lips. "I'll be okay."

"In a few short hours, it will all be over," I promise her.

She's still doubtful about what will happen, I can't tell her or she won't take part, but I know it won't be easy on her.

"I hope so." She leans her forehead against mine. "I can't lose you, Rian."

"You won't." I take her face in my hands. "Ever. I'm yours."

She smiles sweetly. "And I'm yours."

"Even before you knew it," I tell her. I've loved her longer than she will ever know.

"I had better get dressed." She slips from my hands, and I hope her love is strong enough for me that she will forgive me for today.

I have no idea if the talk with my father helped. I haven't seen him, and Catherine isn't around. A part of me hopes he kicked her out. My father and Willow would be better off without her.

"I know I keep asking this, Rian, but are you sure?" Willow is fidgeting with the envelope in her hands that contains the tape of my confession.

"Yes. Just hand it over and walk away. That's it."

"Then what happens. You tackle him and get it back?"

"Don't worry about the after." I glance in the rear-view mirror before turning off onto the road that leads to the airstrip. "He said he would have the paperwork?" I ask again for the tenth time.

"Yes, and I know I need to look at it first before I hand over the tape."

"Make sure it's signed, or it's not worth any more than the paper it's written on."

"I will."

I glance at Willow as the barrier lifts, and she wrings her hands.

"Thank you for trusting me," I say as we park.

She shakes her head but smiles. "Sometimes, I don't get it."

I turn off the car and face her. "Get what?" I check my phone for the time. We have twenty more minutes before this all goes down.

"Just the way you see me. The way you protect me." She shakes her head again. "I just don't get it."

"I've always been drawn to you, Willow. No one could blame me." I lean across and place a kiss on her lips. "You're beautiful."

She smiles into the kiss.

"Are you ready to do this?"

"No."

I laugh at her answer.

"Yes."

I press one final kiss to her lips. "That's my girl."

We get out, and I don't look at her as she walks back to the barrier. I glance at the rooftop but can't see anything. Dean better be in place, or I'll hunt him down.

I text Blitz. "Are you ready?"

"Yes. I'm in position."

"All you have to do is retrieve that envelope and his phone. That's it. I'll give you the signal when."

I push the phone in my pocket. I hate walking so far away from Willow, but I can't afford to have Lacy see me. When I stop, I can't make out her features; she's that far away. But she paces as she waits. I check my phone. It's two-thirty.

I glance up at the roof again and still can't see anything. Dean wouldn't have himself visible anyway. I let my mind rest on that thought. Lacy's car drives down the road, and my stomach twists as it slows down close to Willow. He doesn't get out, and that makes me nervous.

"Come on, get out."

Willow doesn't walk over to the car; instead, she seems to stand five feet away.

"Good girl." She needs to make him get out.

They must be talking as Willow stands where she is. After a few tense moments, I curse him as Willow walks over to the car and leans in. She straightens with a large white envelope that she opens and checks. I don't think Dean could make a kill shot through a car window, and especially with Willow standing in the fucking way. She looks behind her, and I curse her for that. The car starts, and I can imagine Lacy is already suspicious. Willow hands in the brown envelope, and he takes it, but she's still blocking him. I have no idea what is happening, but as he starts to drive slowly, Willow is walking fast alongside the car.

Her body language appears as if she's trying to pull away but can't.

The fucker. I'm moving as fast as my legs will allow. He can't leave with that tape. Blitz springs from his position and tears after the car. Willow's wild gaze shoots behind her, and the fear in them has me pushing harder. She's searching for me, but through her haze of panic, she can't seem to settle on anything. She's trying to pull away, and I can hear her shouts. I can't make them out.

The air crackles, and I know that feeling when something unnatural is ripping through the space around us.

Willow's scream has dread pooling in my stomach. The car slows, and Willow slumps to the ground, her hand is handcuffed to Lacy's—his dangles out the window.

I grab the chain link fence and pull myself over it before dropping on the asphalt. The car still drags Willow, and Blitz reaches it first; he jumps in the driver's side and stops the car.

I pull Willow off the ground. Blood covers her face, and I have no idea where the wound is. Her hand comes free as Blitz uncuffs her from the inside, and I pull her into my chest before laying her out on the pavement. Blitz joins me.

"He's dead." He doesn't ask if Willow is.

I wipe the blood off her face and don't see anything, her chest rises and falls, but the blood soaks her cardigan. Pulling it down, she groans. The bullet tore right through her shoulder.

"Get me a car now!" I put pressure on the wound, and Willow cries out.

Blitz leaves, and I stare down at Willow. Her chest isn't rising as fast now, and her skin has a gray hue about it.

The hum of a car in the distance has me pulling Willow off the ground. The moment Blitz joins us, I get her in the back seat.

"I have the tape and his phone," Blitz speaks.

Once Willow is in, I grab him by his shirt. "Get rid of him and the car." I push him away, and he starts to run to Lacy's vehicle.

My phone rings in my pocket, and I pull it out. My hand is coated in blood as I climb into the car and drive.

"I couldn't get a clear shot." Dean's voice has me looking up at the roof as I drive past.

"You're a dead man."

"Rian, if I didn't take the shot, he would have gotten away; you told me to do what was necessary."

"I told you not to hurt her."

"She'll survive; her shoulder was parallel to his head. I had to. I was following your orders."

I close the phone as I turn onto the road. Right now, I can't think about that.

"Willow. Can you hear me?" I rotate the mirror to try and see her. Her stillness has me stomping down on the pedal as I tear through the streets. I'll never forgive myself for putting her in harm's way.

CHAPTER THIRTY-FIVE

WILLOW

"Let me get that."

"Mother, I'm fine."

My mother ignores me and brings a glass of lemonade to me on the couch. She's been fussing over me ever since I got shot. At first, it was kind of nice since I never had that. But after a few weeks, between the fussing and all the questions about what happened, I've really had enough.

I stuck with my story that I didn't see the attacker, and he had stolen my purse. I didn't sound very convincing since no bullet could be found, but since I didn't press charges, nothing was done about it.

I take the drink. My shoulder is still stiff, but I had been allowed to take it out of the sling.

Henry enters the room, and the air between him and mother is heavy. He still hasn't forgiven her, and the only reason she's allowed in, is to see me. I hate that they couldn't work through it, but Henry couldn't get over the lies.

"How are you feeling?" Henry doesn't enter the room but lingers at the door.

"I'm good. I was just about to go for a walk if you want to keep my mother company." I rise, and my mother narrows her eyes at me, but she doesn't tell Henry not to stay. That gives me hope.

"I can't. I have other commitments. I just wanted to see how you're doing."

"I'm fine, Henry." I can't help the disappointment that enters my voice. My mother stands and plasters on a smile. I wish she wouldn't do that. I wish she would let her pain show, and maybe, just maybe, Henry could move past this.

Henry leaves.

"You should try to talk to him," I say.

"He doesn't want to talk to me, and I don't blame him."

My mother has moved back into our old house. Aran's been living there all this time. I wonder if he told her that he tried to run me over.

When the air grows heavy, I sit on the edge of the couch. "I won't be staying here much longer."

"Oh, things not going well with you and Rian?"

Why did she sound so joyful?

"No. Things are actually great." My lips tug up when I picture him. "We are moving into a house that he renovated." I'm picturing the indoor greenhouse. "It's really beautiful."

My mother forces a smile and stands. "Must be really nice to have everything laid at your feet."

The dig I feel at her words is like an actual elbow to the ribs. "I think I finally deserve some happiness."

She picks up her clutch. "I better get back. I'm sure Aran is waiting for me."

This is her first time mentioning him. "Do you know he tried to run me down?" I'm feeling angry with her bitter tone. I wish my mother could just be happy for me.

"Yes. I don't know where you both got your murderous gene from." She sounds so flippant about what she's saying. Like she's referring to our hair or eye color.

My stomach twists. "Maybe it's too much bottled up anger."

My mother's smile is carved sharp at the ends. Her vicious tongue getting ready to sprout more hurtful words.

"Catherine." Rian smiles at my mother, it's more of a grin, but I pretend not to notice how much he seems to gloat when he walks to me and places a kiss on my lips.

"Were you just leaving?" He wraps a strong arm around my waist as he faces my mother.

"I was. But I wanted to invite both of you to a family dinner at my home."

My mother regards Rian before her gaze moves to me. Why had she not said this to me before?

"Will Aran be there?"

A short laugh bursts from my mother's mouth. "Of course, he's family."

"We will let you know." Rian answers for both of us, and I'm happy with his answer. Maybe my mother is trying to mend things, or maybe she's just fighting for control. Either way, I know I need to get on with my life, especially this life with Rian. I didn't think I'd ever get a chance at happiness again.

My mother tightens her long fingers around her clutch. "I'll be off."

I see her to the door, but she doesn't say anything else. I don't think any mother and daughter relationship is perfect—but I'm most certainly *not* the exception to the rule. I did, after all, take my father's life. Things will always be strained. I just need to learn to live with that reality. As far as Aran trying to kill, maybe it *is* in our genes.

"You look lost in thought." Rian steps up behind me and wraps an arm around my waist. I inhale the unique scent that is Rian.

"I was just thinking about my relationship with my mother."

Rian spins me around so I'm facing him. "I think she really likes me."

I'm ready to swipe at him because of the cheeky grin he wears.

"My mother would rather eat a shoe than ever say she likes you." I can't stop the laughter in my words as I picture her eating a shoe.

"Well, I will be the bigger person and say she's bearable under all that crazy."

"What a compliment."

Rian pulls me tighter. "I've lots of compliments for you." He presses a kiss to my lips.

"Rian." Blitz is in the hallway, and I detangle myself from Rian. He just nods at Rian and walks off. I don't ask. I never do. I accept that a life with Rian will come with many secrets.

"I'll be gone for a few hours, but when I get back…" He presses another kiss to my lips, and I can taste the promise on his tongue.

"What will you do?" I tighten my legs at the thought of having Rian; I can't get enough of him.

"You'll have to wait and see." He plants one final kiss on my lips before disappearing down the hall and out of sight.

I smile at the empty space. Now I have Rian, and I know everything will be okay. He had freed me from all the chains that weighed me down. I know I have so much more to figure out about myself. Too many years of suppressing who I truly am didn't make this easy, but with Rian, I know I'll come to terms with my life and everything in it.

RIAN

Blitz stands beside me as I stare down at Fox. For weeks I've had him locked up in this room but he won't break. That's why he's my right-hand man. But nobody is unbreakable or untouchable.

"I've come to the conclusion that you are a heavy hitter within the Rat Pack. Heavy enough that no one has stolen from us since we captured you."

Fox turns his head away from me, and Blitz steps in, landing him a solid punch to the jaw. I don't want Fox beaten to death; I want a confession. I want the fucker to look me in the eyes and tell me how he betrayed me and, most importantly, why. There is always a why.

Fox spits blood out onto the floor. "I heard you got Willow shot?"

Irritation flows through my veins. "She's doing great. For a smart man you aren't very careful with your words." I would never forgive myself for putting Willow in harm's way, but I know I instructed Dean to do whatever it took to take Lacy out. Willow's injury is on me.

"Just shoot me. That will be the end result, anyway."

He's taunting me. This is what makes Fox strong. He knows how the game goes. He knows withholding the truth gives him the upper hand. He'll die either way. I've been torturing him for weeks and he just won't break.

"I have a real fondness for pain. Not just pain inflicted on the flesh." I nod at Blitz and he steps forward and hits Fox in the jaw again. When Fox's groans of pain die down, I continue. "I like the type of pain that fucks with your mind. That's the beauty of the world, Fox. There are so many types of pain."

"What are you talking about? Just kill me already." Fox's bloodshot eyes close as he leans against the brick wall.

"You have no value on your life."

"Yes, I do." He opens one eye. "I just know how this ends."

I grin. "That's where I think you are wrong."

He sits up and I see real fear trickle into his system.

"We all have something that becomes more important than we are."

Fox shuffles his broken body closer to the wall.

"Blitz, what is it for you?"

"My sister."

I nod at Fox. "And you, Fox?"

"I have no one."

I waggle my finger at him. "I'm very good at detecting a lie. You're lying."

"Rian, I've been by your side..."

I cut him off. "You betrayed me."

"I just wanted a little extra on the side." He shrugs.

"You stole from me."

"Take it all back."

I rise slowly and Fox crawls to my feet. "I already have." Every part of the Rat Pack was dismantled.

"Please, Rian."

I kick him off of my shoes.

"You tell Blitz every detail, every member, and your mother will live. Lie once and she dies."

His sobs tell me it's a done deal.

"Do you want to really know what's more important to me?" I pause at the door and turn to Fox. It doesn't matter what he says, he'll die today.

Blitz leans against the wall, his fists clenched.

"I would have done anything for you. I was like your fucking shadow." Fox closes his eyes, and his breathing becomes labored. A slow smile crosses his face. It's not the kind of smile that's from joy, it's the kind from pain. "All I wanted was something like you had, all I wanted was to be like you." He opens his eyes and I see something deeper there that I didn't see before.

I kneel down and nod my head, joining the tips of my fingers together I rock my hands. "You had everything. You had my respect, but not anymore. The moment you stole from me was the moment you died Fox." I rise slowly.

I give Blitz a nod before leaving the room. Fox's sobs follow me out the door. Once we have all the information, he will kill him and then Blitz will take his place. It will show Blitz exactly what happens when I'm betrayed.

I smile as the final piece falls into place for me—and now I'll go shower so I can be with my girl.

EPILOGUE

WILLOW

SEVEN MONTHS LATER

"I need to get dressed."

Rian's large hands rest on my swollen abdomen. I'm glancing down at the crown of his head as he talks to our unborn child.

"Catherine and her son are coming."

"Our baby's nana and uncle are coming." I correct.

Rian ignores me. "Now, they will say some nasty things, so I want you to cover your little tiny, precious ears."

"Rian," I warn, but too much humor enters my voice. Every day he talks to my belly. The thought of being responsible for a tiny human is terrifying, but when Rian looks at me with so much love in his eyes, I know we will get through anything.

His lips touch my stomach, and my body reacts to him. Rising, he takes my face in his large hands. Moss-green eyes consume me. "If they annoy you, I have bombs strapped to their chairs."

I pull out of his hands. Goosebumps spread across my skin from standing here in my underwear. "Don't even mess about that, Rian."

Ever since the family dinner at my mother's months ago when Rian found out about my brother trying to kill me, Rian has wanted his revenge. We had a huge fight, and I haven't seen my family since. This is a make-up dinner. I want them in the baby's life.

"I'm not messing."

I drag the black dress over my bump and glance at Rian. His gaze is focused on my stomach.

"I won't let them hurt my family." Rian's words are razor-sharp, and his eyes have a predatory gleam in them.

I pull up the straps and turn away from him. "Can you zip me up?"

His fingers touch my bare skin, and my spine straightens at the contact. "They are my family."

"That's the only reason they are alive." Rian's voice has me focusing on the wall; he would kill them in a heartbeat.

"All you have to do is give me a nod."

I spin around, cutting him off. "I love you, Rian." My hands go to my stomach, and Rian's gaze falls to my hands. "But for this baby's sake, we have to make peace."

He works a muscle in his jaw. "Fine. For you."

I smile at him and stand on the tips of my toes, planting a soft kiss on his lips. "Thank you." I know how hard this is for him.

"Blitz is coming for dinner too."

I'm ready to protest, but Blitz is like family to Rian. "Okay, I'll set the table for one more."

Rian's hands tighten around my waist. "I'm doing this for you, Willow. I need you to know that."

I nod. He has no idea just how much I understand that.

The night my brother had tried to run me over, he had been as drunk as me. He was still struggling with the idea that I had killed our father. I couldn't blame him. I'm surprised he agreed to come tonight.

"I know."

Blitz and Rian sit on either side of Aran, and now I see why Blitz was invited—to terrify my brother. The meal is strained, but I knew it would be. After our last meal, I didn't expect this to go smoothly.

"It suits you." My heart flickers at Aran's words, and a slow, deep-rooted smile grows on my face.

"You think?" I reach down and rub my stomach.

Aran's smile makes me unbalanced. It's how a brother should see his sister. Not as a monster, but as a female who is carrying his unborn niece or nephew.

Rian's large hand touches my knee, and I love that he is there for me.

"I know we've had our moments."

Rian clears his throat and removes his hand. I know what he's thinking, that 'moment' is the wrong word, but I'm so proud of him for staying quiet.

"But I want to try." Aran's gaze dances down to my stomach and towards Rian. "For the baby."

I glance at Rian, who's staring at Aran with a smile that's razor-sharp and would have anyone scrambling from the table.

Aran doesn't move. "I can make things right. I should have done something..."

I shake my head as emotion rushes through me.

"I should have protected you and mother."

"Yeah, you should have." Rian's words are like jagged glass. "Instead, you let a ten-year-old do a man's job."

Aran rubs his jaw. "I know..."

"We all have done wrongs, not just you." My mother's voice grips everyone's attention, and it's like a physical shake. Eventually, she's going to admit that she did wrong too.

She sips her wine before plastering on what I have come to know as her false smile on her face. "Neither of my children are innocent."

Her words are like a slap in the face. I don't want to fight, but she's rubbing me the wrong way. "What about you?" I grip the table so I don't move from the spot.

Her brows rise nearly into her hairline. "Me?"

The question has me snorting. Of course she would be righteous.

"Willow's right. You had your part to play in all this, just as much as I did." Aran's defense has me sitting back in confusion. I've wanted this from him, his help, his understanding. I've wanted him to be a brother, but I really didn't think it would happen.

My mother is smiling at Aran, it's calculated, and it looks like she's trying out a new smile for the first time. "Very well. We have all done wrongs." My mother's gaze swings to me, and she raises her glass. "To new beginnings."

I pick my own drink up. Aran and Blitz follow suit, but Rian doesn't move.

"Before we get all pally-pally, I want to say something." Rian's chair scrapes along the floor, and he stands with his glass in one hand, the other hand rests heavily on my shoulder.

"This girl means everything to me."

My heart swells at his words, and I reach back and place my hand over his.

"I think you know, Catherine, what I'm capable of."

Rian's words have my stomach hollowing out.

My mother's jaw tightens, and she tries to smile, but it looks almost painful. "I know exactly what you are capable of."

I look to my brother, and his gaze is fixed on me. I have no idea what he is making of this. Blitz, on the other hand, is nodding at Rian.

"I've let a lot slip, and trust me; I don't let things slip. So if either of you..."

I squeeze his hand, begging him not to go any further. Rian hesitates, and I have a moment of relief. It's very short-lived.

"Causes her to shed as much as one tear; I'll be digging your graves."

I close my eyes and wait for world war three to start. Silence descends around the space, and I open my eyes.

Aran raises his glass. "To treading on eggshells."

Blitz sneers beside him.

"To Willow," Rian says.

"To Willow," echoes around the room, and Rian sits down.

It's funny how the rest of the night goes. Everyone is careful with their words, but a part of me doesn't mind that it's controlled. I spent my whole life filtering every action for my mother, every word. So, having her do it for me isn't such a bad thing.

"Are you okay?" Rian asks me while the rest talk. I take his outstretched hand. He raises it to his lips and presses a kiss there.

"I'm always okay when I'm with you," I answer honestly.

Having Rian at my side is like having my own personal army right beside me. His strength radiates and wraps itself around the three of us. I touch my stomach again and smile.

"You get more beautiful each day."

My cheeks heat at his words. Some days I don't feel beautiful, but the moment Rian looks at me, all my insecurities vanish.

He leans in. "I love making you blush."

I try to suppress the smile that threatens to escape. "I know."

My gaze meets his, and he brushes the softest kiss against my lips. It reaches all the way inside me, and I feel it stitch my damaged soul back together.

Each word, each kiss, heals me.

Love really does heal all.

THE END

I hope you enjoyed *Pitchblack*.

Sinner's Vow is the first book in the Murphy's Mafia Made Men Series.

Read Aidan and Raven's story.

You can download HERE:

https://author-vicarter.com/products/sinners-vow-1

Or scan the code:

PITCHBLACK

Or read on for a sneak peek:

SINNER'S VOW
CHAPTER ONE

Dread drips down my spine in a slow trickle—my stomach clenches. On either side of me, doors line a long, daunting passage. Intentionally, I'm sure.

I'm positive my father revels in intimidating visitors as they shuffle toward his study at the back of the house, the ticking of the grandfather clock taunting them with each step.

The ticking that haunts me now.

For each hand movement accompanied by a tick, I'm another step closer to my doom. Father never calls me to his office for anything good. The last time he called on me, I ended up in the hands of the Bratva.

Raven, you can do this, I remind myself as I place one Jimmy-Choo-clad foot in front of the other.

A half-strangled laugh echoes back to me, and I press my lips together. Even as my fight-or-flight response kicks in, I keep moving forward.

Because, just like all the times before, I know I have no other choice.

You could run.

I shiver and grip the sides of my dress. The memory burns in my mind of what happened the last time I ran, not from my father but from my ex-husband.

I had run home to my father, pleading with him to save me from the beast of a man he'd given me to. It had been a risk, but I didn't know who else to run to. He'd put me in that situation, and I knew there was no escape unless my father granted it.

That day, my father held me as I cried bitter tears on the shoulder of his navy jacket. My sobs jolted my body, and I didn't notice him withdraw his phone, dial my husband's number, and tell my husband to come and collect his wife.

Knock, knock, knock. I've reached the dark wooden door that leads into my father's lair.

"Come in." My father isn't a man you ever keep waiting. My fingers sprawl across the door that I push open, and I step into his office. Olbas Oil tickles my senses. The white cloth handkerchief at my father's elbow is where the strong smell emanates from. My earlier breakfast curdles in my gut.

Three large chandeliers cast light down on the crown of his head. He shuffles paperwork on his mahogany desk. As my gaze travels across the bookcases that soar above my father, I find my calm by looking at a paper dove that Louise had made for him years ago. I have no idea why he kept the present from Louise, but right now, it's what I'm seeking—a moment of calm before the impending storm. I hope this time I'm strong enough to withstand the force of whatever he unleashes on me.

"Raven—"

I pull my gaze from the bookshelves and look his way. Maintaining eye contact isn't easy. His blue eyes always appear clouded, as if there's a madness lurking.

I keep my hands firm at my side, though I want to ball my fingers into fists so I don't fidget.

He gestures toward the adjacent chair. I descend into the brown leather seat before folding my hands onto my lap, waiting for the blow from his words.

He doesn't so much as blink as he leans forward and steeples his fingers on the desk. "You've won your freedom."

I release the breath I've been holding, and without being able to stop myself, I slump into the chair. My lips drag down, and my vision wavers. It's over.

Tears spill, and I'm smiling. I'm smiling with a fierce pain in my heart. God, the price I paid for my freedom had been branded into my flesh, literally. My ex-husband used his belt as his form of punishment.

"Thank you," I find myself saying through quivering lips. I'm crashing from exhaustion. I'm crashing from being relieved from an overwhelming crushing feeling. I'm free.

Free.

"Once you marry Aidan Murphy, you are free to leave this home. You can start over wherever you want."

I'm staring at the gray-peppered crown of my father's head, my vision as clear as a cloudless hot summer's day. His black fountain pen glides with fluid motions across a piece of paper.

"Excuse me?" My voice comes out strangled, pained, heartbroken.

Without flinching, he repeats his words as he continues to write. He pauses when I don't respond and glances up at me. "I need you to retrieve information from Aidan Murphy. Once you do, you have won your and Louise's freedom."

A whimper spills from my lips. The last time I extracted information from Victor, my first husband, it almost cost me my life.

"You said the last time that if I got you the information, we would be debt free." I'm speaking out of turn. I know I've crossed an invisible line even before my father looks up at me with fire in his eyes. His fist comes down with a heavy thud on the table, and I grip the arm of the chair so I don't jump.

"It helped," he grits out. "But it wasn't enough. Yes, you did well. You kept a roof over Louise's head. You say you want to give your sister a better life, but do you mean it?"

Louise. My Achilles' heel.

The information I obtained for my father gave him millions. Where did all that money go? I want to accuse him of returning to gambling, but I also value my life.

"Once you get the information from Aidan Murphy, you can leave him. Finances will be set up for you and Louise. I'd suggest you pull yourself together. Aidan Murphy may one day rule the Irish Mafia. He won't want a weak woman at his side." He returns to his work, dismissing me.

I'm so beat down that I don't at first comprehend the dismissal. When his gaze darts to mine, my brain stalls, mentally repeating his words before I rise. He has taken everything from me. I'm ready to walk away, but I can't. Not this time. I raise my head in defiance.

"No." My pulse builds to a tempo that's more fitting to a dramatic ballad grand finale. The part where the heroine dies, or the moment the hero realizes he's already lost her.

My father rises in one swift motion. He's a large man, over six feet tall, with massive hands.

"I wasn't asking, Raven."

"I don't understand." I blink tears.

His lips curl into a snarl. "You're a woman. You aren't meant to understand the ways of a man. Just get the information from Aidan Murphy, and you have your freedom." My father settles back into his chair.

"Or maybe he would prefer someone younger." My father's mouth curves into a smile. "Louise is very striking."

My stomach roils. His words should terrify me; instead, they make me want to tear the world apart. "You will not go near Louise."

My father ascends and steps around his desk with a raised hand. I fear what will come next. I've pushed too far, and I will pay the price.

The impact of the slap doesn't just burn my jaw; the force sends me sprawling to the floor. The ridges of the wooden floor dig into my palms. My hip takes the brunt of my fall.

I'm staring at the dark wood, panting and shaking. I want to get up. I want to defy him. Maybe he senses the rebellious nature in me. His fingers plunge into my hair, and my scalp burns as he forces my head back.

"Apologize."

I want to say no again, but as his gaze fills with brutality, I know this will end with me injured and still shipped away to marry a stranger. But, for one moment, it's brief. My defiance feels so good.

"No." My heart palpitates as I try to crawl away from my father before he can unleash his wrath upon me. The abrupt opening of his study door stops his assault.

My face continues to burn from the slap he planted on my cheek. I take in shiny black shoes before traveling my gaze up black slacks all the way to George's green eyes. My bodyguard isn't looking at me. A muscle tics in his square jaw.

George captures my father's attention. "I do apologize, Mr. Collins." He glances at his wristwatch. "I'm here to collect Miss Raven. The car is waiting."

My lungs constrict painfully. No one walks into my father's office unannounced, and George follows the rules. So why did he enter without knocking? Or did he knock, and I just didn't hear the sound?

I push off the floor. My arms tremble as if I'd been lifting weights.

"Get up," my father barks as he returns to his seat behind his desk. I hate him. I hate him so much. As I stand, my tongue flicks out, licking the blood off my lips.

When I'm upright, my father pins me with a stare. "The car can wait. Have one of the servants clean her up first," he says to George without taking his beady eyes off me.

My heartbeat thump, thump, thumps. George said the car is waiting. Am I leaving right now?

"Miss Raven." George's brash words have me pivoting toward him.

"I hope you show Mr. Murphy more respect. I'm sure his hand would be far heavier than mine."

I hunch my shoulders at my father's words. I want to rebel. I want to tell him I hate him, but I place one foot in front of the other until I pass George. The office door closes as George falls into step behind me. We walk down the long corridor, and I wrap my arms around my waist to try to shake off the growing fear.

"You shouldn't antagonize him," George whispers.

I take a peek at the forty-year-old man who has never spoken to me. I wonder how long he had been standing outside my father's office door. Responding would be pointless. George steps in front of me as we enter the ornate foyer of the house. We walk past the enormous staircase to the first floor, where I sleep. I'm looking around for my sister. I want to check on her, but no one is in sight to even ask about her.

When we reach my bedroom, George opens the door but doesn't enter. No one is permitted into our sleeping quarters. I had a hand in designing my room. The gold leaf that adorns all the matching white French furniture pulls the room together. It's a mix of contemporary and old world. The large black chandelier over my bed sends light dancing across the gray silk duvet. I find my gaze ping-ponging around the luxurious space. It's my haven, where I seek solitude on the hard days. I often thrash out my pain in my quarters and try to heal myself by decorating the space. I won't return here. I shake off the sense of loss and walk to my open closet.

I need to pack. My stomach squirms in pain, and I scramble for my calm, which in this moment, I can't find. I'm leaving again to marry yet another man. Will he hurt me as Victor had? A part of me wants to curl up and find a corner to hide in. I want to bury my head and let the time pass.

But gathering some possessions and saying goodbye to Louise spurs me to my walk-in wardrobe. I freeze as George greets my father on the landing. My dread grows as I spin around, fearing he's come to finish what he started in his office.

My father barges into my room and slams my bedroom door behind him. When he spins the lock, I know it's to keep George from interfering with whatever is about to come next.

I won't have anyone to save me this time.

Other Books by VI Carter

VICIOUS #1

RECKLESS #2

RUTHLESS #3

FEARLESS #4

HEARTLESS #5

<u>THE BOYNE CLUB</u>

DARK #1

DARKER # 2

DARKEST #3

PITCH BLACK #4

<u>THE OBSESSED DUET</u>

A DEADLY OBSESSION #1

A CRUEL CONFESSION #2

<u>BROKEN PEOPLE DUET</u>

BREAK ME #1

SAVE ME #2

ABOUT THE AUTHOR

V i Carter - the queen of **DARK ROMANCE**, the mistress of suspense, and the high priestess of *PLOT TWISTS*!

When she's not busy crafting tales of the **MAFIA** that'll leave you on the edge of your seat, you can find her baking up a storm, exploring the gorgeous Irish countryside, or spending time with her three little girls.

Vi's Young Irish Rebels series has been praised by readers and can be found in English, Dutch, German, Audible and soon will be available in French.

And let's not forget her two greatest loves: ***coffee and chocolate***. If you ever need to bribe her, just offer up a mug of coffee and a slab of chocolate, and she'll be putty in your hands.

So, if you're ready to join Vi on a wild journey with the mafia, sign up for her newsletter and score a free book! Just be warned - her stories are so **ADDICTIVE**, you might not be able to put them down.

What Readers Are Saying

Editorial Reviews

"Vi Carter has once again blown my mind with another outstanding story. She never fails to create a masterpiece with memorable characters that leap off the page. This book is complete perfection."- USA Today Bestselling Author Khardine Gray

Vi is one of those authors who never disappoints. She weaves **LOVE** & **DANGER** effortlessly. ★★★★★ stars

I definitely recommend this book. It is **SUSPENSEFUL** and exciting. I enjoy reading Vi Carter's book. ★★★★★ stars

How to Keep in Touch with Vi Carter

Visit Vi's website: https://author-vicarter.com/.
Join the newsletter: t.ly/yZWbX
Or scan the code below:

On Facebook, Instagram, TikTok and YouTube @darkauthorvicarter and
on Twitter @authorvicarter
Or scan the code below:

www.ingramcontent.com/pod-product-compliance
Lightning Source LLC
Chambersburg PA
CBHW051253210726
48287CB00002B/486